RED DIRT

E. M. REAPY is an Irish writer and tutor. She has an MA in Creative Writing from Queen's University, Belfast. Her work was featured in *The Long Gaze Back: An Anthology of Irish Women Writers*. *Red Dirt* is her debut novel.

RED DIRT

E. M. REAPY

and bound by CPI Group (UK) Ltd, Croydon, CR

Day received financial assistance from the Arts Co

Head of Z Ltd
Clerkenwell se
45–47 C Green
Lo HT
WWW.HEADOFZEUS.COM

For Helen and Joe

ME

Me and Shane moved to Perth about two months back. In Melbourne before that. Pretty much taking caps and drinking goon all the time, until we blacked out or puked or scored women more wasted than us. Waking up in random hostels in St Kilda or in Aussie houses cramped with Irish immigrants to keep the rent down. Young ones like ourselves. Younger even. Was turning out to be worse than the way we were back in Ireland. Off our faces all the time and running too low on dollars. I didn't want to go robbing. It was supposed to be a fresh start here.

Shane's mam bailed him out once with a grand but we blew it in a weekend with Thai girls and a two-day session in a plastic Irish pub run by the biggest scumbags you could ever expect to find in Northside Dublin. They were legal and stuff in Australia but I got the sniff of fugitives off them, that they could never go back home or they'd be arrested on landing. Should have tattooed *Crimewatch* on their shoulders instead of the big tricolour flags and Fighting Irish leprechauns.

We drank it all away there with them.

I couldn't ask my parents because we hadn't a bean with the recession. Auld lad went bankrupt. Builder who got greedy and thought he could develop a site that was way beyond him. What a cliché. One of the main reasons I left Ireland was to get away from the small town cunts who kept on about us, sneering at my folks. Me auld lady crying every day, verging on a breakdown.

Couldn't be dealing with that.

Anyway, we were down to our last bobs and heard Western Australia was how to go, get into the mines as machine operators or truck drivers and be laughing all the way to the bank with our two-grand-a-week wages. And it really was. The mining boys would be back from three-week swings telling us about how soft the job was for the amount of cash they were earning.

This skinny Corkman engineer who had a stammer got me and Shane interviews for an iron ore mine in the Pilbara. Even for us having no college we could still get in up there. But we'd to do an alcohol and drug test after the interview, and I have to say, we failed it magnificently. The Aussie interviewer asked me if I was 'fucking serious?' when he looked at the results.

'You've wasted my time, mate. Out,' he said and opened the door of his office. I reckon we'd have failed the medical and fitness tests the same way if we had gotten to do them.

We gooned ourselves silly that night. Eleven dollars for four litres of wine in a silver piss bag. Pure depressed. Sitting out in the smoking area of the hostel. Loads of Frenchies and Germans at the next table. Goddesses with brown eyes and long, tanned legs, talking gibberish and laughing. At us probably. Then we met Hopper, real name Derek Finnegan, from Dundalk, with a thick broad accent who pronounced

TH like D. Dem and dere and dose and dat. He joined us drinking and told us the craic. He'd 'taken a long way over here' from Adelaide. But back in Ireland he was a major fuck up. Borderline junkie. Skipped court.

'What ya do?' Shane asked him, his eyes wide and a smile creeping in the corners of his mouth.

'Set fire to a playground.'

'What? Why would ya fucking do that?'

'Ah, it's all in the past, lads. D'ya know when you'd be out of your box and you'd kind of lose the run of yourself.'

'But a playground?' Shane asked.

Hopper looked at his hands and took a deep breath. 'It was an awful abused playground where we'd hang around, tinning, shagging, shooting up – a total shitehole. I was on lighter fluid and I had visions of all these kids syringing themselves and being worse off than us. I remember being a kid myself and I'd a bad auld time of it. Parents. School. Social workers. Everyone hated the Hopper. Always out to get me. Bastards. I was only a child.'

He paused so me and Shane nodded fair enough at him.

Hopper went on. 'So there I was, getting upset, kneeling in front of a slide. A dirty, yellow, plastic thing. I punched it hard and cut my knuckles. A bit was sticking out of it. How could a kid slide down that? He'd tear open his arse. I got so mad. I threw a bit of juice on it and sparked her. But ya see, it somehow kind of spread. The fire. I suppose with the rubbish thrown on the ground and that. I'm not sure. Sirens and smoke. Me only half with it. I didn't run. I let them arrest me. I ran later when my head cleared.'

'To here?' I asked.

Hopper shrugged. 'Look. It's all in the past now. Ye want to try some acid? I can get it off this Kiwi chick I know. Crazy wan with piercings everywhere. Will I put in for ye?'

I didn't even have to look at Shane.

'Yes, sir.'

*

'You get homesick?' I asked Shane.

He was flicking through the *Quokka* classifieds. Someone had told him that's where we'd find work. Every so often his eyes would go bigger and he'd circle an advert with his pencil. I was lying on my top bunk, thinking about the new Irish that had moved into the dorm the night before. She was above Shane's bed. Milk-bottle skinned, Qantas-smelling, sad-eyed *cailín*. She could have been a million Irish girls with her splash of freckles and highlighted hair. Her new Penneys summer clothes unpacked and put away neat into a locker. Cheap and hopeful.

I heard her crying when the lights were out. I wanted to get out of bed and comfort her, rub her back, tell her that we're all better off being here but her snuffles in the bunk across from mine set me off.

I missed it too.

Small things. How the young and auld fellas would be out the back of the church on a Sunday morning with cheery bloodshot eyes talking about football and pints. The smell of turf burning. The taste of McCambridges dosed in real butter, Purple Snacks, Supermac's chicken burgers, Club Orange.

The rain.

6

The awful bollocking rain that soaked us and quenched us.

Shane put the newspaper down and bowed his head. 'Homesick. Yeah, I do be bad. Miss me sister's kids the most. They won't know me. I'd be like our long lost uncle in America from years ago. Only now it's Australia. I'm the one none of them will know. I'll send them packages though once I get work. With nice bits and pieces. Like the Americans used to. With clothes and Tim Tams and Ugg boots and that kind of shite. After I get set up. They'll like me even if they don't remember me.' He smiled and paused. 'I miss it all the time really. When I think about it. But what can I do? Have to just say fuck it to homesickness. This is it. This is where I am. This is what was forced onto me.' He picked up the paper again.

'Yeah,' I whispered. 'Fuck it.'

*

John Anthony came to the hostel on the Thursday and immediately threw his bulk around. He'd a strong Donegal accent, a buzz cut and two sleeves of tattoos. Mostly Republican or Catholic shit: on his left bicep – a man in a balaclava holding a rifle; on his shoulder – a huge green shamrock; and on his wrist – red rosary beads with a cross that fell onto the front of his hand. He'd names, skeletons and Celtic designs inked everywhere else.

I noticed a big dented scar on his shoulder blade, like something had taken a bite out of him.

He caught me looking.

'You want a piece of this?' he asked, his eyebrow raised.

'What?' My face started burning.

'You like the fellas, do you? A lads' lad?'

'No, Jesus. Fuck off. Not at all. It was just – just – the mark you have, I was wondering where you got it?'

He looked down at himself, pointed at the dent. 'This one?'

I nodded.

'Let's just say, we gate-crashed a wee march. And let's just say, if you think this is bad, you should have seen the Huns.' He looked away and laughed. 'No more quick-stepping or drum-banging for them.'

Two Japanese girls came to the doorway of the kitchen and posed for an iPhone photo. They were doing peace sign fingers to the camera.

'So what's the story with the bitches here? Are they all chinks, hey?'

I tried not to roll my eyes in front of him but I'd no time for racists. My auld fella had loads of Polskis and Brazilians working for him back in 2007. Before he went bust. They were as sound as the local fellas. Sounder even. They put up with the shite off us and kept at their job. Rose above it. All the shite we've to put up with here. *Green-niggers. Lowest of the Whites. No Irish Wanted.*

'Here, I heard a rumour that you and your boy couldn't get in the mines. I've got another job. Can ye drive?' John Anthony asked. He opened the fridge and poked through the different reusable bags with name tags on them until he pulled out a steak.

I knew it didn't belong to me or Shane. We shared a bag and the only thing in it was a half-tub of butter and some gone-off ham. Rooting through the other guests' stuff was an automatic expulsion from the hostel so we didn't bother and anyway we found that if you hung around looking starved when the Irish girls were cooking, they'd give you a bowl. Irish girls will never see one of their own go hungry.

'I don't think you're allowed—'

'I don't think you're allowed,' he copied me with a high voice and did this mincing dance with his arms. 'I'm not allowed what?'

The blood dripped off the steak onto his palm and the floor as he held it high in front of me. I thought he was getting ready to smash me with it.

'The food. It's not yours,' I said and took a step back. 'Or ours. If it was ours, you could have it.'

John Anthony looked around the kitchen and then wiped his nose with the inside of his arm. 'Who's gonna stop me?'

I shrugged. Checked around too. Didn't recognise anyone. 'No one, I suppose.'

'Exactly.'

He picked a pan from the shelf above the sink and greased it with someone else's sunflower oil. 'So can ye? Drive tractors and that?'

'Yeah, course we can. What's the job?'

'Be working for the harvest. Mangos. Driving around the farms. That kind of bull. Fourteen-hour shifts. Twenty-five bucks an hour. It'll be cuntish enough but it's only for a month or so, it counts as regional work and when we've finished we'll all have enough saved for a good Christmas dinner in Bali or Sydney or New Zealand.'

John Anthony was a bollocks but we really had no money

left. The hostel rent ran out on the Saturday. I looked at the oil sizzling and coughing splats around the pan as he pounded the steak into the middle of it.

We'd go.

What was a month of tractor driving? Nothing in the grand scheme of things.

*

Hopper wanted in as soon as he heard about it and it was agreed he'd take the fourth seat in the car. We were all drunk at the time but I thought I saw his eyes well up a bit when we told him he could have it.

We'd a going away party in the hostel on the Friday night, a big sesh and I slept with a girl from London who was beyond sexy. She'd a navy polka-dot dress on her and a way of saying my name. I could feel the letters on her tongue before she sprung it out in her Cockney accent. So I was with her and I didn't know if anything went down between Hopper and John Anthony. Maybe nothing had.

As we gathered our crap from the room at 5 a.m., I whispered to Shane, 'What was the craic after I left?'

'Did you not get enough crack off yer wan?'

'Piss off,' I said and launched my shoe at him. 'Did I miss anything?'

'I can't remember nothing after the vodka and the spliffs.'

He was happy. He was whistling and shuffling as he packed his rucksack, leaving clothes that were torn or stinking in a pile between the bunks.

'You'll need them for the farm,' I said.

'Nah. Got my hi-vis for that.'

Shane had splashed out fifteen bucks on the fluorescent orange and navy construction top back in Melbourne and hadn't got to wear it. I smiled. I was feeling happy as well. Maybe the farming would be another fresh start for us. Out in the countryside. Clean air. Healthy food. Could be some nice girls too. The London one said she'd be texting me but I knew that I wasn't the only one who'd have her attention. A girl like that was spread between many fools.

We checked out and met John Anthony in the car park to fill up the boot. He was wearing mirror sunglasses and a white t-shirt that had 'I'm drunk but you're still ugly,' written across the front in black letters. His car was a twelve-year-old maroon Holden Berlina Wagon. Decent motor for travelling.

Hopper was ten minutes late and Shane convinced John Anthony to wait for him.

'Here, ye listen, it's my fucking car so it's my way or the highway. Understand?'

'Yeah.'

Hopper came out with a ragged bag about half the size of ours. He wore an old Celtic away shirt, the NTL black and green one from seasons ago. It was too stretched at the collar and fell loose and wrong on his neck.

John Anthony muttered, 'State of this fella.'

'Travel light?' Shane asked.

'Don't need much more than my jocks and a couple of t-shirts,' Hopper said and scratched his head.

I took a look at him and realised how filthy he was. He'd stamps from nightclubs fading on his wrists and his nails were blackened. On his chin was a smatter of yellow spots, raw and angry. His moustache was wiry, like dark pubes. I imagined his bin juice breath and stood in front of the passenger side so Shane would be in the back beside him.

John Anthony rubbed his hands together. 'Alright, let's do this bitch.'

*

We were almost out of the city, the handful of Perth skyscrapers shrinking in the wing mirrors when Shane piped up.

'Eh, John Anthony, you're taking the wrong road.'

John Anthony looked at me, frowned and looked in the mirror to Shane. 'Eh, Shane, no I'm not.'

'You're supposed to be on the North West Coastal Highway,' Shane said.

I checked the signs. I hadn't a fucking clue which road we were taking.

'No, I'm going on the Great Northern Highway, can you not read?' John Anthony's Adam's apple bobbed as he swallowed.

Shane jumped forward. 'Are you messing?'

John Anthony didn't react.

'But there's nothing that way. That's into the outback. If we go the coast, we'll see the coast. We'll see the Indian Ocean. The beaches. Whales and dolphins. Hot women in bikinis.'

'Who gives a fuck?' John Anthony said.

'But we could see the Pinnacles and later on, Monkey Mia. They're famous.'

John Anthony didn't reply. He pouted and sniffed and turned the radio louder.

I looked back at Shane. He nudged his head forward and nodded at John Anthony. I shrugged. Hopper was staring out the window with his hands in his pockets. The sun was rising, white light blazing the sky around it.

Shane took a breath, leant forward and was about to protest again when John Anthony snapped the radio off and pulled sharply across the lane to the hard shoulder. A big van behind us swerved right and honked.

'Here, is there something wrong with you? We're going the shortest cunting way and that's it. Do you want to add another five hours to a day and night's driving to see some fucking sand?'

Shane's face went a bit pink.

'Well, do you?'

Shane folded his arms. He started and stopped himself twice before saying, 'It's just 'cause we're going north anyway. Be cool to see some sights on the road trip, like.'

'It's not a road trip. It's a fucking commute. Now wise up.'

Shane liked doing tourist shite. He made me go with him to loads of things before. Old Melbourne Gaol where they hung Ned Kelly, the dodge. The place was smelly and expensive but the death masks were cool. In Perth, Shane dragged me with him to the Fremantle Markets and to St. Mary's Cathedral. A fucking cathedral. If we'd had enough cash, he'd have made me go out to Penguin Island. He liked telling his auld lady the things he'd seen down here so she could tell the neighbours and sisters and in-laws about it. I heard him on the phone to her. He was babyish, pure mammy's boy. If she only knew.

John Anthony pulled back onto the road, the indicators

briskly ticking. 'We're going through the inside. It's the shortest way.'

He turned the radio on again.

*

Sometimes I could see Hopper in my wing mirror without him seeing me. Something about him gripped me. He was pathetic with his weaselly arms and dirty skin but he had some security in himself that I couldn't understand. I wanted to know where it came from. I wanted to know how to get it. If he could have it, I definitely should, the fucking cut of him.

He hadn't said much on the drive except ask John Anthony for a piss stop which he begrudgingly got. We pulled in at a dusty roadhouse and Hopper ran around the back of the cabin that said toilet. John Anthony had a smoke and me and Shane got out to stretch our legs.

'Why's he gone behind it?' I asked.

'The poor bastard,' Shane said and creased one side of his face.

John Anthony shook his head and blew smoke at us. 'He's a donkey, sure. We might as well swap for a while, Shane? Sound?'

Shane agreed to take over. I was tempted to get a few beers but then I'd have to battle John Anthony to stop again when the liquid went through me.

Hopper came bounding back to the car with a plastic bag. He opened it and offered us multi-coloured ice lollies.

'Cheers, Hopper. When did ya sneak into the shop?' I asked and tore the wrapper off. It was odd I hadn't seen him pass. The ice pop was melting already. 'And why did ya go round the back of the jacks?'

Hopper slurped at his lolly. Sticky orange drops fell onto his hands and he wiped them off his jersey. 'Didn't want to go in it. D'ya know when a place is too small and ya don't want to be getting your mickey out in case ya'd keel over inside from breathing too fast? Someone would find you with your lad in your hand and be talking about you to everyone and bring them out for the laugh at you?'

I gave Shane a face and looked back at Hopper. 'No?'

He raised his shoulders.

John Anthony bit down on his ice pop three times and it was done. I had a big grin, watching him, praying to fuck he had brain freeze but he just slapped the car and told us to get back in.

*

We were about nine hours from Perth. John Anthony was resting in the back and didn't notice Shane pulling in until he had done it.

'Ah come on, what now?' John Anthony said.

'We're at the 30th Parallel South,' Shane said, his eyes bright. 'Class.'

'The what?'

'It's like the Equator. But lower. Just give us two minutes, John Anthony,' Shane said and got out.

I laughed and followed him and we went to the sign. Hopper came behind us. John Anthony got out and banged the door shut. He walked over to the sign and examined it.

15

'Where is it?' John Anthony asked.

'It's an imaginary line of latitude,' Shane said.

'Imaginary? Give me strength.'

'Can we get a photo?' Shane asked.

I had the camera but I couldn't remember where I put it because I was too steamed when we packed up in the hostel.

'I can take a photo,' Hopper said and whipped out a flip-top silver phone.

Shane laughed. 'Is that from the eighties? What level in Snake can you get to?'

'Not sure. It's an indestructible mobile. Swear. Got no coverage out here but it does have a timer. Give me a minute.'

We stood around the sign. Shane read some of the graffiti and John Anthony kicked the rusty coloured sand and grit on the ground. Hopper went to the car and set the phone up on the roof of it, facing us. He ran back quickly, laughing. He jumped in between us and wrapped his arms behind our backs, pulling us closer together. 'Quick, we've only ten seconds.'

His excitement even made John Anthony smile. We waited for Hopper to check the photo. He gave a thumbs up and we went back to the car.

*

Late in the afternoon, John Anthony and Shane switched again. We were sweaty and stone cold bored from the travelling. No one was talking anymore. It felt like the awful flight from Dublin to Melbourne. Only worse. We weren't being

16

fed by beautiful air hostesses every two hours, didn't have a supply of free booze and no new movies to watch. Only thing to see was grey road, gigantic desert and a withering evening sun.

In the distance, a road train came over the horizon. A big fuck-off truck carrying three huge trailers behind it. We'd heard about them and knew we were definitely in mining country now – the Pilbara.

'I'd hate to try reverse her,' Hopper said.

'It wouldn't be too bad except the blind spots,' I said.

'But I can't even drive.'

John Anthony pressed on the steering wheel and twisted around. 'You can't even drive?'

Hopper shook his head. 'Nah.'

'What? Why in the name of Christ are you coming up here with us?' John Anthony turned to me. 'Did you know?'

'I never asked.'

John Anthony hit the car door with his palm but kept his eye on the road. 'So what exactly were you going to do during your tractor driving job, Hopper?'

Hopper's face didn't change. 'I didn't know what job it was.'

'For crying out loud,' John Anthony said. 'What sort of merry band of gimps are ye?'

'It's only a fucking farm. He'll be able to pick fruit or carry pallets or something,' Shane said.

'Aye, aye, only a fucking farm—'

'John Anthony,' I interrupted him. The road train was a lot closer now. 'Don't think the road is big enough for that and us.'

The truck was coming at a good speed. I sensed the vibrations from it underneath me.

'Plenty of room,' John Anthony said.

'No,' I said, more solid this time. 'Pull in. Let it pass us. I don't think there's enough space. This is a single lane.' I could picture the exact gap between our vehicles when they met. It was too tight for comfort.

John Anthony sneered and sped up the car. The truck got louder as we advanced towards it, it towards us.

'Pull in,' I repeated.

John Anthony kept going. The truck gave us a warning honk.

'Pull in, for fuck's sake.'

The other driver flashed his lights and honked again. His front cab was yellow with neon-blue splashes.

It was too close. The sky was dusky pink.

It was too close. My body went hot.

'John Anthony,' I shouted, 'give him some space, if he swerves he'll jackknife the load.'

The lads agreed from the back and I checked my seat belt.

The lorry's headlights were on us now. I could nearly smell the diesel off its engine.

'Pull the fuck in!' I screamed at John Anthony.

He waited till the truck was less than fifty metres in front of us, its engine and cargo booming before he veered into the dirt track beside the road, losing control of the wheel, the car spinning and shuddering till it stopped, dust rising. And then there was a loud thump.

'Ye-haw,' John Anthony said and clapped his hands.

'What was that?' I asked.

'That was living, boyo. Fuck. I'm throbbing with adrenaline,' John Anthony said. He hollered again.

'No, John Anthony, what was the noise? The bang?'

The sand was settling. I got out of the car and walked around the front and covered my mouth.

John Anthony leaned out his window and shouted 'What?' over at me.

'You hit it,' I said. I bent down. It was panting and breathing shallowly. There was blood.

The car doors shut and the lads walked over to me. We peered down at it. A small kangaroo. Its side bloody and its paw twisted funny.

'You're a fucking asshole, John Anthony,' Shane said.

John Anthony had his hands on his hips.

'What were you playing at?' I asked.

'Back off. Look, I didn't mean to hit it. I didn't even see it.'

'Too busy being Mad Max.'

The kangaroo's breathing had a whistle in it. He purred every so often.

Hopper knelt down and checked its pouch. He rubbed its head. 'Can't leave him this way.' He looked at us.

Shane had his hands up. I stepped backwards. I wasn't going to mercy kill a kangaroo. Not a fucking hope.

'What do we do?' Hopper asked.

No one answered. The sky was melting to navy. I scratched my stubble.

'Since ye're all pussies,' John Anthony started.

Shane interrupted, 'You're the one who hit it.'

'I always keep a knife on me. In case things get out of hand.' John Anthony reached down into his right pocket and pulled out a black rectangular shape. He clicked a switch. A blade shot up and shone.

'Where are you going to get him? The temple? Would that go to his brain?' I asked.

'I'll go for his gullet. Best place,' John Anthony said.

'Fuck. I'm not watching this. Give me the keys. I'll drive for the next while,' Shane said. John Anthony threw the keys at him and Shane walked back to the car with his shoulders tensed. Hopper's eyes looked watery again.

'Don't be a bunch of fucking bleeding hearts. They shoot thousands of kangaroos every night here. Scourge. I'll be doing the Aussies a turn.'

John Anthony took a deep breath. He stood over the kangaroo's head and tried to measure where the blade would have to go. The evening was silent except for some birds in the distance cackling and the click of the cooling engine.

'On three,' John Anthony said and raised his knife. 'One.'

Hopper winced. He put his hand on his shoulder, his elbow jutting out.

'Two.'

Hopper did the same thing with his other hand, bracing himself. The little kangaroo was shivering.

John Anthony roared and upped his arm, ready to thrust his knife down but in that moment, the kangaroo's paws scratched at the ground and the pads of his feet found a grip. He moved out of the way of the knife and shuffled on the ground as John Anthony speared at nothing.

'Jesus,' Hopper said.

'Instinct,' I said.

'The wee gobshite,' John Anthony said.

The kangaroo was using its feet to propel itself further away from us. He staggered upwards off the ground, leaning to one side, limping. He took unsteady small steps for a moment before scampering off, hopping lopsided in the fading light.

*

We were an eternity in the car. The city, normal people, decent radio stations and streetlights seemed distant memories. This was deep outback with nothing but brush. The straightest road to nowhere that didn't twist or turn for hours. The odd railway track. The odd small village with buildings unchanged from the time the Brits ruled the Aussies and tried to 'culture' the indigenous.

I didn't know if we were friends anymore. Or what friends were. Or what fun was. I couldn't even replay riding yer one from the hostel. It was too long ago. I tried to conjure her face up, her mouth and body but I only saw the wonky kangaroo.

John Anthony slept. His snores sounded like a broken chainsaw. Shane had driven all the way nonchalantly, at a consistent speed, getting off the road if we met trucks. At Newman, we stopped at a petrol station and ate some fried chicken with salty chips. Tomato-sauced the shite out of them. It was the middle of the night when the lads switched again.

'I'm done, John Anthony,' Shane said. 'Not swapping back. We'll need to stop somewhere and sleep properly if you want me to drive again.'

'No. I'm good to do the last leg. Only a few hours in it,' John Anthony said and supped on his energy drink. The sickly sweet smell of it wafted.

Then Hopper brought it up. I don't know why the fuck he left it so late.

'I have that acid ye know.'

'What?' I said and woke out of the snooze I was going and coming from.

'Will we take it? There's another six hours in the car, like,' Hopper said.

John Anthony looked at me and sighed.

'Is it alright if we do?' I asked him. Anticipation had me wide awake now.

He stared at the road ahead, the night bursting with stars. 'How long does that shit last?'

I turned around. Shane was grinning as Hopper used the light from his phone to unwrap some tin foil.

Hopper wiped his nose with his sleeve. 'I don't have any liquid, just tabs. Should be mild enough. Three hours maybe. Five max.'

Shane dropped his straight away. 'Been driving all fucking day. I deserve this.'

I reached back to Hopper for mine. He was holding an edge of it by his fingernails.

John Anthony didn't try to stop us or go mental. He said in a calm voice, 'Do what ye want but be fit for when we get to that farm or I'll fucking kill yis.'

I put it under my tongue.

*

Stars bursting out of the night like spores from a flower like cum onto a London girl's stomach like joy out of that perfect moment of ecstasy like colours everywhere even in the black sky of colours and stars and the stars about to explode about to spread their silver onto us and paint us silver and we'd be silver in the colours of life and night time and sex would be colours green and white and gold of home and love would be a colour and it is a colour like Ireland 'cause it's all the one sky so we're really at home still we'll always be at home and I feel joy right now bursting out of the stars they are bursting out of me.

Farm work. In this beautiful, big, beautiful, massive countryside. Under these same stars. The same ones as back home.

No worries, mate.

*

The waves of the trip washed over me but they drowned Hopper. John Anthony was enjoying it more than any of us.

'It's Wolf Creek land here in Western Australia,' he said and chuckled. 'Wolfy, Wolfy with his shotgun and his laugh. Out to eat Little Red Riding Hood and backpackers. Or Dundalk gobshites.'

I looked back at Hopper. He had lost his face with the acid. His jaw was distorted and his eyes bulgy. The sweat was glistening on him.

23

'Why ye changing colours so bad? Why ye echoing at me? Yer on my side though, aren't ye? For when he comes. Ye won't give him to me. I mean me to him. Ye won't save yerselves by giving me to him?'

'Jesus, Hopper, calm down. Breathe like,' Shane said. 'This LSD is a bad batch I reckon.'

'I think Wolfy is coming straight for you, Hopper,' John Anthony said and screeched laughing.

His laugh cackled and groaned in my ears, going up and down in pitches. Stop. Sounds like the *Lord of the Flies*. Lord of the Fleas. The bed bugs. Chewing at us while we slept. Stop it. Munching on our white skin. John Anthony with antennae and eight mottled legs. A thick shelled body. Eggs hatching underneath him. More fleas.

I didn't know if I was talking out loud or not. I didn't want to panic. John Anthony stopped laughing. I looked out at the stars again. They were bringing me home. Not listening to the teasing in the car. Like my mam crying when they snubbed her at mass. When they snubbed her in Centra. In the golf club. On the street.

Mam, I'm sorry. I'm sorry for leaving you.

I'll come back to you in the sky, I'll bring you over here with me. We'll look after each other. You can make me dinners and I'll bring home money from farming to buy some nice clothes and face creams for you.

My head was roasting and the wave washed over me. I took a deep breath and tuned back in to the others.

John Anthony was talking about when the psychopath killer from the movie tricked the backpackers at the petrol station. He talked about the petrol station we had stopped at earlier in Newman. 'Aye, d'ya remember when that bit of petrol spilt onto me legs? When I got the paper towel to wipe it, there was this wee weird Aussie with a Crocodile Dundee hat watching us. I wonder if he's got a Crocodile Dundee knife?'

Hopper was looking out the back window and scratching his ears. 'Ye wouldn't give me away though?' He chanted it. Yewongehmawaydoh. Yewongehmawaydoh. Yewongehmawaydoh.

His chant reminded me of a show I'd seen with these two American chicks pretending to send psychic connections to each other. They were absolute fucking liars. Fooled no one. I started to laugh remembering them and Shane joined in though I don't know what he was laughing at. Maybe we had psychic connections?

Hopper looked even more terrified. 'Not you two as well?'

He tapped the door handle, there was a sound of it opening, a dull thud and the wind from outside as we drove. John Anthony braked hard, skidding, tyres squealing. It took me a second to realise what Hopper'd done because I thought I'd imagined it. I looked into the backseat. He was definitely gone.

'Did he just…?' I asked, my heart began raving against my chest.

'Fucking header,' John Anthony said and turned the car around.

*

Why would Hopper jump out? What was he playing at? Why would he jump out? I was being pumped with pins and needles.

They seared around my body, going in through my fingers and making my hands numb and cold. They rushed to the back of my neck, my shoulders, across my chest and spread down like a giant waterfall inside. I looked at myself and I could see the rushes lighting up where they gushed. I was glowing.

'Are you okay, man?' Shane asked. 'You've been standing there looking at your hands for ages.'

'Have I?'

'We need to find him. He's gone in past those trees.'

Hopper. How did I forget him? We called him from the road. The gum trees were bare and crooked, like skeleton arms stretched wrong. Like paws.

John Anthony roared into the nothing. 'Hopper, get your hole back now. Stop wasting my time.'

I found Shane and gripped his forearm. 'Do the trees look like that kangaroo we hit earlier?'

'What?'

'Where his paw broke? Are the events connected? Everything's connected right?'

'Ah here, you keep a hold of me okay? Till this passes. Okay?' He shouted, 'Hopper.'

We couldn't find him. Not a fuck's clue where he was. It was so dark. My feet crept beside Shane's further and further into the forest. When my body temperature felt normal again, I had a moment of clarity and let go of him.

What were we going to do? I shouted into the woods. 'Hopper. Derek. Finnegan. Dundalk. Fuckface. Come back will ya, we were only messing.'

Shane called me over. 'Don't go off like that, we'll lose you too. Stay close.'

26

'Sorry,' I said. 'Jesus, Shane, what are we going to do?'

He took a deep breath. 'I don't know but I don't think we can stay out here. Not with all this catastrophe around.'

'Catastrophe?'

'Yeah. Can't you feel it?'

'Yeah.'

I turned and shouted Hopper again. I wasn't right in the head for this. Everything was so black. Crickets blasted through the silence, millions of them clicking like flamenco dancers. I imagined the grass snakes, cobras, the Huntsman and redback spiders ganging up on me and circling around my feet. My runners grew out of shape and stamped down on the crunchy forest floor and I panicked shouting for Hopper to return before they stung or bit us all.

*

'Get back to the car,' John Anthony said. He grabbed my sleeve and dragged me. 'Get inside. You too,' he said to Shane. 'Now.'

I sat into the front seat and rubbed my fingers through my hair, rubbed my eyes and neck.

John Anthony slapped the steering wheel after he got in. 'Look lads, we haven't a lot of options here. We can't go for help because we'll forget where we were. I'm not leaving either of you two here and neither of ye are fit to drive and leave me here. Whatever way you look at it, Hopper is fucked. He's off his head and he's in the bush. He could have fallen by now or got eaten by a kangaroo. The temperature's below zero and in the morning it could go to fifty.'

He phlegmed up some spit, wound down the window and launched it onto the road. 'Nobody really knows that he's with us. The hostel people, yeah. But where will they be in a week, in two weeks? We'll be farming. Who will notice when he's gone? Who even knows where he went? Or his real name? We can't spend any more time out here. We can't. We're putting ourselves in a cunt of a situation if we do.'

I got a drumming in the pit of my stomach. Shane looked like he was nodding. A nodding dashboard dog. A bobble-head Jesus. I looked out the window, so much darkness I felt dazzled by it. Blinded by it.

'Ye can stay here and face the same end as him. Or wait for some hick Aussie cunt to get ye. Them or the heat or the wildlife. Take yer chances. But I reckon we go, hey. The three of us. If Hopper gets help, if he's not on Abo land, well it's all the better. We're not going to see him again. His brain and memory is so cheeseholed I doubt he'll remember us or this. And,' he paused and squared his shoulders up, 'it is my car.'

In the bush, the trees were enemies harbouring poisonous plants and predators. How weird it was the way the weather plummeted and soared in Australia. Making us sick. Killing our immune systems. Aboriginal lands were protected. If they caught a white man on them without a permit they could probably shoot him dead. Them poor Aboriginals, darker than Africa. I'd shoot us too. The hillbilly Australians would make us squeal like pigs if they caught us. Slash us open. Barbeque us. This place was hell. It would destroy us one way or another.

I swallowed the saliva that was flooding my mouth. John Anthony was probably right. He was probably right about Hopper not knowing us and nobody knowing him. Why did Hopper even come?

Maybe he wasn't missing, maybe he was outside the car, watching us. Sure it was his gear. He gave it to us. He was the one who'd done it before. He knew what would happen.

I looked in the rearview mirror. I craned my neck forward to look closer out the windscreen and made binoculars with my fingers to concentrate, scanned around. Hopper was there somewhere but I couldn't see him. The darkness swayed and swelled and made shapes I didn't want to figure out.

The hairs on my neck bristled.

I turned round to Shane. We didn't speak. He was grave and serious like he was about to go to a funeral. He pressed his lips and nodded. I nodded back to him and started scratching my arms.

'Drive,' I said to John Anthony.

'Really?'

My breathing was thin. The antennae were floundering on his head. I tried to blink them away. I couldn't.

'Drive.'

*

As dawn slunk in, clouds were a frothy grey and I was coming down a bit. The sky reminded me of being in Achill on a long weekend. Skagging and slurping rum on the beach. Rain drizzling. Bonfire dead. Grey Atlantic. The doom of it. The chill.

29

Shane was asleep across the back seats but his legs were twitching and feet were tapping. He probably wasn't asleep at all.

John Anthony had his godawful sunglasses on. He pulled down the window and a while later took his arm in and cursed the sun for burning his skin. 'I'll look a right bollocks now on the farm with two different coloured arms.'

I wanted to cry about the night before. I wanted to laugh at it. At the fucking state of it. Doing what we did. Mostly, I wanted to sleep but my brain raced with dark imagery when I shut my eyes. Scratching claws on windows. Me being pinned down centre stage in a circus. The ring master releasing his big cats on me. Mam bolting upright in her cosy bed, intuition stealing her from her sleep in the middle of the night.

Shane finally woke and he looked hollow. He started, 'Lads, I've been thinking, I've been thinking we need to turn round.'

John Anthony sighed. He didn't want to hear it. 'Look, let's build a bridge and get the fuck over it. If you don't want to – I'll kick you off it. Understand? Hopper was a fucking loser and it's out of our hands. We'll meet this farmer, we'll start the work, we'll have a new life. So shut it and move on.'

My eyes were burning.

We moved on.

*

We drove up the fields. We drove down them. Tall, dark-green mango trees in exact rows. Fucking zillions of them. People worked there, hurling the mangos off the trees into nets, laying them into the big blue bins. Getting paid badly by the bin. We brought the bins back to the packing sheds for the mangos to be washed, sterilised, sorted, packed, stickered, boxed, palleted. We were getting well paid by the hour.

A handful of the workers in the fields were backpackers, but a lot more were illegal Asian migrants, off the boats and on the farms. I started being able to tell the difference between Indian and Indonesian, Thai and Chinese, Taiwanese and Vietnamese – stunned that I ever thought they looked the same.

We had a supervisor, Henk, who you could talk to for a while before you noticed how plastered he was. He was mid-fifties and a big block of an Aussie. Square face and shoulders. His arms were like orange leathery logs and his chest was as broad as a fridge. On the third day, we realised he was giving us fake jobs when we were finished what we were supposed to be doing.

'Go out and change the tyres on the forklift, swap them with the one in the corner.'

'Go bring the old boxes to the recycling compartment and fold them down.'

'Sweep the yard and wash it with the power-hose.'

'See that forklift in the corner, swap the tyres to that one in the yard.'

We did them though, we kept doing them. Henk's eyebrows furrowed every time he thought up something. When we returned enthusiastic, he sighed.

'Bloody Paddies.'

But he didn't hate us. Not at all. He told us how he'd a convict great-grandfather. A thief. A Pom hater. Bushranger.

Someone who ran with the Kellys. He said the Irish were a noble, industrious race who could tell stories and warm the coldest hearts. He gazed into the distance, his eyes moist, and sunk his Irish coffee, the steam still coming off it. I couldn't look at any of the others or I'd have laughed.

A week into the job, Henk rounded up me, Shane, John Anthony and a French-Canadian called Philly.

'Right, boys. I've had enough of this. We're going on a little trip.'

Me, Shane and John Anthony walked to the courtyard and stood around the ute. Philly and Henk were behind us. Shane played with his phone.

John Anthony didn't look at us until Shane went, 'Well, John Anthony. How's things anyways?'

He swallowed and licked his bottom lip. Nodded his head. 'How ye, lads? How's it goin'?'

We both said grand and left a silence hanging in the air.

Philly was talking in broken English to Henk who said yes and no and when he got to the driver's side said, 'Bloody heck, what's wrong with you young people? Pull your head in, son.'

We hopped inside. Immediately sweat pools gathered on my forehead, the back of my neck and my balls. I pulled down the window and squirmed in my seat.

Henk started the engine, the radio blasted a local country and western station and dust rose from the ground as he booted it down the drive.

Philly asked John Anthony the time but he was ignored. He asked again.

John Anthony turned to me, 'This juck can't talk.'

32

I flinched, wanting to separate myself from John Anthony, from his comment. I told Philly the time and whispered at John Anthony, 'He can talk. Didn't you just hear him fucking talk?'

'Nah,' John Anthony said aloud.

'Because his English is poor?'

'I can't listen to that.'

I flicked a glance at the tattoos written in Irish on John Anthony's arm and shook my head. Decided against the argument with him. I looked out the window till my blood cooled.

Henk drove around the farm, which was no lie about the size of Co. Leitrim. It would take two-and-a-half hours to navigate. Perfect rows of trees. But Henk was on a mission. He slugged from his hipflask as he steered.

'Now see over there? See, past that hill, that there would be a good place to hide.'

He showed us seven 'hiding places' around the farm and by the end we got the hint. Even the French-Canadian nodded that he understood not to be coming back annoying Henk whenever our work was done. When we were done, we were done and had the rest of the shift to hide.

*

Me and Shane separated rooms and we hardly ever spoke to John Anthony. Mostly, we just worked.

But at the weekends, the Saturday evenings and Sunday full days, we skulled goon together like it was water in the Great Sandy.

After dropping the acid on the way here the flashbacks I got were scaring me. I doubt it was to do with the drugs. I would be about to sleep and I'd see poor Hopper, the ugly Dundalk head on him, his council estate life, his junkie buddies, his trying to make a new start down here. We were all chasing the dream. None of us any better than the other.

I kept hearing the sound of the tyres on the road after I told John Anthony to drive. If Hopper had been watching us, the squeal would have made him think that we were racing to get away from him. To abandon the fucker in the middle of nowhere in a country that was mostly nowhere to us.

I couldn't say it to Shane. Couldn't say it to John Anthony. Couldn't finish a sentence. Because we could never go back now. Not after three weeks of being here. Three weeks of pushing it down, deep down in the swamp of memories, down with the bullying we did in secondary school to fit in, down with the lies we told to girls to get our fingers inside them and their mouths on us – the cheating, robbing, battering, screaming, shameful stuff we'd done in the past. The swampy pit of I fucked up.

Jesus, had he family at home? Someone who loved him? Were they looking for him? Or worse, was nobody looking?

Me and Shane acted like nothing had happened but there was always this loom around me. Like a fucking hangover. It was a Hopper-shaped shadow and a sick feeling in my gut that we messed up too bad this time. In a religious way. It wouldn't be auld pairs or guards or the media giving out and making villains of us. This time God was raging. No one wants to scrap God, like. No one wants their piss soaking their face as they go into the wind. But I couldn't say anything.

No one else was saying anything. Best thing to do was forget about it. Forget it. Forget it. Forget it.

Drive up the fields. Drive down them. Have a laugh with Henk about AFL. Say Gaelic football is a superior sport. Try and shift the Lucy Liu lookalike. Save. Take pictures of the farm and throw them on Facebook, show it was kind of the same but really different from home. Look forward to the chance of the ride, the alcohol, the relaxing on the Saturday up at the farmhouse.

That's where we were when it happened. Week three over. Gathered around the big kitchen table. Half-eleven at night. Boxes of goon and mixers. Cigarettes overflowing in ashtrays. iPod blaring out dubstep. Banter. Dancing. Showing off. Stories from home. Stories from travelling Oz. Mostly backpackers but some of the younger Asians were hanging out too. John Anthony was singing 'Come Out, Ye Black and Tans' in the corner, his earring catching the light as he bounced his head around. Henk was beside me at the table, showing me pictures of dead rabbits on his phone, going on about hunting, inviting me out with him and I swear to fuck the feeling came before it even happened. I went all dizzy in my stomach and I looked over.

There he was. Standing in the doorway.

Hopper.

Just like that.

*

I said it to Shane but he said he saw nothing. Still, he was slugging quicker from his beer stubby after I mentioned it.

35

When John Anthony saw us panicking, he beckoned us over with a raise of his head.

'What's going on here, hey?' he asked. His accent cranked up with the alcohol.

I could only talk in a small voice. 'I think I saw Hopper.'

'Wha-?' John Anthony made some noises and shook his head. 'How in the name of Christ could he find us?'

I shrugged.

'What the fuck do we do or say if it was him?' Shane asked.

The dizzy was spreading in waves through my body. I wanted to bend over and spew but just looking at the ground made my head go in swirls.

Should we apologise? Should we just give him a bottle and a cigarette and go fair play, man. Dundalk's Bear Grylls.

'Look it, if he's going to get thick let him get thick,' John Anthony said and patted his right pocket. 'So where is he?'

I looked back and scanned the table and the room. He was gone. There was only the black doorway into the hall, lights off to keep mozzies away from the gaff as much as possible. I rubbed my eyes and checked again, this time getting a better look-out point.

'He was just there, wasn't he? I saw him, I'd swear on it,' I said.

The backpackers were playing Ring of Fire at the table, cheering and chanting. Someone had to skull the goblet from the middle. I grimaced at the thought of it. Some amount of shit tack alcohol mixed in it, goon, cheap rum, cheap vodka, cheap lager, cheap cider. Jungle juice. I went past them to the doorway, peered out left and right.

Darkness.

36

*

I woke with cracked lips. Stretching out of the bed, I felt round for the bottle of water I kept beside it. I'd go for the cure soon. The Sunday morning was usually a continuation of Saturday night but with beef sausages and toast instead of Doritos and pizza slices on the table.

I thought back on Hopper's appearance as I drank the water. It was him, it had to have been. Maybe I was relieved in a way. He survived, the cunt. But like John Anthony said, how did he get here? This place, hundreds of miles from a big town, wasn't exactly signposted well. All sorts of doubt started growing roots in my head. No one could find us here. Henk met us in an outhouse which had a small shop, forty-five miles away, to direct us. Hopper was on foot? No. Couldn't be.

None of it was making sense.

I tried to think about Lucy Liu, maybe have a wank over her but I was too distracted. The doubt sprouted other things.

Hopper looked spooky. Or was that the beer goggles? He looked pale and sunburnt all at once. He looked wrecked. But he was shaven. Clean.

Shane knocked on my door and I jumped. He opened it a bit.

'Are you gooning?' he asked.

'You can come in, you know. You don't have to knock.'

He stepped into the room.

I looked at him. He was the polar opposite of Hopper. Shane was the All-Irish boy, thick dark hair, clear skin that had taken a healthy tan. He was well built and looked strong, though I wasn't sure if he was decent in a scrap. We somehow never got into them because Shane was handy at talking us out of arguments. He was handy with the women back in the cities too, if he didn't get too wasted. If you saw him before he hit the booze or drugs, you'd think he was a right neat prick. He'd the look of a fella that drank litres of milk.

'What ya do after that last night?' Shane asked.

'Fuck all. Skulled a few more. Went to bed. Wasn't feeling it, ya know. Any craic?'

'Not much. Same really. Think Henk scored that German one with the birthmark. Steffi.'

I laughed. 'Really? She's hot. Old Henky's got the moves.'

'Fucking straight he does. I hope I'm that much of a player at his age. He's the right idea. Supervise a load of backpackers out in an isolated place. Be extra nice to the women. Sooner or later, one of them will get cabin fever and fall for you.'

He was smirking. A silence descended and neither of us were brave enough to break it. I picked up my phone and pretended to check the Premiership results even though I fucking hated soccer and it would take ages to load the internet.

Shane took a deep breath. 'Hey, look it, I'll just say it. Are you sure that was him last night?'

'No, I'm not a million per cent, but it was awful like him.'

'D'ya think he's holding a grudge? Because we—' Shane paused. He wouldn't say it.

I sighed. 'I don't know. Why is he here?'

'He probably had absolutely nowhere else to go.'

Australia. Nowhere country.

'I'm kind of glad in a way. Have been feeling like shite about leaving him. Do you think if we just maybe talked to him, he might forget about it?'

'Maybe he doesn't remember anyway?' Shane said and I nodded, pretending to think it was true.

'I've a bottle of Jimmy under my bed. Have been saving it but I was thinking maybe I'll give it to him instead,' I said.

'Really? Maybe we should drink it and give him one from it?'

'Jesus, that's a much better idea.'

I went to the shelf and got two cups down. They were chipped and had kittens in Christmas hats on the front. I poured us a large one each.

*

By the time we left the room, I could feel my eyes going. The world getting the edge taken off it. A lovely whiskey gauze on instead. Sure Hopper wouldn't give two continental fucks as long as we'd be his friends. When we first met him, he'd the look of desperation for people to hang out with. I knew it because I had it before and that's how I met Shane. He'd it too. We were all mad lonely here. And as long as we were sound to him and guided him around the farm, got him in with Henk who'd show him where to doss work and give him fish he caught for dinner, we'd help him out and it'd be okay.

Once he got paid, nothing would matter.

That mini brown envelope with dollars wadded into it.

That was the stuff they should be handing out in suicide wards. Big, fat, bulging cash-in-hand. I used to collect mine, smell it, pocket a fifty and give the rest to Henk to hold onto for me until the harvest was done. We had nowhere to spend it but I didn't trust the other workers. It would be so easy to rob someone's savings from their room. So so easy.

'We'll apologise too,' Shane said. 'Won't we?'

I stopped and thought about it. Sometimes apologising meant too much. Made too much out of something. But if we didn't apologise, maybe Hopper would think we thought it was no big deal. Just fucked off on you in the middle of nowhere. You buzzing off your head. Left you freaking out like a turf sack of mongrels drowning in a lake. Our half-arsed looking for you. The decision for us to go. My decision for us to go. No big deal. Yep, no big deal at all.

So we went to find him, whiskey grinning and open arms. When we walked around the farmhouse, we reminisced on some of the craic we used to have back in Melbourne. The Great Ocean Road trip we went on with this bunch of girls that knew Shane from home. They were primary school teachers and though they were straight edge, it was probably some of the best couple of days I'd had in Oz. We only brought two slabs between the six of us so I didn't bother drinking at all, nothing worse than getting the thirst with nothing to quench it. The girls would do these silly kiddy sing-along things and though you'd be smirking at them at first, mortified for them, they were infectious and you'd join in eventually. None of them were lookers but they weren't mingers either. I'd never have tried it on with them even though I was half-crazy about the three

40

of them by the time we got to Adelaide. Sad thing was, they were the kind of good girls that'd love you so much, they'd be wasting their time on someone like you, and you'd completely fucking destroy them. Use them as a leg-up and look down at the mess they'd become. I couldn't do that to those lovely eejits who sang about animals and told me stories about Cú Chulainn and said I should give them a shout when I go back home. When. Yeah right.

Shane polished off his drink and we'd only a cupful left for Hopper. I took Shane's mug, filled it and laid the empty bottle by a potted plant. When I looked up, I saw John Anthony watching me rise.

'Well. How are the boys? Yer on it?' He was sniffing and wiping his nose so much that a thought to ask him for some coke or K or whatever he was snorting raced across my mind but I knew better than that. John Anthony was one of those 'I'm anti-drugs unless I'm distributing them' type pricks.

Shane didn't know better than me. '*Sneachta*? In this fucking desert, really?'

'What?' John Anthony straightened up and put his chest out.

'D'ya want a tissue or something's what I meant, for your nose?' Shane asked hoarsely.

John Anthony took another quick sniff, blocked his nostril and forced snot out onto the ground. He did it to the other side. A true gentleman.

'Tissue me hole. What ye doing?'

'We were going to have a look for Hopper,' Shane replied.

I wanted to just walk away.

'What ye make of last night?'

I ignored the question. John Anthony's eyes were on me. I itched my fingers.

'I fucking asked yis, what ye make of last night?'

Shane toed the ground like he was waiting to break into a jig.

'What's your point, John Anthony?' I blurted.

'What's my point? What? You don't answer a question with another question.'

'What are you trying to get at? Just fucking say it,' I said.

He stared at me again. 'You've got an attitude so you do. You go around trying to be some sort of altar boy, trying to stay on the fence of life, Mr Bland Bollocks. Sucking up to Henk every fucking opportunity you get. You're nearly coming out his mouth you've crawled so far into his hole. Bullshit so it is.'

I opened my mouth to reply but John Anthony put his hand up and continued, 'My point? I was the one who was dealing with Henk. I was the one who sorted this job out and I got – not only you – but you as well Westlife – I got the pair of ye this sweet fucking number. I brought ye here. No thanks. I helped ye out. No thanks. I said nothing. Ye – not me – ye took drugs – not me – and ye decided that we'd bolt it on that clown of a lad. I—'

He raised his arms and pointed at himself, 'I did not request Hopper's company for the journey or this job. Now if he's back and he's angry, or he's feeling a little bit hard done by, well his problem's not with me, isn't that fair to say?'

He picked up the empty whiskey bottle and passed it between his hands. 'So I'll be telling wee Hopper as much as soon as I see him.'

42

'Wasn't it your fucking car though?' Shane said.

John Anthony tapped the bottle off his front teeth. 'Here, d'ya know what the worst thing is?' He waited for us to acknowledge his question. 'The worst thing is, I've seen yer bare souls. Yer off yer tits vulnerable bareness and ye are yellow, two-faced, townie shitebags. Go. Get out of my fucking sight before I break an arm on ye.'

My blood surged. I wasn't sure if I could take him, even with rage. I knew my limitations. Back in Leaving Cert, a couple of us fell out with a few lads from the next village over. I didn't know if it was to do with a girl or an eighth or a fucking football match. A scrap was arranged. Supposed to be down the tracks on the Friday after school. It was fairly stupid, handbags stuff. We fucked off and went to the chipper after. No one was hurt. But later that evening, I went smoking with one of the lads and walked back home stoned. A couple of the pricks from the other village were at the short cut to my house. I don't think they were lying in wait or anything, they were just having underage cans off the street. So I'd a choice to make and I went for it. I kept walking down the short cut. They jumped me from behind. Fucking stamped all over me. It was embarrassing. I cried. And it wasn't for long either, two or three minutes I'd say. But when a couple of lads are leathering ya, it can feel like some eternity. I hadn't fought back. I lay down and took the beating.

When they left, I stayed there for a good length just looking at the sky. It was cloudy. My teeth were sharp and I couldn't stop tonguing them. The auld lady was going to have a calf. She'd be making a pure scene, calling cops, fussing. That's what I thought about. I got up and went home. Snuck in the back door. Washed meself. Went to bed.

I took a couple of deep breaths and looked at John Anthony's big ugly fists.

'Come on, Shane,' I said. 'Let's leave this cunt to it.'

*

It was hard to sleep. The bed was too stiff. The pillow was too soft. It was too hot with a sheet over me. It was too cold without it. Could hear a mosquito whine around my room. His wings flapping four hundred beats per minute. Him looking for blood to suckle. My fucking blood. I turned on my belly to ignore it. I turned back. I punched the pillow and folded it under my neck.

What could John Anthony even say to Hopper?

The truth. With his spin on it. Everyone's version of the truth comes with some persuasion of their own views. I mean, me and Shane could tell him the truth too, from our slant. Like we didn't want to go but it was scary out in the bush. We didn't know what'd happen. We were fucking tripping as well. And it was a split-second decision. John Anthony had been putting the pressure on.

The truth is never really the truth.

I looked out the window. Everyone's light was off in the courtyard but the TV that hung from the wall at the smoking area was on, glowing blue and yellow. I wanted it to make a storm out. Pour torrential rain. Howling winds and forked lightning. Muck everywhere. Or someone to just have a shower in the communal bathroom. Listen to them wash. Soap up. Water dripping off them, echoing as they were getting clean. Or to be swimming. Like back in Group 1, training in lanes and they said I was good. Galas around the country. Community Games. Green goggles over my eyes, chlorine in my throat and be pushing myself, butterfly stroke. Ready for the tumble turn. Ready to be upside down and to propel myself from the wall towards the finish of the race. After the turn, head above water. Adrenaline. The noises, the whistles, the spectators. The beats of the other swimmers' limbs under water. The beautiful taste of air.

Or a shag.

The Londoner and the primary school teachers and the Thai girls and me. I closed my eyes and thought about all of them, trying to get hard but a mozzie got me. Right on the shin. I cursed it for being the only thing to suck on me in a long while and scratched the bite brutally.

Fuck.

I wanted something badly and I didn't know what it was. I tried to sleep again and kept sighing. Maybe another drink would help. Or reading? I had a book somewhere. I pulled my rucksack from under my bed. Normally, we had to be on the fields for 5.30 a.m. but every Monday morning Henk drove to the outhouse and a couple of the girls went with him to sort out the big shop, so I wouldn't get caught if I was late. I just wanted a bit of sleep after the headfuck of a weekend. I spilled the rucksack on the ground and saw the green shamrock pin my mother had packed as a good luck charm. Euro coins trickled across the floor and when I picked them up, they looked so strange and small in my hand. I rubbed the map at the back of them and calmed. The alloys in the coin heating. Metal in the air.

Like most things in life, problems are usually solvable by the simplest solutions. I put the coins back into my rucksack and kicked it under the bed.

Simple. We'd have to find Hopper before John Anthony did. We'd blame John Anthony for everything.

*

I scanned the house for Hopper the next morning. Everyone was in grabbing a quick brekkie. Black & Gold cornflakes, bread and loads of mangos. Mango chutney. Mango yogurt. Mango juice. I didn't like the taste of them. I buttered a slice of toast and walked around the kitchen. There was lots of scraping of plates and slurping of coffee and chat about the day ahead. I checked outside in the smoking area and behind the house. No sign. Henk wouldn't be around for a few hours so I couldn't ask if he'd picked up another Irish lad yet.

I said hello to Shane when he walked in bleary-eyed and his hair arseways from bed. He was the worst morning person I'd ever met, going into four weeks in the job he still struggled to wake up. He grabbed a mango juice and gulped it down.

'Story?' he asked and wiped his mouth and chin.

'Keep an eye out for Hopper won't ya, I think we need to talk to him before John Anthony.'

'Why?'

'Because we need to get to him first. Hopper's not that stable. I'm not sure I want to be on his bad side. If we get to him before John Anthony,' I said and took a bite of my toast.

'We can blame John Anthony?'

I stopped chewing. 'Yeah. We can tell him it wasn't us. He'll believe us over him anyways.'

The noise started dwindling and people went out to work. I was happy now that Shane was on side, even if there was no sign of Hopper. I spent my whole shift checking for him at the different areas and when I'd to collect bins, I asked the backpackers and workers if they'd seen the new Irish guy, kind of thin, brownish hair, gold rings, a bit smelly-looking, but none of them had.

Henk returned at afternoon smoko. The Aussies called all breaks smokos, even if they didn't smoke on them. Him and the girls were unpacking the big shop.

'How's me boy?' Henk asked, whacked me on the back and pulled me in for a bear hug.

The rum was coming out through him with the sweat.

'Hi, Henk,' I said, tearing away. 'Had a good time of it?'

He swept the room with his hand. 'These ladies are exquisite company.'

Some of the girls smirked and I noticed one of them looking at me, not smirking, just eyeing me.

'Henk, I got a question for you. Is there a new Irish lad here today? Did you get him over the weekend? Just he's our friend from Perth and we'd like to show him around.'

'New Irish bloke, nope. Got enough of a handful with you three. There is a Sheila,' he paused and pointed at the starey chick. 'Fiona, here, say g'day to your kinsman.'

'I know you,' is all she said and she eyeballed me.

Terror rippled through me. Had I rode her?

'I know you from back home.'

Oh fuck. Worse again.

'Well, that's grand. Welcome to Mangopolis. So Henk, I think that a new Irishman is here.' I turned my back on her while I spoke to Henk. Didn't have time for being the *Céad Míle Fáilte* committee right now. Though she was behind me, she was still fucking boring through me with a look.

'No. No more Irish. You three men and the little lady.' Henk laughed.

Maybe he thought Hopper was foreign because of his accent. 'Henk, you sure? Has a new lad started, small, lean, browny hair?'

'No, boy. I bloody said no. Didn't I? I'll never understand the need for relentless questions I get from you lot. You young people are worse than feeding lorikeets. Now out to work, son, smoko is over.'

*

'Wait, wait!' Fiona shouted after me as I jogged back to my machine.

The afternoon was heavy with heat. I wiped my forehead with the bottom of my t-shirt giving Fiona a flash of my white stomach.

'What ya want?'

'I know you.'

'Yeah, yeah. So you keep reminding me.'

Her body was slim. Her fair hair was to her shoulders. She'd a small scar in a broken circle on her cheek and her eyes were sparkling blue in the sun. She put her hand on my arm. I looked at it.

'You're the builder's son, yeah? My dad worked for your dad.'

My stomach sank. 'Look, Fiona or whatever your name is, I'm not my father. I didn't mean for people to lose their jobs and homes. Don't drag that shit halfway across the world.' I pushed her hand away.

'No, wait,' she said and put her hand on my shoulder this time. 'It doesn't matter, what happened back there. Everyone went mad. Everyone. The whole country. I know your mam. She used to visit the nursing home, even after she quit, even when yer family got really really – with the developments and all...' She trailed off. 'It was nice of her though. My gran is in there. Alzheimer's. Completely gone in the head. Her memories. She liked your mother. I love my granny. Isn't it mad the two of us are here in Western Australia, instead of the West of Ireland? The times, eh?'

I got pangs. She spoke like home and looked like home even though she had a good tan. She'd that Irish girl thing, the friendliness radiating off her.

'Here, fuck off with your giant speech. I've got stuff to do.' I climbed into my tractor.

*

Yer one had put Mam in my head over Hopper. That guilt was different. Mam's emails saying 'Skype soon, pet?' or 'Will you send on your new number?' or 'Let us know you're okay.' I loved her, but I couldn't give her an inch or she'd be hassling me the whole time. Mam and her worrying. It never ended.

49

I remember when she used to come home from the nursing home. This was well before the Boom. I was in primary school. She always smelt of hospital and boiled food.

She left the job when we moved into the new house. It was a five bed, had a Jacuzzi, a bar, a games room and a basketball court just for me, which I only played in once ever with my friends. She acquired her posh accent.

There'd be no point ringing her now, for a while anyway until this Hopper mess was sorted, because she'd only get it out of me. She could pick up what was bothering me just from my voice and interrogate the shite out of me until she knew what was going on.

I drove up the fields. I drove down the fields. I looked out for Hopper.

At the end of the shift, Fiona was waiting.

'You'd want to have some manners, young fella,' she said to me.

'Long day. Not interested.' I waved her off and walked towards my room. I needed a scrubbing and some food.

She followed. 'Look, I don't know anyone here, except you, and I don't really know you but I know your mother is nice and so there's a good chance you are.'

'Cromwell's auld lady was probably sound too.'

She stalled. Dust rose from the ground. 'Did you just compare yourself to Oliver Cromwell?' she asked.

I paused and looked at her. Her lips were plump. Her nose was a bit uneven. I could smell her ice cream perfume and I tried to keep my eyes from the flesh of her legs under her denim shorts.

'I suppose I did, yeah.'

'Fuck off so,' she said and walked away from me.

I looked back at her and smirked.

*

She was sitting in the courtyard, wearing a hoodie and scratching away at a sketchbook when I'd finished my dinner. The TV showed some shite American comedy, the actors had big white smiles and delivered punchlines to fake recorded laughter.

Fiona didn't say anything when she saw me coming but nudged her head in acknowledgment before she went back to her drawing.

'You alright?' I asked.

She chuckled but didn't look at me. 'Why wouldn't I be?'

I put my hands in my pockets. 'Dunno.' I went to look over her shoulder but she closed the book before I could investigate.

My fingers found lint at the bottom of my pockets. I rolled it around, feeling awkward as fuck. 'Earlier – I – you caught me at a bad time.'

'You're grand. Whatever.' She eyed me and something about the way she looked gave me that tremor again.

'Don't be like that. Fiona, wasn't it?'

She nodded.

I said, 'Sometimes,' and stopped. I sighed. I didn't really want to tell her but knew that I had to. She'd stay sulking otherwise. 'Sometimes when home is brought up, I go funny. The way things went with the buildings.'

'You're grand,' she said and got up to leave.

I put my hand out to stop her. The cloth of her hoodie

was thin but fleecy. 'No, wait. Stay where you are.'

She didn't move.

'Stay,' I said and nodded. 'Will you stay with me?'

She didn't move.

I sat down and she sighed before going back on her seat. When she was settled, I asked, 'What's your surname anyway? And which part of town are you from? Did things work out okay for your father? Are you okay? Are things okay for ya here? Your room and that? The work?' My voice was gone fast. I gulped. 'I'm sorry.'

She touched her neck and pursed her lips. She wasn't listening to me. 'I'd love a decent cup of tea.'

I laughed. 'That's Shane's chat up line, I'll warn ya now. "I've Irish teabags and a pack of condoms." It works some of the time too.'

'And does he?'

'Does he what?'

'Have the teabags?'

'Does he fuck.'

*

We sat for hours that passed like the snapping of a finger, small talking about nothing much, joking over even less and drinking the piss tea from the kitchen.

She checked her watch. 'Damn. I gotta head to bed, not used to this place or getting up early.'

I nodded and dragged myself away from her. 'Sound.'

She shouted at me as I walked down the courtyard. 'I'll see you soon?'

I gave her a wave yes.

'*Oíche mhaith*,' she said.

'*Oíche mhaith*,' I repeated and plunged my hands in my pockets again.

I tried to remember exactly the sound and look of her laugh, to stamp it onto my brain and I was half-smiling as I went to sleep.

*

Next day, I began hounding Henk and the workers about whether a new Irish lad had started and Fiona started hounding me at the breaks and end of shift.

She latched onto me.

I sometimes wasn't sure if she had a thing for me or Shane. Obviously, like all the women, she asked me if he was single. Shane the Superstar. He always won out so I didn't really compete.

'Yeah, he's single. Go for it,' I said in a flat voice.

'I actually might,' she said and looked cheerful.

But I knew she liked being around me. She came over to me first, she spoke to me first, she checked things with me first. Maybe it was that we were both from Mayo and Shane was that touch exotic, alien even, being a Galwegian.

But it was more than that. She was drawn to me.

It had been so long since we'd a girl as a friend that one of us wasn't deliberately trying to hop.

Fiona said mad stuff like, 'you show people how to treat you.' Her philosophies made me laugh and made me think while I was on my own, driving.

I found her more refreshing than any of the people I'd met on the farm. More than anyone I'd met in Australia really. But I'd never say that to her. Especially if she was going to try Shane. Wasn't going buttering her up for him to eat. Fuck off. But still I hung around for her or she hung around for me.

She was making the days go faster.

*

Me and Shane walked to the courtyard and heard some shouts. We quickened our pace and saw John Anthony, Henk and an Indonesian worker in a circle arguing. We got close enough to hear the action without getting involved in it.

'Henk, believe me,' John Anthony said. 'This article doesn't know his arse from his elbow.'

'He try kill me.'

John Anthony made some high pitched sounds and sighed. 'He wasn't working. He was lazing in that tree. I didn't think the branch would break.'

Henk stopped him. 'Shut your beak, boy. This is the third complaint. Intimidation. Do you know how much a new cherry-picker would cost me?'

I beamed at Shane.

John Anthony was clasping his hands in a begging way. 'They needed a shaking, Henk, that's all. You can't have an eye on everyone and this crew were doing no work. I wasn't trying to hurt them or make them fall off the tree. They were up there chattering. Bunch of monkeys.'

'Tractor hit tree. Me in branch. He shout. Branch crack. He laugh. He say, up, up, fuck up you work now. You work for me.' The Indonesian mimed the events as he spoke them.

'Alright, alright, son. I follow. You can go,' Henk said and pointed towards the farmhouse. 'And you? We'll see how you like being the one in the trees.'

John Anthony took a step back, his mouth wide open. 'What?'

'You heard me, boy. You're on a week's suspension from driving. You'll be picking the fruit instead.' Henk took a notebook out of his back pocket and scribbled something. Then he noticed us and beckoned us over.

John Anthony stamped on a passing cockroach. Me and Shane edged over to them.

'Which one of you is out near the nursery?' Henk asked.

Shane coughed. 'Me. I am.'

'Show this boy out to the fields tomorrow and allocate trees.'

Shane pressed his lips.

'What? Henk? You can't be fucking serious with me?' John Anthony asked with his arms out wide.

'Boy, you haven't seen the half of it. Shane, I want you to report back to me. No slacking off. On my farm, we practice empathy, it's how we keep a system like this running.'

John Anthony took a deep breath and blew it out. He turned and said, 'Fucking drunk cunt.'

Henk caught him by the neck. 'What was that?'

John Anthony squealed. 'Nothing.'

Henk seized him tighter. 'Better be nothing, boy.' He shoved him away.

John Anthony skulked off.

Shane was smiling but he'd his hands in his pockets and was looking at the ground. I knew from hanging around with him that he was nervous.

I struggled not to burst out laughing, but as soon as John Anthony was out of sight, I exploded. 'That'll learn him.'

Henk whipped out his hipflask and offered us both a slug. 'He has a fucking attitude, that boy. I'm doing him a bloody favour.'

*

On the Friday lunch break Fiona told me how she was looking forward to the Saturday night. I think we hyped it a bit too much but she said this wasn't the first farm she'd been on. She'd briefly done pumpkins in Victoria and worked in a garlic factory. She said she'd already got the second visa sorted.

'Are you stone mental?' I asked. 'Why are you here?'

'I kind of like the work. The picking. As long as there is work. In Ireland I was a boring letting agent stuck in an office, complaining about the shite they were complaining about on the radio. Everyone fucking complaining. Then with the crash, I'd nothing and spent the days applying for jobs and trying not to be more depressed. Here, I'm outside, chatting to loads of new people. Getting a tan. Getting some cash. It's a great life.'

'I can ask Henk to get you put in the packing sheds, better pay.'

'Ah, no, I'm okay for money now. Have saved. I prefer picking.'

'What about the bites?' I often saw the pickers comparing their red swellings on smokos.

Fiona smiled. 'From the green tree ants? The weaver ants? They're amazing. You know how they got no bees here in this part of the world? So the ants pollinate the mango trees. They work together in a colony, building up to like a hundred and fifty nests between trees, recognizing each other by smell and eating all the pest insects.'

I whistled and drew a circle around my temple with my finger. Crazy lady. How did she even know that? And the humidity outside was shocking too. Though our tractors were old and shite, we'd get some breeze driving back after dropping off the fruit.

'Days off in these isolated places, they're worse than any of the rag weeks I've been to,' she said. 'Everyone goes wrong, like.'

John Anthony was sniffing when he saw her with us. We'd been staying out of his path all week since he got suspended.

He sometimes smoked at work and he made these elaborate inhalations and talked while smoke was coming out of his mouth. The more I thought about or looked at John Anthony, the more certain I was that I despised him. He stood beside Fiona and asked me who she was.

'I'm right here, ask me yourself,' she said.

He didn't make eye contact, he went red and said, 'So who are you?'

She told him her name and where she was from and asked him where he was from and asked him if he knew a list of people that she knew from Donegal. A customary thing but she was gone to town on it. She was asking him about people that she didn't even know the name of, just they were from Buncrana or Gweedore or Letterkenny or had red hair or she'd met them in the Blue Campsite at Oxegen and they were sound.

'I didn't say I was the Donegal census collector.'

Shane stood and checked his wrist. 'Well look at the time, isn't someone supposed to be up a tree?'

'You're a wee ballbag,' John Anthony said.

Fiona gave him a huff. 'Shouldn't talk like that.'

John Anthony's eyes opened wide. He glanced at her before jumping his view between me and Shane. 'Oh look it, another fan for ye. Is she sucking Henk off too?'

Fiona looked stunned. Her neck and cheeks flushed.

'Apologise,' I warned John Anthony.

'Hah,' he said. 'Have her. Sometimes I'm ashamed to be Irish when I see the likes of ye.'

He quenched his cigarette by crushing it into the ground and hocked a good ball of spit.

'Yuck,' Fiona said and he did it again, this time it landed close to her feet.

Me and Shane shouted at John Anthony but he bulldozed in between us to walk to his field.

'My tree awaits.'

I had to hold Shane back from going after him. But he wasn't putting up much resistance. It was more for Fiona's benefit. He crouched down beside her and asked if she was okay.

'I knew I got a bad vibe from him. Was just playing around with the Donegal thing.'

'It's not your fault. He's a shithead. Hope he gets gate from here soon.'

'Actually, no,' she said and pushed herself off the ground. She stomped down after John Anthony. I couldn't help the grin that came on my face watching her. Hands on hips. Calling him to turn round. Her about a quarter of his size.

We watched as they had an exchange. She kept her hands on her hips and he had his arms folded. She nodded her head and waved her palm over to where we were and John Anthony put his hands in his pockets.

He said something back to her.

'Wasn't that Pirate Queen from round yer parts?' Shane asked me.

I nodded.

'D'ya think she's a descendent?'

I laughed and kept watching as John Anthony put his head down and offered his hand out to Fiona. She let it hang for a moment and shook it. She gave him a closed mouthed smile and strolled back to us. John Anthony went out of sight down the fields.

Shane woo-hooed her. 'Did you get that ape to apologise?'

She shrugged. 'Ara, he's probably not the worst.'

Shane bit on his bottom lip looking at her. She curled her hair behind her ear. I tried not to sigh.

'So, is there any more Irish here or just ye guys?' she asked.

'Just us really,' I answered.

She nodded. 'You know what the Aussies say about us? They say we're good workers but we just disappear. One day, on site, the next, vanished. I've fucked off from a few places myself to be honest.' She started tracing letters and shapes into the red dirt. 'So who's Hopper anyway?'

Me and Shane traded a glance.

'Why?' Shane asked.

'Because ye keep talking about him and you, you're always inspecting the place as if there's snipers about. A few days ago I would have thought you were special but now I realise it's because you're looking for something. Someone. Who is he?'

Shane put his hands in his pockets. I looked at the holy medal on the chain around Fiona's neck. St. Christopher. When you're travelling, you make gut judgements on people. Like Shane, my gut said – he's one of your own. But John Anthony, my gut said – kind of a wanker but had something we needed. Fiona – one of your own but try not to fuck her or fuck her over.

'Hopper's this fella we're waiting for. I thought he was here last weekend but haven't seen him since,' I said. 'We're waiting for him to show again.'

'I thought ye were going to give me a big story about some madness that had happened.'

Me and Shane looked at each other.

The sun was on the rise over the mango fields and we'd only another five hours of work left.

*

Henk asked me to help him with a job at the sheds. We'd to throw out an old machine and install a new one. They had engineers on site and I asked why couldn't one of them do it?

'Flaming heck, here we go again with the questions.'

After the machine was in and operational and noisy as fuck when turned on, and we were sweating like absolute lunatics, Henk said we were going to the river to cool off.

I grinned. That had been another fake job so he could get me out fishing with him. We went in the ute. On the ground of the passenger seat, he had left a five litre bottle of water and an esky filled with tinnies.

'Don't be shy, son. Grab us a beer.'

I stuck my hand in the icy water and passed one to Henk. He opened it with his teeth and sang while he drove. It was only a dirt road so it didn't matter that he wasn't going straight. The river was half an hour from the packing sheds which were twenty minutes away from the farmhouse. He had shown it to us through the window in our first week but we hadn't got out to explore it.

'Over there on the right is the river, ace place to hide.'

But now, I got to see it up close. It was a vision of Australia. Shaded swamp, flies buzzing, birds, virgin grasses, big heavy-leafed trees, sun lighting the water, the fields. A smell of earth and riverbank and forest. The sky endless blue.

Henk rubbed my head and said, 'Now, son, get the spare rod, bring the esky over and let's take a breather.'

*

We caught seven flatheads. Henk thought they were shite and was disappointed with them but I was buzzing from it. They were so much heavier than they looked. Plus I had got fairly merry at the river and was in love with the whole situation. Dossing, fishing, boozing. A perfect afternoon. Henk told me about Strayan waters and some of the lunkers he'd had in his time. Barramundi. Giant trevally. A baby speartooth shark that he released again, because the nipper was 'endangered'.

Henk was even more emotional when he told me about a half-brother in Darwin who he'd reconnected with over the last three years after the man survived skin cancer. 'Good can always come of bad, son.' He also had a daughter who worked in Brisbane. His grandson was 'a little galah' but he'd die and bloody commit mass murder for the kid if he had to. Henk loved his grand statements and gestures. When he asked me about my family and my Australia, I fobbed him off by bringing the subject back to the great outdoors.

'Kakadu, that's the place to go, son,' he said and took a gulp. 'Before you leave, make sure to spend some time there. You gotta see the billabongs in the Banggerreng.'

I just nodded along and pretended to know what he was on about.

'I get homesick for Ireland,' he said later when we were going into our sixth tin and the evening breeze came.

'Did you live there before?'

'Nope. But it's in me blood. When I hear your talking, you and the boys, I pine for my ancestors.'

I couldn't brood over ancestry because the mozzies were out at dusk and they loved my Irish blood as well. I slapped my arms and face and legs constantly, tormented. They were even going for my eyeballs. Henk eventually noticed this and said we'd get some grub in and would barbeque our catch the next evening. I drowsed in the ute the whole way back. Instead of dinner, I had two slices of bread and went to bed early. The fish would be a treat tomorrow.

The sleep in, the feast, Fiona's first piss up with us. The weekend was shaping itself nicely. If we could fucking find Hopper, I'd go as far to say I was beginning to enjoy this mango life.

*

Shane knocked hard on my room door in the morning. He came in and his cheek was puffy, the start of a black eye was forming.

'Here, where were ya last night?' Shane demanded.

'I was out fishing with Henk and went for an early kip. What happened to your face?' I sat upright in the bed and could see swells on my own skin from the mosquitos.

'John Anthony hit me.'

'Were ye drinking?'

'No, it was after work. He was hanging around, waiting and when he saw me alone he cornered me.'

'Why?'

Shane sat at the end of my bed. He opened the curtain and a blinding white ray came through the window. He closed it again. 'He said you and me were asking for it. That we were plotting against him since we got here. Making Henk hate him. Making the new women hate him. He said he'd find you later.'

Who the fuck did John Anthony think he was?

Another knock at the door.

'Who's there?' I shouted towards it, angry, thinking it was him.

'It's Fiona. I'm coming in,' she said and let herself inside.

She was holding two plastic bags filled with silver goon pouches and a Tayto six pack. Shane brightened up as she pulled the crisps out.

'Where d'ya get these?'

'My friend gave them to me before he went back home a few weeks ago. I've been kind of saving them for other Irish people. To share the joy. No one else would appreciate them.'

I got out of bed in my jocks and grabbed her head and kissed it. 'You're a legend, Fiona.' I took a pack and had a look at the cover before opening. I sniffed inside and smelt teenage discos, lunchtimes during Junior Cert, buses home from galas, hangover porn days. I ate the crisps slowly, letting them melt on my tongue.

'What happened your eye?' Fiona lifted Shane's chin towards the light and inspected him. 'Did he catch ya with a ring or something?'

'Yeah. John Anthony, you know, that idiot Nordie from yesterday.'

Fiona took the kitten Christmas cups off the shelf and poured me and Shane some white goon. She took a plastic cup out of the bag and poured herself one.

'Right lads, there's something ye're not telling me. Let's have it. If we're friends, we're friends. If not, I'll go now and ye can enjoy yer drink and we'll leave it at that.'

We were awkard for a moment but I took a mouthful. And once I started it all came tumbling out. We went back to the hostel where we met Hopper, even told her his backstory. She sat there and didn't react. She poured us another goon each.

'It's a bad act,' she said. 'To be honest, it's a fucking very bad act. But I don't understand. How did he get to here? Why haven't you seen him since?'

I said I didn't know. It was borderline impossible.

Shane said he had three whole weeks to walk it. Maybe he was a power walker. We laughed nervously. It wasn't even funny.

'Maybe he's a ghost?' Fiona said. Then none of us said anything for a while.

*

Henk had the barbie going at 6 p.m., we were well on it at that stage. Smoke came off the flathead on the griddle. On the side tray were some cut-up tomatoes, onions and lettuce and on the table beside the barbeque were loaves of bread, slabs of cheese, sliced mangos and potato salad.

Fiona and Shane had been flirting to no end in my room and I was expecting them to at least shift before dinner was eaten.

We were standing around the TV waiting for the food to cook. Shane was telling Fiona about underage county finals he'd won, cars he had souped up during the Boom and the famous places he'd been in Australia. She seemed impressed.

'I'd have been nowhere except the pub,' I said, 'if it wasn't for Lonely Planet over here.'

Shane smirked at me and I left them to it.

I went by Henk and asked him if he needed help. He declined and clinked my cup with his schooner. No sign of Hopper, which I'd come to expect though I kept looking for him. No sign of John Anthony either. Good job. Fucking gobshite.

The hot Asian chick said hi to me and giggled. I winked at her. Philly was by the smoking area and I gave him an elaborate '*bonsoir*,' and bowed at him. He put his hand up.

Fiona and Shane grabbed us seats at the round table. She pointed at a few white lads and asked if any of them were Hopper. We said she'd know him if she saw him. Henk announced that the food was ready. There was a big upsurge with lots of bustle and laughter as a queue formed. Henk threw three big chunks of fish on my paper plate and joked with me.

When we got back to the table, Fiona asked, 'Did ye ever eat raw fish?'

'Nah,' I said and Shane shook his head. 'Is it nice?'

'It's an acquired taste, I suppose.'

Someone got their iPod and blasted out *Bob Marley's Greatest Hits*. I rubbed my belly and looked at the stunning orangey-pink of the sunset and at the different people around me, eating, talking, chilling out.

This time of year in Ireland. Frost. Rain. Always. Winds that bit. People as grey as the sky. Wearing 700 layers of clothes but still having runny noses and chattering teeth. Shit closing down, companies laying off, everyone signing on, stuff half finished, half falling apart, scandals. Politicians. Bankers. Builders. I wondered if my auld lad had sorted his life out, had got past the shame of the bankruptcy. And Mam. Maybe I would give her a call tomorrow. I squeezed some more white from the goon pouch into my cup. Maybe I'd talk to both of them this time.

'What we going to do about John Anthony?' Shane asked when Fiona went to get another portion of potato salad.

'What do you mean?'

'He can't be hitting us and threatening us. We have to show him he's not the fucking boss of us.'

I sat and stared at Shane, the black eye was well on its way, greenish-blue underneath and a fatter eyelid than the other.

'We should jump him,' Shane said. 'He's not about so he's either in his room or he's scoring. And I doubt it's the latter, the way he speaks to women. The two of us could take him.'

Fiona was zig-zagging and hello-ing her way back to the table.

'Okay. But she doesn't need to know. She'll conk soon, she's a wreck. Wait till she goes to bed. Then we get him,' I said and we changed the subject before Fiona sat down.

We'd have to go for it now, together. Otherwise John Anthony'd hammer me if he got me on my own.

*

As predicted, Fiona crashed. About half an hour after dinner, we carried her down to her dorm. She tried to lob the gob on Shane before we put the bedclothes over her fully-dressed body.

She gazed with drunken amour. 'D'ya not want to? I do. That's a big deal for me. A really big deal.' She hiccupped.

'Not tonight, when you're sober we'll talk,' Shane said and kissed her hair gently.

'Ya dashing bastard,' I said.

Fiona was mumbling and said to wake her in a while, before we went to the nightclub and we laughed. I took off her sandals and put them by her bed. We switched the light off and left.

Outside her room, we hatched a plan as we drank.

'We lure him out,' I said. Shane nodded. 'If I knock on his door and provoke him, he'll come at me. You have to be ready for him.'

I'd wait. Plant one on him unexpected. Shane would join until we got him on the ground.

'We kick the fuck out of him,' Shane said.

'If he fucking ever, ever messes with us again…' I noticed how slurred my words were coming out.

'Or Fiona,' Shane said.

'If he fucking ever, ever messes with us or Fiona again, he's going to be – yeah.'

Shane agreed.

'Another drink?' I pressed the goon pump and filled our cups. I needed the courage.

'Cheers.'

*

We went down the lane to where John Anthony's room was. His was the only light on in the row. At the window, through a crack in the curtain, we saw he had his laptop open. He dipped into a bag of popcorn and shoved a fistful into his mouth. We couldn't see what he was watching but from the noise that was leaking it was definitely a GAA game. Nothing sounded like Croke Park, the commentators and the crowd.

Shane paused, 'Is it All-Ireland time again?'

I looked at his face to see if he was genuine. His eyes were wide and he was frozen with the question.

'Shane, the All-Ireland was almost two months ago, we were in Perth watching it. In Northbridge, remember? The day after we beat the Aussies in the rugby?'

Shane blinked for a second and shook his head. 'Oh yeah. Yeah, course I remember. Dublin. Jesus, my brain. Mad.'

'Okay, focus. Are you ready for this?'

'Are you?'

I paused. 'Not really. Here, piss me off.'

'What?'

'Piss me off,' I said and tugged him away from the door. He pushed my arm. 'What ya mean?'

'I need to get more psyched. Make me mad.'

Shane looked blank for a second. 'She likes you.'

'What?'

'She likes you. She does. But she wants me.'

I sniffed. He stared at me.

'She wants me. My cock.'

I ground my teeth.

'You ready?' Shane asked.

'Yeah, let's go.'

He rapped on John Anthony's door. I was leaning back into the wall behind me to be inconspicuous, my breath sped up and my legs went heavy with dread and rush over what we were about to do.

*

You can plan things all you want in life, down to the perfect last detail and still it won't turn out the way you expected.

Yeah John Anthony came to the door and his head turned sideways a bit when Shane threatened him. Yeah I jumped at him from the other side and landed a thump onto him. But it didn't knock him down, it only pushed him away. He stood and for a moment he was still. Then he erupted. He wrestled me to the ground and belted me in the head at least six times with his quick fists. Blood gushed out my nose.

Shane launched on top of him, but that only made John Anthony's weight crush me even more and clatter the back of my head against the ground, completely stunning me. I didn't see stars like in them old cartoons, I saw flashing glaring white lines coming off every shape distinguishable in front of me. I groaned but couldn't move. I tried to feel the ground under my palms and push myself up but I couldn't. I don't know how long it took for me to stop seeing white-hot lights everywhere.

It finally faded and I turned and saw Shane was on the ground too, further away. I saw John Anthony's knee rising in the outside light and coming down. Shane was sputtering and moaning. Where was everyone? Had they not heard the noise? I drifted away from Shane's cries and the GAA inside John Anthony's room, my hearing went down the lane, back to the main farmhouse where the iPod blared a strumming guitar. The mango farm choir doing a group sing-along. Fucking Wonderwall by Oasis. Behind that all the insects whirring and buzzing, the nocturnal birds hooting, the possums and crickets and frogs and geckos. I zoned back in. John Anthony kicked Shane in the head, in the side, in the stomach. Spit was exploding from his mouth as he shouted down at him. I sat and wobbled upright.

The lyrics of Wonderwall drowned my headspace.

Then John Anthony's voice came into my mind, menacing but clear, 'I always keep a knife in my pocket. In case things get out of hand.'

I stumbled towards him. He was baring his teeth and something human was gone from his eyes as he pounded Shane, he was pure beast.

I composed myself and reached for his pocket, hoping with all my life, hoping. God please God, Jesus, Mary the Virgin, St. Patrick, Zacchaeus, fucking all of ye up there, help me. I stuck my hand in, grabbed the knife from it and flicked the blade.

He was already turning, acknowledging what was happening, I had to go quick.

The blade. My hand was shaking. I drove it towards him. His neck.

I plunged it in.

The side of his neck.

My face got splattered by his blood, hot and pumping out of him.

He held his neck, the handle of the knife and fell in slow motion to the ground. Shane was looking up at me.

John Anthony stayed down. He gurgled.

He stopped making noise. I didn't move. I couldn't.

'Oh holy fuck,' Shane said. 'Oh holy fucking fuck.'

*

'I'm going to get Henk, okay. Stay, okay?' Shane said.

I did what I was told.

I looked at John Anthony. He was dead. I killed him.

Henk came striding down the path with Shane limp-running beside him.

'He's dead. I killed him,' I said to Henk.

Henk made some sounds and put his hands on his hips and ran his fingers through his hair. He took a swig out of the hipflask in his breast pocket.

He said, 'Get the ute, now,' to Shane and threw keys at him. Shane shuffled back the lane.

Henk touched John Anthony's forehead and said, 'You young people. I'll never understand it. You could be out hogging or shooting or spearfishing but instead you attack each other.'

Rest of it was sketchy. I couldn't keep with it.

Wiping my face. Blood. Headlights, ute, Shane, driver's door shut, Shane squeezes my shoulder, heave, we heave John Anthony into the back, insects crawling on the headlights, crawling on him, Shane says he'll clean, go, go will ye.

Henk driving, Shane in the rearview mirror, a blanket or something, farmhouse slipping away into the distance, fucking Wonderwall, headlights, Hopper!

Hopper there!

There in the trees, stop, go back, Hopper, nothing, I thought it was him.

Henk hands me his hipflask, he tells me more – drink

72

more, son. Hopper, he's there, I swear to God he's there, I saw him, by the dip in the track, he was just standing, my nose, my nose is broken, I can't touch it, it makes me cry.

We pass the packing sheds, Hopper's walking down in front of the ute, he's looking at me, he's looking in the window at me, Hopper, I shout again.

Henk brakes, you need to stay calm, mate, calm. But it was Hopper, Henk. He's not a ghost. Is he a ghost? I think I killed him too. I fucking killed him too.

*

It's cool by the river. Henk does the work. He says Mother Nature will sort it. I know he means the crocodiles or the dingoes.

Henk puts his hand on my shoulder. I'm looking down at the river slap against the bank or imagining it because I can't see much. It's black out.

'Son, life is made of incidents. They test a man's courage, his morals, his faith. I don't think you struck out from a place of evil.'

'We disappear, Henk,' I said. I was still entranced by the water.

'What?'

'We disappear. Us Irish. That's what they say about us. As workers. We work hard but we disappear.'

Henk waited. The moonlight lit his face.

'We all have to go, Henk. It'd be the only way. If the lot of us fucked off, no one would notice one of us gone. That'd be the only way. We'll go tonight. Us and Fiona.'

Henk drove us to the nearest town. It took over four hours. Fiona was sobering and clueless.

'Where are we?' she asked. 'What's going on?'

'We left,' Shane said.

'Why?'

'It's okay.'

'Something bad's happened,' she said in a dreamy way then gasped and quickly sat up straight. 'Shit lads. What happened?'

Shane hushed her and pulled her close to him to go back to sleep. 'It's sound, just trust me.'

'Where's my stuff?'

'We packed it, it's fine,' Shane said and kissed her hair.

'But—'

'Fiona, please,' I said.

The way she looked at me was haunting but eventually she nodded and tucked herself into Shane.

Me and Shane were silent. I was dying to sleep but I couldn't. It was weird because I could see Hopper everywhere, not John Anthony. Henk drove fairly well. We only met one other car on the road before getting to the town.

We got out and Henk hollered at a truck driver that had parked beside us. He spoke to him for a few minutes then returned. He said he had arranged a lift for two of us with the truck driver who was going to take a quick nap. The other one would have to wait and get a bus when the station opened at 8 a.m.

Henk helped us get our stuff out of the back. He kissed Fiona, shook Shane's hand and pulled me in for a massive hug.

'What about – you could post – I...'

I wanted to ask him about my wages but I couldn't. I couldn't make the sentence tactful in my head and I couldn't risk pissing him off.

'Son, you just forget about this. I don't need police snooping around the mango farm. So you forget about this, leave it behind you. You're young. Leave it. Enjoy your life.'

He wet the shoulder of my t-shirt with his tears. Then he let go.

*

Shane got us three cups of coffee in the small petrol station down the road. We were sitting on our rucksacks and morning was torturing us with its brightness. Shane had a proper shiner now and he was pressing his lips real tight to stop them shuddering. He had a tremble in his hands.

'I've been thinking. I've been thinking, I'll be the one who gets the bus somewhere. I'll get the bus to somewhere I can get a flight. Gonna go across to Sydney. Good few of my cousins are there. I – I can't do any of this anymore. Ye take Henk's trucker lift to Perth. You know, it's not because of – it's just I have to, like – I have to go.'

He kissed Fiona on the lips for a few seconds. 'Look after him,' he said.

He nodded at me and I nodded back.

He took a drink of his coffee and turned away from us

before I'd see him cry. He walked down towards the petrol station again and I watched him go.

He was the best friend I ever had.

*

The trucker was a heavy-set man with a thick Australian country accent, he said far like 'faaah.' He offered us some from the bags of crisps, cookies, chewy sweets he opened and even when we declined he made us take some.

'Need a doc, boy?' he asked when he saw me grimace blowing my nose. The back of my throat had the tangy taste of fresh blood and it was making me nauseous.

'It's okay, I'll get it checked in Perth.'

Fiona was pale and quiet. She scribbled at drawings in her sketchbook. One of the farmhouse and the orchard around it. She was good, I could clearly see my room, Shane's room, the courtyard, the smoking area, the laneway where I murdered John Anthony.

The roads were dead. The trucker played Kiss and Cat Stevens. Sometimes he switched to radio, to Triple J, and they played 'Brother' by Matt Corby every few songs. His voice cooing made my chest tighten.

I tried to sleep and when I'd eventually fall into something, I didn't dream of the lads, I dreamt of sitting at the kitchen table at home. The auld lad eating lamb chops, Mam fussing all over him, fussing all over me. I dreamt of the ground being marshy from rain and the little drops on the windowsill as I looked outside to the grass. I dreamt of the stove and warming myself by it and I dreamt that I could go back in time. I woke up whimpering to Fiona stroking my hair and telling me it was going to be alright.

She didn't ask any more questions. She made some small talk and she made me eat during the truck stops. I was bruised. Broken.

Because I'd been a bit shitfaced, it sometimes felt like it hadn't even happened. That I didn't go for his knife, that I didn't thrust it into his jugular.

Why didn't I stab him in the face? Or the hand?

Sometimes it felt like it wasn't even that much of a sensation, to have taken a life. It was like cheating on a girlfriend. Bad thing. Unfair. But happened in the spur of the moment. You move on. Did that mean I was a sociopath? Would I kill again?

I didn't know. My body creaked and was sensitive any time I moved, it hurt in at least five places. My head split with questions. I hoped Shane wasn't feeling as shite as me. We had to take a stopover for the trucker to get a long sleep. Me and Fiona tried to get comfortable in the front seats when he went into his berth.

*

After we'd been back on the road for a while I saw a sign.
PERTH 500KM

I was relieved that we could be in a city and figure out what to do. We couldn't talk properly while this Australian man was driving and singing and eating all the time.

Fiona was colouring in a different sketch.

'Did you do that?' I asked her. 'Or did you buy it like

77

that?' It looked like a postcard of a sunset but bigger. It was class.

'I drew it. Met this lovely older Australian couple a while ago who looked out for me. Really kind people. I know they'd never take money off me so I want to give them a gift. Something thoughtful.'

Thoughtful. That was Fiona. I wondered when was the last time someone could have said that about me.

'Where you going in the city?' the driver asked interrupting us.

Fiona looked at me blankly.

'Em, I know a hostel, me and Shane stayed in it before. It's on the other side of the bridge, out the road a bit. I'll show ya.' My mind couldn't come up with anywhere else. If we checked into a double private room and decided in the morning what to do, it would be okay.

*

The trucker dropped us off at the backpackers just after midday. Fiona did the talking inside. I made eye contact with no one.

We went to the room and got into the bed together. She snuggled into me and she was so warm and soft that I nearly wept again. We passed out. A couple of hours later, she said she'd make us some dinner.

Left in the room, staring at a damp stain on the wall, I decided on some things.

I would give up drugs and I was giving up binge drinking. Just one or two drinks from now on.

I decided that I wouldn't turn myself in over John Anthony or Hopper.

But I would do something really good though, for the world, like volunteer or something.

Fiona came back with a plate of steaming spag bol. The portion was enough to feed three people.

'Here, eat this mister,' she said.

'It's so fucked up, Fiona,' I said.

She stayed quiet for a moment. 'Are you going to talk about it?'

I just shook my head and sliced at the spaghetti. I devoured the dinner. There was sauce all over my face and I wiped at it with the back of my hand. My nose was still excruciating but Fiona had an inspection of it and said it definitely wasn't broken, just a bad bruising.

'You'd know if it was broken, that's for sure,' she said and touched the bridge of her own nose.

'I can't look at it. I can't look at meself,' I said. Except for the mushrooms that she had mixed in with the mince, the plate was empty when I handed it back to her.

She didn't say anything. She gave me a sorry smile, took the plate and left. I sighed and lay back down looking at the stain and ran through the list of what I would and wouldn't do again.

*

Fiona came back to the bedroom different. It was her body language or the way she wasn't saying something. It was completely obvious she was holding back. It wasn't a fearful distance, it was more a protective one.

'What's going on?' I asked and sniffed, more blood globbing together and going down my throat.

She went to her rucksack and opened one of the compartments. She took out a washbag.

'I don't know how to say this without sounding strange.'

'Ah come on, Fiona. Hasn't everything since we've met been strange?'

She got out a baby wipe and started taking off her makeup, rubbing it around her eyes and over her cheeks.

'Okay it's strange because I've never met the lad. But ye told me I'd know him when I saw him. I don't know why I think it but I think Hopper is downstairs, in the common room.'

I was frozen.

'Look I could be wrong. I've never met him except for what ye've told me. I just, my instinct, I don't know. Maybe this is fucking mental. I don't know,' she said and flicked the wipe into the bin.

I pulled a white t-shirt over my head, trying not to have it touch my nose. 'I'm going down.'

*

As I walked down the stairs, each step sent an impact into my body, each impact punched my bruises, I effed and blinded but still I went as quickly as physically possible.

The commotion of another backpackers' evening about to set in, hostel revelry and cheap partying hit my ears and sounded unbearable.

Still I kept going towards it, the din getting louder and louder. I walked to the common room and stuck my head in from the doorway. It felt like I was going to get the runs. My insides were squeezing and opening and wrenching.

In the corner with his back to me. A shiny blue tracksuit top. Knee length black shorts. Same height. Same hair but longer, it needed a cut, strands rested on his neck.

Hopper's face at the doorway of the mango farm kitchen changed in my mind to Philly the French Canadian's, it changed to Shane's, it changed to the Germans' and Scandinavians' and English lads' that we never talked to, a white face. Anyone's face.

Bile threatened. Bile mixed with blood mixed with guilt mixed with something I couldn't pin. Like fear or hate.

I looked over at him again and his body went hazy and I wiped my eyes. Hopper? It was him.

Was it him? It was the same stance. The same build. The druggie vibe. Had to be him. If he saw me and knew me, he'd ask about the farm. About the others. Was it him?

I should step into the room, go over, check properly but

everything went blurrier. The thick sensation in my gut was rising, burning my windpipe.

Something was forcing me. I had to move. I rushed back to the bedroom.

Fiona was sitting on the bed, 'Was it him? Your Hopper?'

I nodded yes at her. I paused for a second and shrugged. 'I don't know.' Sweat was soaking my back. Everything was swishing yet hyper real. 'I don't know anymore.' My voice was cracking.

'Hold on, where are you going?' Fiona asked as I lumped my clothes and charger into the rucksack.

'Have to leave. Get out of here. I can't be here. He'll remind me of – Fiona – I won't be able to forget that I – what I did – oh fuck, why'd I do it?' I pushed her out of the way and tried to puke into the sink but had to catch it with my hands instead. Red. Bolognese.

Why did I do any of it?

Leaving Ireland. Leaving my parents. Leaving Melbourne. Leaving Hopper in the woods. Leaving Shane.

Fiona was rubbing my back as I retched over the toilet bowl. I never wanted her to stop. I spat and went to the sink. I soaked a towel and mopped my face and forgot about my stupid fucking nose and yelled when I pressed the towel against it.

'Okay, it was him, yes?' Fiona was still stroking my back. She took the towel away from me and wiped my face and neck gently with it.

'I imagined him, Fiona. I used to see the shithead every-where I went. I was obsessed. Am I fucking losing it? Am I losing my mind? The stuff that happened, the stuff I did, it wouldn't have happened if I had known Hopper was fine. I don't think it would have anyways. Not like that.'

She soothed me and wrapped her arms around me. I dragged her down to the floor so I didn't have to see myself in the mirror. Just tucked my head into her shoulder. My hands clasped around her waist feeling the slight curve at the top of her arse, my middle fingers able to touch across her lower back.

Fiona said, 'When I got here, I travelled around first. Had a big holiday. Thought I'd get a job easy but I didn't. My parents loaned me money and they have fuck all. They've been scraping since the recession. Since before it. So I went to get the farming done, hoping things would be okay. But there, I completely ran out of cash.' Her voice changed to a slower tone. 'It was bad. I was so skint. I'd nothing. I was stealing off my roommates. I agreed to something pretty low. I don't want to say but I went somewhere in the bush with men and it was bad and I'm still trying to get over it.'

She was shaking.

'But I'll get over it. I have to. I know you're lost. I see it. I feel it. I can feel it every time I look at you. Things are going to be okay though, they have to be.'

'No. No, they won't,' I said and forgot everything else she'd just said. My breath fluttered. 'I fucking stabbed John Anthony. I stabbed him and watched him die. What if his friends from the North come looking for me? You know the ones I mean. Everyone knows them lads even if nobody mentions them anymore. What if they get wind of this?'

She took a noisy inhale. 'You – you stabbed him? Christ.'

'What if Henk has told the police already? Or Shane? I

don't even know what he did to clean up. I never even checked.'

'They won't have. They were involved too.' Her eyes were big and sad. 'We're all involved now.'

I cringed. 'No. Not you, you're not.'

'Then why did ye bring me?'

I wanted to tell her the truth. I brought you to save myself but I sighed and said, 'I'm going to go,' in a low voice.

It was only when I felt the tears gathering underneath my chin that I realised I was crying.

'Where?' she asked.

'I don't know. I'll look for some work somewhere, maybe in Margaret River, I don't know.'

'I'm coming with you. You're a fucking mess. You can abandon me when you get your shit together. Maybe when you feel like stalling. That's a promise. You're not okay. You're not fit to be alone at the moment. When are we going?'

'Once I pack, I'm moving,' I said and she locked her fingers with mine for a moment.

*

As we left the hostel, forty minutes later, there was a nip in the night air. Fiona was on her mobile, trying to arrange a car for us. We went by blocks, by sushi parlours and pie franchises, parks and pubs, past shiny buildings and perfectly gridded streets. My feet were unsteady but I knew I would crawl away, scuttle louselike away if I had to.

The rental car place was making things way too difficult. They wanted an Irish driving licence, an international licence, a credit card, the dates and place we would return the car to. And after all that, they wouldn't let me book because I was under twenty-five.

Fiona shrugged apologetically, 'I'm twenty-four still.'

We stopped by an internet café and looked at ads for secondhands up to a grand. We found a dented '95 black Mondeo sedan and enquired. The guy said he'd give us it for five hundred dollars if we paid in cash, asked for nothing off him and didn't even dare to complain or attempt to bring it back.

'Sound.'

Quickest sale ever.

I borrowed four hundred dollars from Fiona.

'Did you not save anything up there?' she asked me as she pressed her numbers in the ATM.

All my fucking envelopes of hard cash were now with Henk forever. A pay off for things. For silence. My stomach went weak again. I couldn't think about it.

The car guy knew we were dodgy, calling him this late at night but he delivered the car over to the park where we said we'd meet him. I handed him the wad of cash and thanked him. Fiona inspected the car, frowning.

'It's fine,' I said.

'You Irish in a hurry?' he asked.

'Nope. Well, yeah. We want to see the coast before our visas run out.'

'It's beautiful, the West Coast. Beautiful,' he said as he pocketed the money and handed me the key.

'So I hear,' I said and thought of Shane and the tourist stuff he'd wanted to do.

'You need to renew the rego on that car,' the Aussie said.

'Okay.' I hadn't a fucking notion.

The car stank. Dog hairs on the upholstery. Fast food wrappers stuffed anywhere they could be stuffed. Ashes on the ground.

'It's fine,' I repeated to Fiona. 'You don't have to worry about the mess.'

She was jumpy and checking everything on the passenger side before she sat and positioned herself.

The Mondeo was grimy but working okay. Wouldn't get too far but it would get me away. I turned a few corners, respected the traffic lights and one-ways and found the turn to get us back to the hostel. Fiona looked at me puzzled, her hair loose around her fresh face.

'Why are we here again?' she asked.

I took a breath and felt like such a piece of shite that I actually looked at myself in the rearview mirror. Just to see if my eyes had changed over the past few weeks.

'You've to get out, Fiona,' I said.

'What?'

'I have to go alone. I drag everyone down. I make bad choices. I don't want you with me for this.'

'I'm after giving you four-fifths of the cash, don't fuck me over now,' she said. I was afraid she'd get girl screechy on me.

'Fiona, I won't ask you again, you need to get out. I'm not bringing you with me. I'll pay you back at some stage, I swear on that.'

'I'll ignore this. I'll ignore you said this. So keep driving. We go to Margy's, we get some work. Keep going and go now.' Her face was burning but her voice was calm.

Some backpackers stumbled around the front doors, cigarettes dangling, ready to be lit. Music blared from the nightclub up the road. I was looking at everything except her but once again I could feel her eyes boring a hole through me.

'I'll go with you,' she said.

I sighed deeply. What sort of life lay ahead of us? Scrounging around the Aussie landscape. Me checking my shadow all the time.

How the fuck could I involve her in this if it got real heavy?

How the fuck could I run carrying her along with me?

She took a breath in through her nose and let it out her mouth.

I tapped the steering wheel, a frantic beat. I wanted to say sorry but it wouldn't come. She opened the car door, kicking it wide and got out. She took her bags from the boot. I rotated my head, hearing my neck crack as I stretched it each side. She didn't look at me again but she stopped for a second to straighten her posture. She walked towards the entrance. I watched the clouds drift in the vast Australian sky, fogging the night. I said a prayer to no one and grinded the Mondeo into gear.

YOU

You realise that this isn't backpacking.

This isn't finding yourself, exploring new cultures, being breathless with wonder. This is 2 Minute Noodles for breakfast and dinner. Smoking butts. Drinking the leftover goon from parties. Hoping it's white. Red makes you hungover for a day and a half with a plundered stomach and Catholic guilt.

You've borrowed less than a tenner off so many backpackers here now. You know they won't get too angsty about less than a tenner. Makes them look like scabs if they do.

It's your fourth week not making rent, your sixth with no job. The hostel has you trapped. Too poor to stay, too poor to leave. Antonio, the owner, keeps promising you work.

'Soon, soon, I told you. You fucking Irish. Always hassling me.'

The hostel is a seventy-bed in a small outback village. You share a dorm with three Asian girls and a Scotsman. The girls are lovely but you've already robbed them. You watched the drama unfold in another language. A flurry of incomprehensible sounds as they searched around for the twenty. You bought noodles, deodorant and a big Crunchie with it. You did your laundry with the change.

When Antonio has got you all jobs again, you'll pay it back. You'll pay it all back. When.

You've sixty-seven days done of your eighty-eight for a second year visa. But you've been stuck in this hole for over a hundred days waiting. You've picked fruit, broke your back pulling vegetables out of the ground, thrown pumpkins on a conveyor belt stuck to a moving tractor, trimmed vines, swept the outside of a potato factory, cried, cried, got tougher, cried. You sometimes wonder what life was like before this. Clew Bay sunsets back home or sitting on trams in urban Australia looking out at the skyscrapers. Lazing on the white sand East Coast beaches. No dehydrated earth in sight.

*

On Saturday night, there's some sex scandals, some scraps, some craic and you unwind. Forget about how miserable it is. But on Sunday, you're hungover and it's magnified. You're going into your fifth week in the red. How did you let this happen? You can't ask them at home for money. They've already sent you a loan that they had to get a loan for. They've no money. You were supposed to send some back to them.

You've lost half a stone. Your shorts are loose at the waist and baggy at the arse. Your eyes are always raw and stinging.

You go to see Antonio.

'What is wrong with you stupid fucking backpackers? How many times do I have to say it? The citrus season is bad this year. And everyone's still paying for the knock-on of Cyclone Yasi. I'm trying my bloody best to get you jobs but I'm not god of the harvest. I don't know when more work will crop up.'

'But I don't have any money left, Antonio,' you say and try to swallow. 'I can't pay rent.'

You're terrified of being homeless here.

Homeless in Australia. A twenty-six hour thousand-dollar flight away, past the Indian Ocean, South and West Asia, the Middle East, most of Europe to Dublin and a three-and-a-half hour train across the country to the Atlantic coast, to home. You're not a druggie or a runaway. You've had a decent upbringing and a decent standard of life. Of education. When the property market collapsed, you couldn't find any more work as a letting agent. Landlords were renting places out themselves.

Australia was where everyone was going. Australia would save you.

'I need a girl to clean the toilets and fridges. If you do them today and tomorrow, I'll say we're okay for that first week you owe me.'

'But I still owe you another three plus this week's?'

'Yeah, yeah. We'll figure something out. Cleaning bucket and sprays are in the store room behind the common area. Now get out of my bloody sight.'

You walk to the store room with a spring in your step. The sensation of hope is back. The cleaning job was something. It would help.

You pick up the supplies and clean the toilets and fridges. You scoop out old food from the fridge and retch. You scoop out black goo and hairs from the tiles around the toilets and retch. When the day is done, you shower for twenty minutes. The water is scalding. You use the Asians' shampoo.

*

The following days there's still no work. No sign of work. Backpackers with money travel away, go to bigger places – Mildura, Swan Hill, Wagga Wagga – and try get farm jobs, or go west to Margaret River. They say they only pay by the hour over there in decent vineyards.

You can't leave though. You've no money to get out.

A Welsh girl with luscious ginger hair is smoking at the benches. You go over to her and ask for a cigarette. You've never asked her before so you might get lucky. You do. She passes you a Longbeach Menthol.

'What's your story?' you ask.

'What do you mean?'

'You working?'

She pauses, looks you in the eye. 'Yeah, I'm working. I got a job in the potato factory. Admin.'

'You landed an office job here? How?'

'Well, sometimes you do what you have to do.' She smiles.

You're intrigued. You smoke in silence, quench the cigarette and go to check the 'Free Food' shelf in the kitchen to see if there's anything you can muster. Someone has left Black & Gold stuffing beside a nearly empty tub of tomato ketchup. You take both and put them into your food bag. Dinner will be exotic tonight: ketchupped breadcrumb noodles.

What Ginger said is going about in your head. You try and shake it clear but it keeps creeping back. You return to the benches to find her but she's gone so you check the jobs board to get her room number. Twelve. You go down the courtyard in your flip-flops, avoiding the broken glass. You knock. She comes to the door.

'Yeah?' She's got a face mask on now. Grey mud all over except the skin around her eyes and her lips. She still looks pretty.

'I – I just wondered what you meant earlier?'

She sighs. 'Look, I can see you're stuck. Half the people staying here are. I was too. I'm only going to say this to you so don't go broadcasting it.'

You lean in closer, able to smell the dank carpet in the room, the chemicals from the face mask.

'Antonio, being the nice guy he is, will accept alternative ways of paying rent. And sometimes that can get you into the factories too.'

You try to steady yourself. 'What do you mean?'

'Aw, come on. We're both big girls. I bet you've slept with fellas and wished they had paid they treated you so bad? We all have.'

Your ex-boyfriend Malley flashes into your mind.

'I – no. Antonio will – you mean – if I go to bed with him?'

'Yeah. Don't say I told you. He's married you know. I gotta go. This fucking mask is burning me.'

She shoves you slightly and closes the door. You stand staring at the number twelve, the chipped red gloss around it.

You roll what she said over in your thoughts. You go into the bathroom and look at yourself in the mirror. Poke underneath your cheekbones. Gone lean there too. Gaunt. You wash your face, blow your nose and breathe slowly.

You pace the floor. Wash your face again. Check your watch. You hop into your bottom bunk and try to sleep. Listen to some music. Get up. Go back into bed. Check your phone.

Go to A. Dial Antonio. Hang up.

'What are you doing?' you ask yourself. You try to weigh it up again. Antonio is a sleaze. His blackheads are almost popping out of his pores. His fingers are stubby and his fingernails are bitten to blood. He's got a vicious mouth. But this is killing you. You can pretend you're somewhere else with someone else. With Colin Farrell in the Hollywood Hills.

You dial again.

'Hello,' he drawls. He's chewing on something.

You want to hang up. Terror makes your blood pump.

'Hello?'

'Hi – em – hi, Antonio. This is Fiona. From room three. I – I was wondering…'

How do you even ask this? What words do you use?

'I was wondering if we could make some sort of deal with the rent I owe you?'

'You're the Irish chick?'

'Yeah.'

'The black-haired one. Long legs?'

You cough. 'No – no, I've got fairish hair. To my ears. I'm in room three. With the Asian girls.'

Long pause.

He chomps again and leaves you listening to him breathing through his nose. 'Hmm. I'm not so keen. You done a good job cleaning. I might need you to do that again. But you tell your friend with the black hair to give me a call.'

He's about to hang up and you hate yourself for it but you go, 'Please. Antonio. Wait. I can't just clean. I need work. I'll do anything.'

He swallows and bangs his lips together. 'I'll call you back.'

The line dies.

You recall the whole conversation, adding in bits and pieces, what he might have meant, what you should have said. You feel the way you felt when you puked all over yourself on the bus home from the Transition Year Grad, the second time you'd ever been properly drunk. Blue Aftershocks and Bulmers. You feel the way you felt when you were with Malley at a music festival and you tried to pull him out to dance with you. He shoved you off and called you a pathetic bitch. His spit flew in your face as he shouted you down. You were afraid he'd hit you in front of everyone. Them blind-eyed, embarrassed for you. That feeling back again.

You're a fucking fool. And you're fucking ugly. Even that fat old Greek prick doesn't want you.

You bury your face in your pillow and scream.

*

The phone wakes you two hours later. It's Antonio.

'Hey, Irish, you sure you'll do anything? I don't want no more whinging out of you and no turning back either.'

You drench your mouth with saliva and swallow it, wipe your tingling eyes. Your voice gives it away that you've been sleeping.

'Yeah. I don't know how much longer I can survive like this. I don't know what to do.'

He starts chewing something again, the crunch coming over the receiver.

'Good. I got a pal. He's a farmer, okay. It's out in the bush. You live there with him. He'll pay you every week. Now, he's a rough kind of bloke. Very outback. You gotta know this before you go. He did have a wife once so he can't be too bad. You get accommodation, food and two hundred to six hundred bucks a week, depending.'

'Depending?'

'Depending on what you do. How far you go will be your own choice.'

Panic slashes through you.

'I – I don't know,' you stutter. 'I shouldn't.'

'Look, girl, how about I sweeten it by cancelling all your debts here? I'll clear the five weeks you owe me.'

'It's only four.'

'It's five on Monday. Eight hundred and seventy-five bucks wiped clean.'

You stay silent and try to decide. If you could just save for

98

two months, not doing anything, you'd be able to leave and start again. But you can't go out there, he could be a sicko, and if you go you'll be a... But if you stay, what happens? More of this? Going down, further down. Bigger and bigger debts with Antonio, with the other travellers? You can't steal anymore. You don't want to. You hate this. You hate it. Because if you just did it with the farmer a few times, you could get out quickly. Even pay your folks back.

Antonio interrupts your thoughts. 'I'm getting bored now, you keen or not? Plenty of other chicks would be grateful for this chance.'

You take a big breath. 'When would I go?'

'Get packed and I'll collect you in thirty minutes.'

You need to go now or you'll chicken out. 'Okay Antonio,' you whisper and hang up.

You gather your shit from the bed. You take your towel and toothbrush out of the bathroom. You tear the picture of your parents and gran off the wall beside your bunk and squash your shoes and make-up bag into your rucksack. You spray yourself with the Asians' perfume. It smells like Euphoria but you can't tell from the symbols on the label if it is.

You stare at yourself in the mirror for so long that your sight becomes spotted with black and you don't look like yourself anymore. You drag the bag out the front of the hostel and wait for Antonio. You don't say goodbye to anyone. You can't handle the explaining and you don't feel up to lying.

Antonio beeps in his ute. You walk over and he tells you to put the bag in the back. He drives out of the village, playing a Frank Sinatra CD, shouting at the cars in front for turning and not using indicators, for going too slow.

For a while you forget what you're doing and admire the parched desert outback scenery. Bleak, thirsty, stunning.

You see your phone signal is gone, this far into the country-side. Antonio takes a right and a left, drives for miles of farmland. He points at a farmhouse in the distance. 'Your new quarters, chick.'

Panic is mutilating you. You can't back out. You want to back out. You have to back out.

Oh fuck.

What are you doing? You can't do this.

He pulls up outside the house. Four tractors, a Hummer, two utes and a scrap Golf are parked in the driveway.

'How many people live here?' you ask. Dread makes your voice squeaky.

'I don't know. Nothing to do with me. Take your bag. I'll cancel your debts. Hooroo, mate.'

Antonio leans over and opens your door. You mechanically get out and pick up your rucksack, the white flight-sticker still hanging off the straps – Dublin to Sydney.

You haul it onto your back. It's nearly bigger than you.

Antonio honks. His tyres screech with the U-turn. You can see heads in the front room turn to look out the window, through a haze of smoke. One of the figures gets up and walks out of the room.

He switches on an outside light even though you can see. Antonio's ute is dusting out of sight. The front door whines open and the man watches you walk. He's slim and wears a grey checked shirt. He grinds his jaw.

'How ya goin'?' he says. His thumb rests on the waistband of his shorts.

You pull your rucksack higher onto your back and inch towards him.

You're with Colin Farrell in the Hollywood Hills. You chant. Over and over.

Colin Farrell.

Hollywood Hills.

*

You have this disconnect. It's like you're there, you can see yourself, but you're not inside. The man stands, watching you. He says nothing else until you pass by him and put your rucksack down in the hallway. The floor is grubby. You spot a cockroach and gasp.

'Yer Sheila's here,' he shouts into the front room.

There's shuffling and creaking of a chair that has released a weight.

An old man walks towards you. He smells of liquorice and lager. He turns you around. His hand is cold, thin and has liver spots. He turns you back. You're disconnected. You're calm. You're watching the scene. He cups one of your breasts. He raises it.

'Not much milk, eh?' he says and the man who opened the door howls with laughter. His back teeth are rotting.

The old man leans in closer and sniffs your shoulder. The tip of his nose is wet.

'She'll do alright,' he says. 'At least he sent a white this time and not a damn reffo.'

He walks back to the sitting room. The smell of smoke in the house is fresh.

The man who opened the door says, 'You'll call him Mr Fletcher. I'm Rusty. Me bro is Jett. We'll be telling you what to do. Now go make us some dinnies, good girl.'

You nod and go towards where his finger points. He doesn't follow you. You wonder will this be easier than you thought. You wonder why it feels like your voice is stuck in your chest. Under your ribcage.

The kitchen is large. Around the sink, pots are piled up. Food has dried into the bottom and sides of them. The plates are crusty. A fly paper towel is peppered black. Cans of alcohol pyramid in the corner.

A biscuit tin holds a stash of pills and medicines, syrups and painkillers. The old man must be in really bad shape. Maybe he won't be able to— Or do you have to be a whore to all of the men? Do they all get a go? It makes you wince to think about.

That old lady from your hometown, with a hairy mouth and sagged flesh. She hung out in the chippers, not the corners. The midfielder from your year who paid her for sex in the shopping centre car park and bragged to everyone after about how gross it was. You remember laughing at his story, not because you thought it was funny but because everyone else was.

But you need cash. You need cash. Stay disconnected. Stay numb. Get some money. You're here for the money. Stay numb.

In the fridge, there's a stench of old milk. The shelves are littered with onions, mushrooms, red capsicums, garlic cloves and avocados. There's a plate with thick bloody chops. You decide you'll make them a good feed before you do anything else. In the freezer, you find oven chips. You look out the window and see a forest in the distance. The men leave you alone as you prepare the meal, not one of them comes to see what's going on.

The crickets begin their leg grinding and the night drops quickly through the sky. You're hungry but you barely pick at the food, even as it's cooking. If this place becomes a prison, you will starve yourself to death and you get some comfort from this idea. A sense of control over your body.

The kitchen grows more humid from the cooking. You realise you're sweating and wipe your neck and behind your ears with a cloth. The chops spit as you fry them and you watch them shrivel as they cook. You're transfixed.

Where the fuck are you, Fiona? Is this even the real world?

More sweat flows from you and before you reach the sink, life blanks, the room goes black and you're gone.

*

You come to on the couch. The old man Fletcher, Rusty and Jett stare down as you groan. The back of your head feels like it has a cartoon-style bump swelling out of it.

'It's alright,' Fletcher says and hands you a cup of water.

Rusty is eating a crispy, black chop. You stare at Jett and think he looks like Rusty but in a shrunken-down fatter way.

You want to ask if all the food was burned but you're afraid of getting slapped around. The blood is hopping under your skin.

'It's alright,' Fletcher says.

You sit up slowly and your eyes are filled with floating

103

spots. Fletcher shouts at Jett to get you more water.

'She can get it herself,' Jett says like a teenager but if you guessed, he's at least forty.

Fletcher flicks the tip of Jett's left ear and Jett puts his hand up to cover it.

'What you fucking do that for?'

'Get her some fucking water, I said.'

It sounds like they are saying fah-king and it makes you jumpy each time they swear.

Jett seizes the cup from you with such force, you think he'll crush it with his big shovel hands.

Rusty sneers at him as he goes. You don't know where to look now.

'It's alright, girl,' Fletcher says again.

Jett comes back with a cup of water and thrusts it at you. It spills on your lap. Fletcher boxes him across the head.

'You flaming mongrel.'

'What, Pa? Why you being so nice to this one? What's special about her?' Jett asks and rubs his head.

'Get her a blanket, she'll sleep here for tonight.'

Rusty looks confused.

Jett says, 'Rusty, you get it.'

'He asked you,' Rusty says.

You don't move a muscle. You don't even blink. You want the blanket. You want to sleep here. You don't know what's down there.

'She'll cook and clean. That's it for now. She went unconscious. I want her good and ready. Let her get a hold of this place. We don't want it to be like the last time.' Fletcher pauses. 'So that's it for now. Cook and clean. Understand, boys?'

Your eyes are watering from not blinking.

'I fucking said, understand, boys?'

Rusty says, 'Sure, Pa,' and nods his head.

Jett gives you a cold look. He mumbles, 'Yeah, whatever,' and flashes unmatching teeth at you.

*

During the night, you're in their sitting room. It's hot but you leave all your clothes on, even your shoes. You turn on the TV and let the images come through without sound. When you sleep, it's in snatches, falling off that cliff of consciousness, waking suddenly and checking where you are. Still the same.

Your dreams are worse. Night terrors. Kneeling on a bridge. Sharks in yellow water underneath. Malley watching from the shore.

Cigarette smoke curls up your nose.

'Alive yet, Princess?' Jett asks.

You sit up quickly, fully, and wrap the blankets over and underneath you.

'Now, I don't know why we've got this little confusion. You're the girl, sent to be our girl, and yet you're not. Now why is that, d'ya reckon?'

You tense in your upper thighs, in your crotch. Is this it? Is this going to happen? How will it feel?

'I don't know why me old man thinks you need sparing for a day or two because in my opinion, breaking the animals in straight off is always the best way to use them.'

He strokes your cheek with the back of his finger. It's cold but surprisingly soft. 'Now, I don't think you came here without knowing what you were coming here for, did ya, Princess?'

You pull away but he's moving closer. You've got nowhere else to go. He leans in closer. His breath is on you. Dog's breath. He's showing those teeth again. You loosen your arms. Now you regret wrapping the blanket on you. Your legs are trapped. He pushes his mouth onto yours. His weight is coming down on you. But he can't rape you over these covers. You can feel his hard-on against your leg. His kiss is rough and his tongue is probing through your mouth. He's moaning. He stops. He starts again.

You make a decision.

You kiss him back. You go harder on him, meeting his sour tongue. You make some noises, push your breasts against him.

'Oi, mate, this one's a keeper,' he says to no one and tears his singlet off over his head. It ruffles his hair. He smiles. You smile back.

When he goes to unwrap the blankets, you relax. You let him strip them away. He smells faintly of sweat and soap and garlic. He pulls your top and slobbers on the skin on your chest. He fingers your top down further with one hand and with the other he loosens the blankets more and your legs become free. His mouth is on your nipple now. You're confused that you feel a little aroused. He puts his hand down your shorts, forcing it in further and further. You don't mean to but you whimper. His fingers wriggle towards you, pressing hard against you.

He shoves one, two inside. Your breath gets heavier. His eyes are closed. He dips them in and out. He stops. He takes his hand out of you and tastes it. He smiles.

'You're not a dirty one, I know it. Don't need a rubber now, do I?' he says as he grasps his shorts, pulling them downwards, unleashing his bristly pubes, his erection.

It's now.

Now you kick him as hard as you can into the balls. You drive all the force you've got behind it and leap from the couch. He flails backwards and tries to break his fall, his arms reaching behind. He lands on the table but he's too heavy and it upturns on top of him. He roars. You topple the two-seater over as you rush past it to block him from the door. You run out the sitting room to the hallway, eye your rucksack and you run to the door and it's unlocked thank fuck and you run and now you can hear his hollering and noise behind you. A light goes on. You half look back. Jett has pulled up his shorts but is still topless. He's running. He's fast.

Oh God Jesus.

You're going down the dirt track. You're no athlete and you haven't eaten properly in weeks. He's gaining on you. You need a plan. You hear an engine start. You look around. The forest. Down the road. You run but your legs are turning soft.

The ute is pulling out of the driveway. Your body is burning. Your muscles are burning. Your lungs are burning. Your mouth is so dry. You see the trees. The engine is getting louder. Jett is still following. You run through the woods. You stall, almost skidding off the edge. There's a big drop. A river. You look behind. He's almost caught up. You pray. You don't know if the water is deep. Should you dive? You'll fucking maim yourself. You'll crack your skull. You'll lose your bottom jaw. Teeth. Or miss the river and slam onto the ground. Your wrists and shins will be white broken timber jutting out through your skin.

He's too close now. They're too close now. They've probably got guns. They'll probably tie you up and torture you before they kill you.

You take a big breath.

You jump.

*

The impact against the rocks sends a shockwave of pain through your body, up through your head. You take a second, bite down on your lip, massage the pads of your palms which feel burst, flattened. You don't think anything's broken. Or maybe you're too full of adrenaline to notice. They've got a torch scanning down and you duck behind some scrub.

You'll be able to follow the water, you'll find some fish or something. It'll lead you to the Murray River. Where there's a big river, there'll be a big town, eventually.

You freeze suddenly when you see their light veer towards you. You crawl under brambles of a hedge, its thorns claw skin from your face. The lapping of the water is replaced by shouting. It's not far from you.

Jett says, 'You shit slut. I'll fucking get you. I'll take you apart.'

They zig-zag the flashlight again and it misses you by a fraction.

Your heart is racing but your mind is calm.

They shout again. This time at each other. They're arguing. They don't know where you are.

You're still. You become one with the hedge. You think about nothing.

You don't know how long it takes for them to leave. The ute door slams twice and they rev the engine for a while before the vehicle rumbles away. You wait until it becomes a far-off hum before moving.

You look at the star-freckled sky.

You think about nothing. It's all you have. All you are. All your stuff is gone. You have no money. You have no friends, no lover, nowhere to go. You have nothing.

You stare at the sky and you realise you are free.

You realise this and you say, 'I have everything.'

*

You don't think you've broken anything but the more you walk, the more bloated your foot gets. You walk anyway. The Fletchers will come looking. Hunting. Every footstep makes you weak. You keep going. You follow the river which is wide and loud as it flows.

The sun is high and ferocious so you guess it's around midday. You guess you've been shuffling along, taking tiny breaks, gasping for water for about eight hours. You don't know if you can drink the river but maybe just one mouthful, just one, that can't do much harm?

You bend low, wet your hands and face, they dry immediately. You wet your hair. It stays damp for longer. You sup a drop from your palm. Your mouth and throat sing. More. More.

'Fuck it,' you say and wade deeper into the water, lowering down, gulping great mouthfuls until your belly is jiggling with liquid. The sun is too hot now. It's too bright. You climb up to the forest and look into it. It's eerie, silently full of life. Sun rays break through some of the gaps and light tiny pathways. You stay close to the edge, where you can see the river. You don't want to go into the forest properly. You're afraid of who's on the other side of it. You check around.

You lean against a tree, check the forest again. No one. Would they find you here if you fall asleep? Maybe. You need sleep though. You try to keep your eyes open but you're drifting, drifting low, your head goes low.

You let go.

*

A jagged pain wakes you, thudding down your side. Your face sweats and your mouth gets watery. The pain shoots across your stomach, clasps it from the other side. It jumps. It groans. You get up and fall again after leaning on your right foot, forgetting the old ache with this new one.

'Oh no,' you say.

You get your shorts down on time.

The cramping happens until the sun no longer breaks through the cracks of the forest roof. Nothing is solid. You're grimy and weak. You go down to the river, the fucking prick of a river and wash. You're hungry, there's nothing left inside you. You're hungry. You don't know what to do. You cry and go back to the forest, further down to avoid the trees and smell of earlier.

You're going to die here.

How will anyone come across your body?

You'll be eaten, the birds will take your eyes and the dingoes will ravage the rest of you. How will you be identified? Will anyone even notice you're not in the world anymore?

Your chest feels heavy. Your eyes sting. You lean against another tree and notice the night set in.

The forest isn't eerie anymore. It's breathing. It's watching.

You take off your canvas shoe and hold your foot tight. The throb numbs when you cut the blood supply off. You jitter when insects fly near. You hear twigs snapping. Everything here is natural, except you.

You think about your father to calm yourself. After the buildings went bust, he got a part-time job as a bread man, delivering fresh sliced pan and baked goods to the shops and restaurants. The change suited him so much. He didn't come home sore and exhausted, he came back lively with stories from people around the town.

When you told him you were going to Australia, he tried to smile but his Adam's apple was jumping up and down.

'Would you not go over to London to your sister?' he asked.

'No, Dad, Sydney'll be better. It'll be sunny.'

'London's an hour on the flight from Knock though.'

'Australia's only a day away. You could be sick in bed watching telly for a day. Something inside is telling me to go there.'

'Don't go falling for someone because I won't visit grand-kids that live the other side of the planet,' he said.

If he knew what you did, where you are, what would he say? If any of them could see you now?

Or Malley with his skinny arms and tight fists. Perceptive. Alternative. Someone that always got invited to a party. He was only aggressive to women. That didn't count. He'd probably shout at you for being so stupid. Shout at you because he loved you. You wipe your cheek.

Who are you lying to?

If he saw you now, if he knew what you did, he'd do nothing. He wouldn't care.

A rustle jerks you out of your wallowing and back into the forest. It comes nearer. Your heart thumps.

Shit, it's a big animal.

You sense its presence. You smell its heat. The forest is black but your eyes adjust enough to see different shades of black. Your hearing amplifies.

The creature can sense you too. It's beside you. You stay still. It breathes. You don't want to scare it.

You feel it coming. Feel the warmth from it. It sniffs. It's at your hair, your neck, your shoulder. You don't move. Your heart is booming. It sniffs more, nudges your head. Your stomach grumbles loudly and it moves away, the ground crackles underneath it.

*

The sky starts to leak daylight but your only thoughts are of food. You want food. You don't know what to do about it. Your foot is fat and dead looking. You can't get the shoe back on. You curse and plead but it hurts too much so you leave it off and try walk as far as you can again, further down the river. Maybe a town will come soon. You could get a Red Rooster chicken roll. Or a pie, filled with steaming curry.

You keep walking.

Trudging.

Sighing.

*

You wonder how long it takes the body and mind to adapt to new things. You're so hungry and thirsty that it becomes something that is just there, part of you now. Same with the dull pulsing in your foot. You can't remember what it was like to not feel this way.

You spot a tree with only one ripened orange hanging from it. You rush over and pick it. Hold it for a couple of moments. Feel the weight of it. Look at its naval. Peel it, surprised at how weak your hands are. You get the skin off and put it in your pocket. The citrus scent is more than enough to make you salivate. A juicy, fat, sunny orange. You devour it, eat the fruit, the seeds, the pulp and the rind, the lot.

You remember eating bowls of ice-cream and sliced oranges in your granny's house on a Sunday evening before School Around the Corner, Glenroe and bed. The end of the weekend. Would you ever see her again? She was frail when you left Ireland, her memory in tatters, living in an old folks' home with kind nurses and a big statue of the Virgin in the hall. When you said goodbye to her, she called you your auntie's name.

Your skin blisters from sunburn. Your lips are cracking and bleeding for want of water. You shouldn't drink the river again. Kids in developing countries died from diarrhoea, you saw that on TV. You need water though. The need is giving you headaches. It makes you nauseous. It slows your steps and your thoughts down.

You need water.

You go on as much as you can, try not to collapse. You're wilting. Your throat is closing from dryness. You've stitches scratching your side. You breathe deep and loud as if you're about to sleep.

You don't care if it happens again. Nothing is worse than this thirst. Maybe you'll be immune this time, have a better tolerance. You go down to the river and drink. You sup it greedily and it cools you.

It makes you violently sick.

You continue on, much slower than before. Your body is dry and empty. You have to keep going.

Are you far enough away from them? If you walk a little more today, more tomorrow and the next, surely a town or a village would come? Can't be nothing forever?

You don't drink any more of the water. Instead you sit in it.

You let the current flow against your swollen foot. You're fucking it up more walking on it but what are the options? Go back to the Fletchers? You laugh out loud. When you think about the Fletchers, what you nearly let happen, this hobo crippled trek doesn't seem so bad. And yet, sometimes you think about it in a different way. What was the ride if you're going to be fed and roofed? It could be over in a minute if they were really keen. They'd just use your body for friction, then release. But for it, you'd have had some food, some money. You could get as drunk as them.

You shake your head and guilt gnaws at your chest. These thoughts. You don't know what's wrong with your thoughts. You can't trust them anymore.

Something whacks into your hip as you lay across the bank with your leg in the river. You're blocking it. It's a narrow silver tailed fish.

'Oh!' you shout and grab a hold of it. It resists against you, even though it's no bigger than your hand. It's struggling forward and backwards. You're losing your grip so you fling it onto the grass behind you. You hop over to it. It's still. When you inspect it, it flaps and panics in a fit. It stops again.

'I'm sorry, buddy,' you say. It flurries around. 'Come on. Choke.'

You leave it flailing for a few minutes. When it seems dead, you pick it up and look at its yellowish eyes, its big black pupils. Some cultures eat raw fish. Surely that can't kill you? Surely you'd have a better chance of dying if you didn't eat it? Wasn't there water in their eyes too?

You check the brightness of the sun, looking skyward for a second. Was a fire possible? Wasn't this country all kindling, ready to go up in flames?

You hum and look around. You hop to the edge of the forest and pick up some twigs and bring them over near the fish. Grabbing two rocks you try and channel MacGyver, grating them off each other, hoping for a spark.

'Come on, light, you bollocks.'

Nothing happens. You sit down and sigh and look at the fish.

'Probably going to have to eat you as you are. Hope you taste good.'

You lift it and put a voice on for it, 'I taste alright, you bitch.'

'Hey,' you say.

'State of you,' it says.

'State of you,' you reply.

'Ya slag. Ya fucking eejit. You'll spend the rest of your days out here, on your own, going mad. You deserve it too. So fucking thick.'

'Hey, come on, lay off me,' you say and squint at it.

The fish writhes again, resurrected. You scream. How long can they survive out of the water? You slam it off the ground five times and it bleeds. You didn't know fish could bleed. You never thought about it before. You pick up the rocks and bang them off each other. Twist them against each other. Scrape them. Throw them away and pick up the fish, hit it off the ground again to make sure it's dead. You wipe the grit and muck off it and look for the softest bit of its body. You sink your teeth into its underbelly, just past its throat.

You suck its eyeballs till they pop in your mouth, fishy juice that tastes of the river but juice all the same.

It's the worst meal you've ever had. You get your shoe and hobble along, trying to stay out of the way of the molesting sun. You tongue free stringy skin that has got caught between your teeth and spit it on the ground.

You keep moving. You're gagging thinking about the fish. Just remember something else, Fiona. Irish college. Being in the *Gaeltacht*, chanting '*Amhrán na bhFiann*', over and over until it was memorised. And the *Bean an Tí*, waking her 'guests' at 5 a.m. for breakfast because she had to go milking after. If you didn't get up, she poured water on your head. If that didn't work, she banged a stick off your headboard and threatened to call your parents.

You got your first kiss in Connemara, after a *Ceilí Mór*, with a Wicklow boy who had red hair and so many freckles, his skin was blotched brown against the pale. He was thirteen, a year younger than you. He gripped your hand and you walked around the back of the hall. His teeth scraped your lips but you were delighted with yourself when you went home. You weren't a child anymore.

You limp and remember the other lads you've shifted. Picture their faces. When it comes to Malley, you make him much bigger and taller than he is in real life. You do it so he can be more physical in your memory. So that him being so rough with you could be matched by some sort of brawn.

Last thing you'd heard about him was that he was seeing someone else. Some other fucking idiot had swallowed his charm and would face his wrath soon. Or maybe it was just you who annoyed him? Maybe you were the only one.

You heave a sigh.

How could you miss being with a man who made you feel lonelier in a relationship than you are out here in the wilderness?

But he didn't always do that. Though you could never say it out loud, when you made up after an argument, after he got aggressive or you got crazy upset, it was electric. It was raw and charged passion. You stuck it out for that. For the way he'd be affectionate and promise no more heartache. He needed you. You needed him to need you, it made you feel complete, wasn't that what a woman was for? Wasn't that what a relationship was?

The night that it snowed outside and the water supply got cut off, you lit candles and set the duvet on the living room floor. He sang along to Pearl Jam and said with an intensity that made you tremble that he would die for you.

Big statement.

Empty statement.

Anyone could say something immeasurable like that. He wouldn't visit your family, he accused you of cheating if you spoke to other men, he'd itch his fingers and snarl if you asked him a question he didn't want to answer. But he'd die for you.

He'd die for her now probably. And you'll die here and never be found.

*

You wake early, the dawn just beginning. Your face is wet from lying on the ground. You touch the grass. Dew drops. You lick the beads. You take off your t-shirt and mop the grass with the sleeve until it's soaked, squeeze the drops into your mouth. You do this until the sun dries everything and starts burning the skin on your back.

You check your foot, the bruise has coloured it a dark purple-green. The swelling has gone down or at least doesn't feel as painful. A fat caterpillar crosses over your toes.

You've seen it before on TV, you know the Aboriginal people used to get protein from insects. Bushtucker. You take a deep breath, pick it up and chew it.

Done.

Fuck off squeamish, helpless Fiona. Those days are gone.

The birds hoot as you follow the river. A tree with low branches blocks you and you duck to get under it. Loads of lumps of larvae are stuck on the bark and you pick one off, close your eyes and crunch down on it. Your teeth crush it making juice squirt and leak from your mouth. But you wipe your chin and keep chewing. It tastes nutty. You take another one. And another.

The rays hit the leaves on the trees, everything is neon. The contrast turned up. Bright greens and blues. Yellows.

Australia could be so beautiful.

Your mam would love this forest. She liked bringing you and your sister for cycles in the woods outside town on a Sunday, her only day off in the week. She worked every morning, going to the hotel early to wash pots and peel spuds and carrots and onions for the lunchtime carvery. She left there to clean big houses and offices. In the evenings, she tried to have dinner ready and everything in order for when you got back from school and your father finished on site. She never wanted ye to be poor. She kept you in the same clothes and shoes as the girls from the houses she cleaned.

A lump comes to your throat. Your mam, always trying to give you the best life, and look at you here and what you've done with yours.

Her raw hands and fingers. Her modest smiles when she was in town and met people you knew. She was always aware when you were embarrassed of her. What reason did you ever have to feel like that? To be embarrassed that your mother worked hard? None except trying to look cool for people you didn't even like. You want your mam to hug you now. To take your hand and help you out of here.

The sun goes behind a cloud. A big black turkey with a red head, wiggly yellow throat and black beak struts by you. You consider chasing it to break its neck. But how will you eat it? You're too weak to even think about how much effort that would take and how bloody and feathery it'd be if you didn't cook it.

You walk closer to the forest and look out for fruit or berries. Grapes. Anything. You munch on different leaves, on yellow and orange flowers, hoping they won't leave you sick in your stomach again.

You eat unripe things that you've never seen before. Some have the texture of kiwi fruit, or taste sweet like cherries or sharp like gooseberry. You're constantly sick but you're kind of getting used to that.

*

The next while, you trek underneath the tall, guardian-like trees. You don't disturb the giant webs that lay over paths, you go around them, or if they're spun across the tress, you go under them.

Sometimes you stop to watch the birds, to listen to them, to call out to them, make up conversations. 'Grand day, isn't it,' 'Any craic?' 'None, now, yourself?' You can shout as loud as you want.

You get into the river and let it take you downstream for a while, just floating. But your skin flares and you get out, dry up and hit the shade again. Mostly, you're under eucalyptus trees and other trees you don't know the names of. You don't know the names of anything. It's like this whole new world has been unlocked for you, a world you'd always been in but never aware of.

You make camp to nap at the base of trees or even by the river if it isn't too cold. The insects feed on you. They bite and hover and taunt you.

'I'll eat ye if ye don't fuck off,' you say but they never take heed. You lay and watch the sunset. The purple, gold, pink, red changing into blues; royal, navy, violet, midnight. Once tiredness comes, you sleep soundly.

You wake with the sun.

*

Your eyes snap open and you watch it from where you slept on a flat patch near a bare gum tree. It's at least four foot, slim, brownish-skinned, marble-dark eyes. Its movements, quick and deliberate, aware of everything around. Vibrations tremor through it. It looks smooth, assured. You couldn't move if you tried.

It coils and uncoils and dips in and out of the drier cracks in the ground. Its body is lithe, its scales have flecks of a lighter brown, dark green and black. The pattern curves around it to a soft whitish underside. Its head is rectangular. It doesn't hiss.

It approaches. Swift. Deliberate. Its face is right in front of yours. You look it in the eye. Its mouth opens and a black pronged tongue flashes out and in. You don't know if it's poisonous. You try to breathe.

It moves closer, flicks its tongue again. You don't know if you should strike or jump or scream.

It lifts its neck. Shit. Its body starts rising. You can't look away from it.

Shit. Shit. Shit.

Your senses are all alerted.

Danger.

Now.

'Please don't bite me. Please don't bite me.'

You need to get away. Your pulse drums in your ears.

Its tongue flickers. Its body makes a slight S shape in the air.

You need to get the hell away. You push yourself up on your arms as quick as you can but it springs. It's like a hard punch into your face. It latches onto your cheek. Its teeth pierce your skin. You grasp its body. With two hands you pull it off and fling it as far as you can, towards the river. You look back and can't see it. You touch your cheek. Clear sap and blood on your fingers.

You slap a long legged insect away from your face. Then another. Fucking bloodsuckers. You massage the back of your left shoulder, your muscle is pulled. You get up properly and limp on, holding the wound.

*

If there's lethal venom, how would you know? Would you just drop walking? Would you convulse and puke and turn a different colour with the poison? Would it be metallic, spreading all across your face? But when you touch the bite, it feels like a scratch, it isn't swelling much. Your face is tender when you move your mouth. That's grand. You've nothing to smile about anyway.

All you can do is keep going and wonder what the fuck will get you next.

The sky changes in the middle of the day and with it, everything changes. The air becomes charged, tense. The clouds rush to dark grey and the winds pick up. It's the quickest swing in weather you've seen. Within an hour, a storm begins and torrential rain spits down though it's a warm rain. You keep your mouth open, it moistens your tongue and throat.

The river gets wild under the storm, the trees buckle in the forest. You crouch down in a gap and feel dragged by the winds. Your hair smacks your face. Thunder rumbles and lightning flashes up the whole sky, making it pink. The lightning is forked and bolts of it smash into itself while other bolts hit the ground.

You start to pray even though God probably forgot about you a long time ago.

The river rises quickly. It's not safe. You need to get higher. You wanted water so badly, now it's going to kill you. The ground goes soft and your bad foot keeps letting you down. You fall on your face into the mud.

Is there a point to any of this? Should you stay down and let nature take you? Call this whole thing off? This joke of a woman you are, this joke of a girl.

You sigh and push yourself up and stumble forward.

Not after all this.

Not yet.

The wind bashes you and the river gets higher. You try to get to the forest. Rainwater seeps down, making it hard to get a grip on anything. But you struggle on, clinging and heaving. Finally, you're at the forest's edge. The leaves are pelted with rain.

The river is wider now and alive. Even the marsh land is disappearing. Rainwater stings your eyes and fills your mouth and ears and nose. It drowns them in hisses and glugs. You can barely breathe as you face the storm. But you're refreshed.

You laugh and raise your arms and a feeling washes through you. The storm cleaves the air.

It's terrifying here.

It's fucking glorious.

*

Late in the evening, the storm dies and the forest is glistening with raindrops. You shiver in your wet clothes and try to figure out what to do to dry off. You hobble further through the forest to find a dry patch, or somewhere exposed to hang your clothes and let the air take the damp from them. You keep a watch to the left to see how far away you are from the edge, from the river, in case you get disorientated and lost amongst the trees.

From the corner of your eye, you see the swish of long, dark hair move behind a tree.

Fuck.

'Who's there?' you shout. 'Hey, who are you?'

You've become so accustomed to being on your own that it makes your heart speed to think that someone else is here.

You walk over slowly to where you'd seen it. You tremble from fear as well as from your soggy clothes.

A middle aged lady is bent down, picking mushrooms and putting them in a food bag. She doesn't turn to greet you or explain herself or anything. Her hands have big blue veins bulging as she picks.

You cough. She stays where she is, working away.

'Hey,' you call. 'Hey, lady.'

You tiptoe over and tap her back. She gasps and drops the food bag as she turns, holding her hand to her chest.

'Oh, my, I didn't expect to see someone out here. Girl, you gave me a fright,' she says. She removes two earphones from her ears and turns off her iPod.

'What were you listening to?' you ask. Your voice is high pitched. You sway as you stand.

'Joy Division.'

'I know them. I like them. I do. Transmission.'

'What are you doing out here?'

You lose your balance and clutch onto a tree. 'Yeah. I don't have an answer. Isolation, wasn't that one of their songs? I don't know. What are you doing out here?'

'Calm down,' she says and puts a hand up. 'It's okay.'

'I – the storm – I—'

125

'Okay, relax. Calm down. Take some deep breaths with me. Yes?' She looks older than your mother but her skin is unblemished and pale. She wears a long navy smock over jeans and her feet are in construction worker boots.

You sigh a yes and copy the way she's breathing. After five deep inhalations and releases, you feel your heartbeat slow down.

The woman gathers her dark hair and twirls it around. 'What you doing out here, girl?' she asks.

You shrug. 'I'm lost, I guess.'

Your mind goes empty for a moment and you have to search it. Find memories for how you got here. Antonio's bitty nails on his fat hand holding the gear stick, the curdled milk in Fletchers' fridge, Jett's stained white singlet falling on the ground. His tongue in your mouth. Your chest gets tighter. Your eyes squint.

'Are you okay?' she asks.

'I don't know.'

'Scottish?'

'Irish.'

'Where did you come from?'

'I followed the river. I don't know where I was. Or where I am now.'

Tears brim against your bottom lids.

'Oh, girl,' she says and opens her arms out.

'I'm all wet,' you say.

'Come here.'

She embraces you. You begin to cry into her shoulder. She's warm and you can smell lemon shampoo and sweat off her hair.

'I'm sorry,' you say after a minute or so. You straighten yourself, rub your eyes and face, take a deep breath up your nose clearing and sucking the snot back.

'Don't be sorry,' she says. She looks around. 'I'm just waiting on my partner Geoff. Don't be afraid. We're not hippies either. These mushrooms aren't magic. They just taste good. And they're easy to find after a storm.'

Geoff comes bounding through the trees a couple of minutes later. He has white hair that fuzzes out under his baseball cap. He wears cream slacks and a rugby top. He looks fit but he has a slight limp and when he stands still, he massages his elbows and the bottom of his back.

'Who's this, Dorothy?' he asks the woman cheerfully.

'This is – I don't know,' she says. 'You never told me your name, doll.'

'I'm Fiona,' you say and offer your hand. He gives it a firm handshake.

'Fiona, are you hungry?' he asks.

'Have you anywhere to go?' Dorothy asks.

'I – I don't, not really. No.'

'Look at your foot, love,' Geoff says and points.

'I know, yeah. It's getting a bit better, I think.' You forgot that you're only wearing one shoe. The other washed away somewhere in the storm.

'Your face?' he says.

'Oh yeah, a snake got me,' you say and imagine its lunge again. 'I don't know if it was poisonous. Would I be dead if it was?'

Geoff comes closer and closes one eye to examine the bite with his other. Stray white hairs whisker on his cheeks

127

and his skin is clear and waxy.

'Doesn't seem infected. What did the bugger look like?'

You tell Geoff the details you can remember. He presses around the bite to see if anything comes out. It pinches and you try to stay still.

'You're safe, I reckon. Lucky.'

Dorothy rubs her throat. She exchanges glances with Geoff and nods at you.

'Well, you'll come to the cottage for some dinner?' Geoff invites.

You check both their faces. You haven't seen a human face since…

Geoff and Dorothy are real. They aren't birds or fish or grubs. They seem kind. You don't know what you should do.

'Ye won't give me back to the Fletchers'? Or Antonio?'

'What?' Dorothy asks.

'Ye won't give me back to the men?'

Dorothy's eyes grow wide at Geoff but they soften when she looks at you. She moves closer and puts her arm around you. You fold into her side.

'Fiona, you'll come with us and we'll get you some dry clothes and food. We won't give you to anyone. I promise you, love.'

*

Their car is a half-mile walk away and Geoff offers you a piggyback but you decline and shuffle beside them. It's an hour's drive to their house. It's like you've never noticed what a car looked or felt like before. You touch the seat and window. Smell the exhaust. You are amazed by the road, by signs, by the civilisation of the sporadic houses and cars you pass on the way.

Geoff explains that you're on the Victorian side of the border with New South Wales. When he gives you a map, you look at the outback village where the hostel had been and where you are now. There's no distance between them. Are you far enough away?

You get to their cottage. It's on top of a small mountain. You gaze around. Farmland, vineyards, hills and forest everywhere. You can see a river in the distance. You wonder if it's your river.

The cottage is a four-bed and wooden. Bright and mismatched flowers grow around it. The door sign says, 'Beware of the Dog' and 'Sorry about the Mess but We Live Here' in crazy fonts and patterns. The house isn't locked and when Geoff opens the door, a little white furry dog jumps up and down off his leg, yelping.

They bring you in and make you a cup of strong coffee. It's nice and strange to be in someone's house. You'd forgotten your own family home back in Ireland, a bungalow near the church. Your dad on his chair by the fire watching Reeling in the Years and tutting, 'It feels like only yesterday,' regardless of whether the show was looking back on 2004 or 1978.

Dorothy's house is different but it has that feel of a good place. The feel of a home. The faint smell of cooking, of fruit, of dog. The clutter of being lived in. She shows you pictures of her sons. They are handsome, ruddy men with strong jawlines. Even her youngest, who's twenty-two, is married with kids.

She shows you pictures of her grandchildren and bits and pieces of the artwork they'd made for her – a lollipop-stick-framed painting with scribbly people in a garden, a poem about her typed neat and autographed.

You smile but feel inadequate, twenty-four years old and unable to look after yourself, never mind anyone else.

Geoff busies himself in the kitchen. You hear him open the fridge and the oven, clatter pots and pans. He whistles and clicks his fingers as he prepares the food.

Dorothy puts the pictures back and offers you more cushions. When you've finished your coffee, she sits beside you and takes your hand.

'So, what's going on, girl? Are you a runaway?'

You take a deep breath. Could you tell her?

'Yes, kind of.' You sigh one of those shaky sighs before you might cry. 'I did something really stupid, Dorothy. Really stupid.'

'I ain't a judge or juror, doll,' she says.

You clamp your teeth. Struggle with how to tell her without it sounding awful. She waits.

'I ended up in a house way out in the bush. Just men and me. You know what I mean?'

She nods. Her mouth is downturned.

'I escaped, I didn't stay for long. Before they could…'

She squeezes your hand.

'And they chased me, but I hid, waited for them to go and I walked. Followed the river. I have nothing, I just have myself.' You look down at your clothes, which are threadbare in parts from being wet and dried by the sun.

'How long you been walkabout?' Dorothy asks.

'Don't know. Maybe three days? I'm not sure. It felt like a really long day with scary nights in between. Thought I'd end up in a town, or something. But there was nothing. Just the river, the bank and the trees beside it. I only met ye because the storm forced me deeper into the forest.'

She keeps a hold of your hand. 'Don't worry about anything. My girlfriend Meryl will call later. She's a doc and she'll check your foot. We'll set up the internet after dinner and you can apply for a new passport. You can also contact the police.'

'Why?'

'Because you need to report the hostel man and those farmers.'

'But Dorothy, it was my own fault, like. I asked for help. I agreed to the offer.' Your breathing narrows.

'Well, I'm going to report them. Bloody morons. You were in a vulnerable situation. They took advantage. That's exploitation, love.'

'No, no, wait. I did it, it was my decision.'

'Love, it's bloody trafficking and it needs to be reported.'

'Dorothy, please. I don't want anyone to know.'

'Who do they think they are? Giving us good farmers a bad rep, and you listen to this carefully, you didn't deserve it. No one deserves it.'

'My family are devout and they'd be crushed if they knew. I think it sounds worse than what it was. I'm fine. Please don't report me.'

She stands and puts her palms up. 'I really think you should talk to the cops. You don't have to press charges,

131

but let them put it on file. It could help them in the future if these ratbags are running something.'

'I'll think about it, I swear,' you say and exhale a deep breath.

She gives your shoulder a squeeze and says she'll be back. You massage your temples with your knuckles. How could you report them without acknowledging you consented to it? You brought it on yourself. Dorothy didn't realise that you knew what you'd agreed to.

You look at all the bookshelves they have around the room to distract yourself. Encyclopaedias. Collections. A whole shelf of books by Patrick White. Loads of biographies, history and geography books. You pull down one on nature. Flick through the pages to see if you recognise the plants or trees or fish.

Dorothy returns with a bundle under her arm. She lays it on the couch and unfolds a big red t-shirt and red and white board shorts, holding them outwards for you to see.

'These were my Brett's, but he won't notice them gone. He hasn't lived here for years now,' she says. 'And these sandals are mine. I think they'll be too big for you but you can strap yourself into them. Oh,' she says and taps her forehead. 'I'm a flaming wally, back in a moment.'

She returns with a white bath towel that smells of fabric softener.

You bury your nose in it.

'You'll take Brett's bed for the night?' she asks and leans over the stove.

You accept and look at her, puzzled as she lights it.

'It gets chilly this high in the mountains,' she says.

You go into the bathroom to wash. When you see yourself in the mirror you cover your mouth and have a closer look. You're brown and thinner than you were in that hostel. You guess you're around seven stone. Maybe less. The snake bite tracks in a small circle on your cheek. Your teeth are glowing white against your skin. Your hair has bleached in the sun. There's dirt on cracks in your neck and your skin is peeling in patches.

You touch the toilet paper, pump some liquid soap, open the medicine cabinet and close it again. You brush your teeth with your finger, using their menthol toothpaste. It makes your mouth tingle and your tongue numb.

You shower, lathering with Dorothy's shower gel, the foam is delicious to rub over your body. You wash your hair with her lemon shampoo.

When you get out, you put on some neroli oil moisturiser let it dry on your body. Brett's clothes are soft. You brush your hair, forcing through all the knots. You look in the mirror again, from different angles. You smile at the sensation of being clean but ruin it for yourself by thinking of the Fletchers' house.

*

Meryl is an elderly doctor with an old style medicine bag and stethoscope. She inspects your foot, pressing and massaging it.

'How'd you do that to yourself, love?' she asks as she bends over it.

You look to Dorothy. Her face is stern but she doesn't offer an answer for you.

133

'I tripped in the bush,' you say.

Meryl bandages it properly and recommends rest. It's not broken but it's had a 'bashing.'

When Meryl leaves, Dorothy asks, 'Do you want to phone your parents?' and shows you into the PC room. You dial but the call diverts to voicemail.

'Hi, Mam, Dad.' Your voice is much more formal speaking to the machine. 'I'm just dropping ye a line to say I'm okay. I'll send an email instead with the craic because I don't want to be using too much time on the bill payer's phone. Lost my mobile, sorry, but will get a new one soon. Okay. Bye.'

You return to the living room and the dinner is on plates, steaming.

'Tuck in,' Geoff says.

For the mains, a mushroom and lemon risotto with garlic bread. Geoff and Dorothy talk as they munch, giggling at each other's stories and adding to them. The food is great but it's hard to eat. Your stomach feels small.

You thank them when dinner is done. Dorothy dials up internet on her PC. You apply for a new passport and pretend you'd got information and procedure on how to report the farmers and Antonio which Dorothy congratulates you for. You write your parents the quick email you promised, sending apologies because you've been living and working in a nature reserve with no technology. It doesn't seem like a full lie.

*

A few nights later, you're watching an old movie on TV. Geoff snoozes on the one-seater. The dog is asleep on his lap. Dorothy picks up a notebook when ads are on.

'What do you write?' you ask.

'I don't know. Ideas. Maybe draw some pictures or do puzzles. Sometimes lines of poems. Advertisers won't violate my brain and steal my attention.'

You smile at her. You try to imagine her when she was younger, in a hippie sixties dress and headband, being a poet or an aromatherapist and fighting for women's rights.

She checks if Geoff is still asleep and whispers, 'Fiona, when I was your age, I travelled too.'

'Did you? To where?' you ask and perk up in your seat.

Dorothy goes to the stove fire and adds wood. 'Around Indonesia and the Philippines. Wonderful. You should visit them if you can. In Ubud, I met a man. An American. Handsome. Different. I was bloody sick of Aussie blokes.'

She looks at Geoff, his face soft in sleep.

'This American brought me for dinner, to events, on excursions. I started falling for him. He talked about his hometown in Missouri and I thought it was so exotic. I could see us together forever. I was jumping way ahead of myself but,' she says and pauses, 'us women often do. So he was courting me and I thought he was Mr Perfect but his moods went erratic. He might bite my bloody head off out of nowhere. I ignored it though. Didn't want to see it. One night, he brought two bottles of wine to my guesthouse and we sat inside drinking. We'd never made love. I thought that night, that'd be the night. I was a virgin. I didn't tell him that. He thought I was so rebellious and far out for travelling on my own, I didn't want him to know. We got drunk and he said we were going to a party. I didn't want to go out, I wanted romance in the guesthouse, under the Balinese moon. Monkeys and mopeds noising in the background. He ordered me to put on a dress and make-up. I did it. He drove out of the town to a big villa, built in the jungle. A real impressive place with gigantic glass windows the size of walls. Lots of white people. Expatriates. Some young local girls too. He was holding me by the wrist. Gripping me. I should have known. I did know. I was ignoring it still. He pulled me over to an old bloke, introduced us. The old bloke was nice enough except he kept looking down my dress. "So you want to be famous," he said to me, I said, "No, no I don't," and my American holds my arm so tight I gasp. I said, "Actually, yes. Yes I do," and the old bloke brought us upstairs to a giant bedroom.'

Dorothy looks into the stove fire as she talks.

'Did they...?' you ask.

'No, no they didn't. The old bloke got a camera out and asked me to sit on the bed, pull a strap down from my dress. Pose. I did that one. It didn't seem too hard. Didn't seem like anything bad. They kept telling me I was beautiful. He wanted me to lean back, spread my legs and have the American kneel in front of me.'

She returns to her chair. 'I was tempted, Fiona, it was exciting. It was the most exciting thing that had ever happened to me. This old bloke wanting to take raunchy pictures of me and a man I thought I loved. But it was seedy too and I got scared. I said no and fled. When I got back to my guesthouse, I told the owner that I didn't feel safe, could he keep an eye on my room. But the silliest thing was—'

She holds her notebook again. 'I waited for the American to come back. To tell me he'd been coerced into bringing me. To tell me he cared for me and he was sorry. Of course he never did.'

You watch her scribble. You know what that feels like, to wait on something that you'll never get, the masochism of hope.

*

Your foot is healing. You're healthier and stronger after the week in the cottage. Dorothy and Geoff say you can stay as long as you want and be a WWOOFer, volunteering on their organic farm. It won't count for your second year though.

You break it to them at breakfast.

'I should get the last of my days and get signed off. I've done so much of the visa work, it'd be a shame not to do the last bit.'

Dorothy takes a gentle sip of her ginger tea. 'You leaving us, doll?'

You nod. You know it's a good idea. You'd get back on your feet with three weeks of working and go to Sydney, get a job in property. Or anything.

Geoff strokes his hair. 'Fiona, love, do you eat garlic?'

'Em, yeah,' you say and think about it for a minute. 'Yeah, I do. Why?'

'Well, my brother's wife's cousin has a garlic plant, down in a big town three hours from here. I could make a few calls and see can if we get you in. He'd probably know where the backpackers stay. But Fiona, you'd absolutely, undeniably, totally stink of garlic all the time. You hear me?'

You smile. 'Yes.'

'I'll make the call so,' Geoff says and rises.

Dorothy finishes her tea and gathers the breakfast plates. 'I'm going to miss you. You make me clucky. I never had a girl around.'

'I'm sorry,' you say and get a cloth to wipe the table.

'No apologies. Now, before you leave us, let's go to the village. I'm not sending you off in those,' she says and points.

You look down at yourself in the XL surfer clothes. 'No, no, Dorothy, if you'll let me keep what I've on me, I'll be grand.'

'Fiona, you don't know what we've got in the village for clothes. This ain't no Brunswick Street or Bourke Street Mall.'

Geoff is chuckling and chatting on the phone in the room with the PC. He hangs up, comes out, claps his hands and says, 'That's sorted, love. You'll get inducted tomorrow. They'll put you in a section where you'll have a stool so you can rest your foot. And you're provisionally booked into a small female-only backpackers in the town. I hope you don't mind, it was the one that the factory recommended.'

You hug him.

Dorothy asks Geoff to drop you to the village for retail therapy.

*

You drive down the hillside past miles of small cottages, farms, trees. You ask what the different ones are. Dorothy shows you the River Oak, Red Gum, Blackbox, Coobilah, Silver Wattle.

The village has Victorian style buildings and would have been like a postcard if it wasn't crumbling down so much. On the main street is a small IGA grocery shop, a butchers, a post office and across the road, two op shops and a hotel. It's called a hotel but it looks like a country pub.

'Now we've got Vinnies or Red Cross to pick up some outfits.'

You choose Vinnies first. Charity shops smell the same everywhere. A kind of perfume over old, stale clothes; ancient dusty books. You enjoy flicking through the rails. You find two t-shirts from the 'Dollar Bin' and a pair of black shorts.

Dorothy tells you to get a frock so you try on a dark purple dress that has loose long sleeves and a belt. It makes you less skeletal looking and the colour contrasts nicely with your hair. It seems like vintage couture but only costs three dollars.

In the Red Cross, you find some newish runners for the factory, another three plain t-shirts and a red sports jacket. The Red Cross has undies too, but they're brand new and Dorothy gets you a five pack of white granny knickers. The whole cost of everything from both places is twenty-one dollars. You're speechless.

Dorothy kisses you on the forehead when she passes the bag over.

'I'll pay you this back,' you say.

'You bloody better not.'

*

When you gather your new things into one of Brett's old schoolbags, Dorothy comes into the room and gives you a book.

'A small prezzy. It's only for nippers, love, sorry about that but you might learn something from it.'

You take the copy of *Australian Plants and Animals for Children* and give Dorothy a smile.

'Take these with you too, I've got lots of them. Just to keep you going till your first pay day.'

Dorothy hands you a small bag with cosmetics, a travel toothbrush, moisturiser, shower gel and an unused disposable razor. You notice the green notes. Two one-hundred dollar bills.

'No way,' you begin but Dorothy shushes you.

'Don't start. We're not all ferals out bush. Get on your feet. Get strong. I know what it's like to be bashed by the world. But it's not all bad. I promise.'

*

They drive you to the bus station in the village and hand you a ticket, pre-booked. The bus is due in thirty minutes.

You take the view from the village in again, try to imprint it on your memory. But when you turn you notice it. Black thick smoke clouding the distance.

'What's that over there?' you ask. Dorothy and Geoff turn to look where you're pointing.

'Ah shit, a bushfire. It could spread quickly with that wind. Crikey. Any word of this?' Geoff asks.

Dorothy shakes her head. Her face goes white and she doesn't speak for a long time.

You wonder if it was near the forest where you followed the water.

'It's awful,' you say.

You stand there, until the bus comes, listening to Dorothy and Geoff's stories of bushfires. They look worn and heartbroken as they talk about old blazes that raged, the damage caused and their hopes this one will get contained quickly.

They say goodbye, ask you to write to them. You want to pay them back for their hospitality.

Dorothy says quietly, 'Don't pay us back, love. Pay it forward to someone else. That's the traveller's way. Value yourself. Respect yourself. Look after yourself. Promise?'

'Promise.'

They wave you onto the bus and return their gaze to the horror and trance of the bushfire destroying the land. They stand there powerless to do anything to stop it.

*

The hostel is a large, three-storey yellow building. It's clean and sterile inside with white walls and a chlorine smell. When you check in, the hostel worker gives you a faded lilac single bed sheet, a plain pillow cover, a 'doona' cover that has red and black stripes, a plastic basket with a cup, chipped plate, bowl, knife, fork and spoon.

'This is great,' you say.

'You kidding me?' she says.

'No. It's great.'

She turns her head and looks at you sideways.

Your room is on the third floor. There's no lift. You carry everything up. People going downstairs past you take a good look. They're youngish, in bright holiday clothes.

The hostel worker shows you how to use the key and says rent is every Wednesday or you're out.

'What about this week's?' you ask, your voice shaky at the threat of eviction.

'That was already paid by card,' she says.

'You sure?'

She nods and you think of Dorothy and Geoff and feel protected for the first time in a long, long time.

'Do you know if that fire is still going north of here?'

She looks solemn. 'Yeah. Heaps of bushland gone. They say it started somewhere round this place. It's not even beginning of the season yet. Arson, maybe.'

She opens the door, hands you the key and leaves. You tiptoe over the threshold. An overpowering smell of floral perfume greets you and you are careful not to step on the pile of clothes beside the door. Three girls live in the room.

One is at the mirror, squeezing her spots. One is rifling through a pile of laundry and the other is tapping on a laptop. They pause what they're doing and watch you enter.

The top bunk on the right is free. You wave hi and go

towards it. You put the basket down and throw Brett's bag on the bed. You climb onto the bunk without talking or introducing yourself properly. It's not taking much to make you panicky about being back in a hostel dorm, even if it's a different one, miles away from Antonio's place. The less anyone knows about you, the better.

'Is that all you packed?' the girl at the laundry says. Her accent is quite posh but distinctly Irish.

Your shoulders loosen. 'Where you from? I haven't heard an Irish voice in ages.'

'I'm from Kerry. Gráinne.'

Gráinne has a long neck and pinched nose. Her hair is dark red. She's a briskness when she speaks, like it's wasting her time to think and respond to what is being said.

The laptop girl slams her computer shut. 'Here, what about my accent?' She has a Northern Irish softness to her voice. She wears a grey pyjama top with red love hearts and grey short shorts showing off long, slim legs. Her face is clean of make-up but she is the prettiest of them, even though she looks a lot older than the others.

'Shut up, Louise,' Gráinne says. Louise doesn't flinch.

'I'm afraid, babes, I'm not quite a full breed,' the one at the mirror says in a Cockney accent. 'Mel.'

Mel is dressed in black 'for Amy.'

'I don't get it?' you turn to the others.

'Big fan,' Gráinne says half-whispering. 'Still in shock.'

'Why?'

The three of them stare at you. Louise tells you about Amy Winehouse's death and about some crazed gunman in Norway.

'How did you not hear about these things? Where were you before this?' Gráinne quizzes.

You gulp. 'I just suppose I hadn't really – I didn't really pay attention.' Your face burns.

Louise butts in, 'It's easy for that to happen, pet. We're trying to adapt down here. It's hard to focus on everything.' She gives you a warm smile and opens the door of the small wardrobe in the corner. Inside, dresses choke the space. 'This is where our stuff is,' she says and starts freeing a shelf, 'but you can probably fit all your clothes here?'

You think about your rucksack sitting in Fletchers' hallway. The cockroaches nesting in it. The men going through it, finding your underwear and sanitary products. Finding pictures of your family. The fridge magnet souvenirs from the East Coast. The scrawls of email addresses and phone numbers of people you barely remember that you met on the way. The ones that joined when you were drunk the whole time when you landed in Australia first, when you were blowing all your money.

You nod and get embarrassed again. 'I – I left my clothes with a mate. In Melbourne. Just brought that bag for the farmwork.'

Gráinne says, 'Oh,' and looks pleasantly surprised. 'Good thinking. It's hardly like we needed this, working in that stinking garlic factory.'

You sit up in the bed. 'D'ye work there?'

You want to know more about it.

'Can you not smell it?' Gráinne says and her face crumples.

You inhale through your nose and can get garlic, faintly, underneath the sickly sweet flowers. 'What's it like? I'm starting tomorrow.'

144

Louise says, 'It's grand. Me and Gráinne are both doing canteen jobs as tea ladies so we're not touching it. But still, it fucking stinks.'

Your heart sinks a little bit.

'You'll be okay,' Mel says. 'You get used to it.'

*

The factory is a huge warehouse and has a metal bridge running the length of it with walkways and stairwells to connect all the sections. Fans whizz everywhere but it's still pretty sultry inside. You're put on Section Twenty-Two and your supervisor is a lad from West Limerick called Mitchell Dunne.

'Why 'West'?' you ask.

'So you know I'm not from the city, girl. I'm from the county of Limerick. People don't get that.'

The lot of you are just 'Irish' here in Australia so it doesn't make a difference.

Three others work on your section, Si-won and Amy Park from South Korea and Tommo from Dublin who sits across from you.

Tommo is great fun but how much work he does depends on the severity of his hangover. He's got a chip on his front tooth and dimples when he smiles. When he laughs too hard, he gets wheezy.

You get three short smokos and a forty-five minute lunch break on the work shifts. You catch up with Louise and Gráinne. They've to have teas, coffees and Milos waiting in the big canteen when you get in.

145

'So yer breaks aren't any shorter waiting for the kettle to boil,' Louise explains.

They have it soft enough inside, wiping down the counters and tables, sweeping the floors and washing the dishes between breaks but you don't mind it too much on the line. You do ten hours snipping the roots and stems off garlic mostly. But some days, you have to sort it into nets or for paste. Some of the workers, mainly the backpackers, pretend they don't see anything septic in the garlic that goes down for paste. It's because if they take the rotten stuff out to drop it in the waste shoot, the gunk and wet garlic will cling to their fingers and they'll have to have a couple of showers in the evening to get rid of the smell. You're not too bothered by it, the job is decent overall and you smell of garlic anyway, so you just go with it.

Sometimes, Tommo'd be in top form and you'd be struggling to breathe from laughing so much. If Mitchell isn't about, Tommo does his Dracula impression, 'It burns,' and throws himself off his stool. It's lame but it gets you every time. The garlic rolls past you. Amy Park and Si-won have to do your work. You bring in Double Choc Tim Tams and offer the biscuits to them on smokos to apologise for messing. They don't really mind it, they're just mad to work.

Amy is a hip hop dancer in her spare time, she tells you when you wait for the line to start one morning. Tommo is late again and Si-won is talking to Mitchell.

'Are you really?' you ask.

She nods shyly.

'Will you show me?'

She checks around and nobody is looking so she gets off her seat. She jerks her head, shoulders and arms out and moves them back in, robotically. At the same time her hips twist her body around.

'Amy, that's really fucking cool,' you say and clap.

She puts her head down and smiles. She re-adjusts her hairnet before going back to her stool.

Tommo lands in and winks at you. 'How are the garlic warriors this morning?'

Mitchell pulls away from Si-won and turns to Tommo. 'What time do you call this, boy?'

Tommo's cheery face drops.

Mitchell takes a deep breath.

'The belt hasn't even started, Mitchell. Chill the beans,' Tommo says and right on this cue the warning signal sounds. The belt begins chugging. Within seconds the garlic is at your section.

Mitchell walks away.

Tommo checks to see if he's out of earshot. 'I've a BA, a Postgrad and an MA, so I do. I know they're only in Arts but what has Mitchell, the stupid culchie? Nothing but attitude. Seeping out his big pores along with the fucking garlic.' His Dublin accent grows thicker when he's mad.

'Hey Tommo, I'm a stupid culchie too.'

'You're not stupid, Fiona. Never say that again.'

Mitchell is always fuming with Tommo. He's constantly catching him out arsing around. Even if Tommo is doing some work, Mitchell still threatens him.

'I'll ask them to move you out of this section. I don't give a fuck if we're both Irish,' Mitchell says as he rubs the beads of sweat under his hairline up through his hair making it wet and high off his head. 'Not a fuck.'

You're happy coming home from work and hanging out with the girls, even though you see Louise and Gráinne at break time. Mel worked in the factory before you were here but got a bar job and quit. You can properly relax in the room in the evenings. You don't even do much. You don't need to. It's just comfortable. Everyone has their bad habits, Mel is constantly popping her zits and talking about men, Louise bursts into song in the middle of conversations and Gráinne is so sarcastic it's hard to know when she's joking or when she's being a total cow. You wonder what they dislike about you and try to keep off their toes.

You take turns making dinner for each other. You never tell them about the outback and the things you'd eaten, you can only give them weak smiles when they frown or are grossed out by onions or mayonnaise or fat on meat.

They loan you their clothes and once you get paid, you get some bits – a cheap Nokia, strong sun block, factory boots, a small backpack.

You read snippets of Dorothy's book whenever you can, trying to learn more facts about Australia's environment.

Saltwater crocodiles or 'salties' are the most dangerous species of crocodiles to humans. They loiter and bask in sunshine during the day and hunt at night. They aren't picky eaters and usually deploy the 'death roll' to kill. They seize their prey in an inescapable grip and roll over, throwing their prey off balance, making it easy to drag into the water, sometimes eating it all in one go.

*

Mitchell is running around the place, his shirt sleeves rolled past his elbow. His hair standing tall. He puts his hand on your back gently. You shirk it off like it's burning hot.

'Don't touch me,' you say.

'Hey, girl, I didn't mean to hurt you.' Mitchell is confused.

'You didn't, it's fine. Sorry. I just got a fright.'

'Is it going okay here?' he asks in his lilty accent.

'Yeah, it's grand, Mitchell, cheers,' you say. You feel bad about your initial reaction so you smile at him and ask, 'How's Ingrid?'

Ingrid is his Swedish girlfriend. She sometimes offers you lifts back to the hostel. Her English is crisp and Mitchell is relaxed around her. She's expecting, due at Christmas.

'She's good, girl. Still a bit sick in the evenings. But it seems to be passing.'

'Any word on sponsorship?' you ask.

Mitchell sighs and says, 'Not yet. But we've got buyers coming over from Italy and Greece next week and I reckon if I.can get along with them, I should be elected for the visa. You know, two of the backpackers got it last year so maybe. Fingers crossed, eh.'

You smile at him and return your attention to the belt. He walks away.

'This is probably the height of his career. This and the hamster porno he'll no doubt star in,' Tommo says over

149

the rhythmic shrill of the conveyor.

'I don't know why you're so harsh on him, Tommo. He's sound enough.'

'Do you really want to know?'

'Yeah, go on.'

'Nah, I'm saying nothing,' Tommo says and laughs. He's quickly choked by his raspy cough. He slaps his chest. 'Fucking joints are ruining me lungs.'

'They'll ruin your brain too,' you say.

'Ah, that's well rotted by this place.'

*

The Friday before the buyers come, Mitchell walks around and Si-won lets out a little scream. Mitchell comes to see what's happening. Si-won never fusses. He holds onto his finger tight. He's slit the skin with the trimmers. Blood streaks from the clean nick. You wonder if he'll need stitches.

Mitchell says, 'Look, I'll get you a band-aid but you should know, if you don't cut yourself at least once during your shift, you're not working hard enough.'

Tommo gives you eyes.

Si-won's soft face goes a bit white but all he wants to do is get back to trimming.

About thirty of Tommo's cloves go by as this is going down. Amy Park sorts them.

'She's a sexy garlic assassin,' Tommo says and winks at her.

Mitchell shouts over at him to get back to work. Tommo doesn't move so Mitchell storms over and speaks with his jaw clenched.

'You know what your problem is? You think you're still in Dublin. That this place works like there. Well it doesn't. I was in Dublin before. Awful. Homeless junkies, stuck-up bitches and lads who think they're fucking class at everything. You're not there anymore. You're in Australia and none of your Dublin city bullshit is of use here so get back to fucking work.'

He goes off to get Si-won's plaster.

Tommo starts, 'Here, d'ya wanna know the truth? What happened with us? Why I hate that dope?'

You nod. You've at least forty minutes to next smoko. And you like his mad yarns.

Tommo takes a big breath and says, 'One day, I pissed myself at work.'

He stops and checks your response. You stay still. You want to hear more.

'It was way before you got here. So, yeah, I'm not proud of it or anything. It happened because Mitchell wouldn't let me go. He knew I was hungover to death. He knew me bladder was full from all the water 'cause I was parched at the beginning of work and drank about two litres. I was hopping up and down like Elvis with me legs crossed and me face was sweating. I said, "Come on, please. I'm absolutely busting", and he said break was in twenty and I could wait.'

You press your lips tight and try not to laugh at the image.

'So I'd been waiting. I'd been waiting and waiting and I couldn't anymore. The first drop sprung hot and dangerous and next thing I was proper leaking. A relief and a shame too. It reminded me of a weird experience I had one night in Cambodia with a local girl but that's neither here nor

151

there. So the jeans were sopping and the floor was dribbled underneath me. The heat and wet was uncomfortable. The piss went cold on me skin. I sucked a breath in and called him over. Pointed to meself on the quiet. Said I told him this would happen, I was bleeding dying to go. He sent me home to change me jocks. And as I walked away from my station, he announced it again. Much louder this time so that even the non-English speakers knew something was off and they all looked me up and down and stared. Some laughed. Some gasped. Some just put their eyes back on the line, disappointed they'd become part of the drama between me and him. The routine of their shift broken. I didn't really mind though.'

'Really?' you ask.

'Yeah,' Tommo says, 'Embarrassing and all as it was, I snuck in and changed back in the hostel. Had a good auld chinwag with this girl from the next room. She was sick of picking oranges and had told the hostel owners to go fuck themselves. Wasn't going to bother trying to get the second year. Ireland has to be better than this slavery she goes and asked me why I was finished work so early. I faked a cough and said I'd to get me medicine but I was heading back to the factory. I gave her the nod. Pints later. Got into the van, got it started after a few scratchy attempts and on the way I had a stop in Hungry Jacks for a feed of pancakes and some coffee. Checked me Facebook on the phone. Checked me Paddy Power and swanned back in just in time for second morning break. I wouldn't let him know any of it got to me. I don't think it did really. Life is messy anyway.'

'I suppose it is,' you agree and chop at the never-ending garlic.

*

On the Saturday afternoon, the Irish girls suggest drinking some wine in the room before going down the town to converge at a hotel where they let backpackers in. Some of the other drinking establishments are hostile and have 'Locals Only' signs. You hear stories of backpackers getting jumped and beaten up if they are alone and how hostels with low security have been raided. Passports, laptops, phones, cameras and designer clothes stolen from travellers.

'Why do they hate us?' you ask.

Mel says, as she fills a glass with wine, 'It's 'cause before the second year visa laws changed, the locals did the work that backpackers do. Not the factory jobs, more the farming, you know? They did the work and got well paid. Livelihoods, innit? We came along, desperate for jobs and undercut the locals. Not our problem. The farmers could pay fairly if they wanted to. They could also still employ the people from the area, like. But would you, if you could get cheap workers?'

'I'd exploit the shit out of them,' Gráinne says and laughs.

'Out of us, you mean?' you ask.

Gráinne shrugs.

*

Mel says she loves Irish men.

'Really?' Louise asks with a high pitch in her tone. She grimaces.

'Yep. Can't get enough of them. Love the way they speak to me and the crap they do to charm me.'

She's dating two Irish lads from different hostels in the town and also seeing one of the Italian supervisors in the garlic factory.

You like your male friends from home and Tommo is good craic. But when you think about Irish lads romantically, an image of Malley bullies its way to the fore of your mind. You try to blank it out, like you usually do, but the alcohol won't let you this time.

You remember your last argument. He wanted you to change your outfit for an evening in the pub with his friends, something that didn't make you look so 'mousy.' You had long since abandoned your own friends. He hated them. He said they were manipulating you. You went home and put on your nicest top, a silky royal blue shirt and skinny jeans. You spent ages on your make-up, spritzed perfume on your neck, wore your pearl jewellery and brushed your hair. You couldn't get it to sit right. You changed it from being tied in a tight bun, to down with clips holding it back to wearing it loosely on your face but no matter what way you did it, you looked shit. You knew he'd be disappointed but he texted telling you to hurry so you went back and forced a smile.

You were in a booth near the fire, sitting glumly surrounded by his friends. A couple and two single men. They talked about themselves and how interesting they were. They congratulated each other on being cool. Malley smoked weed in the smoking area, downed pints, ranted about what was wrong with the world. How frustrated it made him to see so many stupid people going about their lives, not realising all he realised. He never wanted kids. He said he'd never bring another human into a disgusting place like this. The couple seemed impressed by his self-sacrifice. You were sad about it. You never knew. You'd always imagined that you'd get married and have a few of your own. That he'd change and mature and be kinder when he was a dad.

When you brought it up with him back in your flat that night, you knew you were playing with fire but you'd had a few vodkas.

'You don't want children?' you said.

He didn't answer. He smoked and put on a DVD.

'I don't want children yet, but further down the line, you know?'

He stared at the TV. His jaw fastened and a vein throbbed in his temple.

'We shouldn't rule it out, should we? I think we'd be good parents,' you say. His silence was spurring you on. You were about to start again when he caught you by the arm and pulled you down. His face was so close to yours, the tobacco stains black between his teeth, his moustache wispy, his navy blue eyes bright with rage.

'Say another fucking word while I'm trying to watch this show,' he said and released you.

You rubbed your arm. It was pink from his grip. 'Why do you threaten me like that?' You were shouting. You shouldn't have shouted.

He sprung and pushed you. You fell back against the wall, your teeth chattered.

155

He returned to his spot on the couch. 'You make me so angry and I'm not an angry person.' He wouldn't look at you. 'Your stupid nagging. See what you make me do?'

You stayed leaning against the wall, fearful that he'd go for you again, fearful that he meant what he said. He kept his eyes on the TV, turned the volume up.

You eventually left, walked around the town for hours, only wearing that blue top. Freezing under the wind and drizzle. You walked back to your parents' house, found the spare key under the flowerpot and went into your childhood bedroom with its turquoise carpet and postered walls. You lay down and stared at the roof.

And you hated yourself ever since for making him hate you.

Tears itch at the corner of your eyes so you try to be present. You take a deep breath.

You focus on Mel.

She has an angular way with her body, though it isn't curvy or proportionate, she juts it out well and holds herself confidently. She wears good-fitting clothes and has a quirky style. Her eyes suggest things that you can't decipher. She has sex appeal and she knows it.

'Does it not get complicated?' you ask.

You couldn't juggle three men.

A flurry goes through your gut – there were three Fletchers back in that farm.

'Nope. It's as complicated as you make it,' Mel says and licks her bottom lip.

'You're a slut, Mel,' Gráinne says and the guilty sensation goes through you again.

*

The girls insisted you weren't going to drink the goon and go wild. You'd sip bottled wine and be civilised. But at this stage you're at least four bottles in and it's all getting mouldy. You try your best not to talk, you know you'll only dredge him up, or worse, confess about the Fletchers.

'Fuck Ireland,' says Gráinne. 'Listen, I tell ye a story, the reason why no one wants to give out about the Celtic Tiger going to shit, is because we were the reason. You, me, you.' She points at Mel, 'Not you.'

'It's true, so true,' Louise says. 'Lads, don't think I'm loaded now or anything 'cause, I'm not, at all, but I bought a fucking house back in the Boom. 100 per cent loan. I was twenty-two.'

'What's happened to it?' you ask.

One of Louise's eyes is going to sleep. 'Nothing happened it. A Latvian family live there now. The rent covers the interest on the mortgage. It's not even paying itself off. Just paying more into the bank. I pretend it doesn't exist to be honest. I don't see it or any money from it. Probably never will.'

You know from your old job at home that about a quarter of a million Irish people have Louise's problem, more even. Imagine if you'd bought a house you couldn't pay back with Malley? Fuck.

Mel tuts and says, 'Man, this is crazy.'

'Well, let me tell you a crazier one,' Gráinne slurs. 'It goes back to it. How we were all involved. My mother got really into it with her business partner, they bought and sold restaurants. But it went tits-up, like it did for everyone. Anyway, Mother got wind of NAMA. Of debt collectors. She'd properly gone bankrupt. Them fuckers, they take everything. But she was a woman with incredible tastes and had the most beautiful pieces. She'd only wear them to balls or formals or fundraisers or launches. Antique jade and emeralds. Yellow diamonds. Black opals. And so, when she heard they were coming she hid the jewellery behind a tile in our shower.'

'What happened?' you ask.

'They came and took everything. Except the jewels. And my estranged father helped her to hold on to the house with the bank, it being a family home not completely in her name. Legalities. It's grand now. Mother is back in the restaurant industry. I think she'll start a new business. Not to the insane levels she had it at before, but just enough to stay comfortable.'

'That's all you need,' you say and Gráinne refills your glasses. 'Just enough to stay comfortable. Enough so you don't agree to anything foolish. By accident. Sort of.' You stop yourself and check you haven't said too much but they aren't paying attention to you. They are eyeing Gráinne's pour.

*

The alcohol makes your brain and body disorientated from one another. Time is blotchy. You look in the mirror at your face, try to put on eye shadow. You have to lean in closer and step back again in order to judge where your eyelid is, where the colour is going.

'I'm locked,' you say. The girls laugh.

Mel zips her dress. It's vintage, stripy and she matches it with brown cowboy boots.

Louise is beside you putting her hair in a high spiky pony-tail, spraying it and adding pins.

'The last time I dressed up,' you say and your brain goes in spots trying to think, 'It was so long ago. Really want to save some money, pay my parents back. Going out was how I spent it all the first time, I never thought. You know what I mean, Louise?'

You turn to face her, your arms are flailing a bit. 'You know how you just don't think? You don't think about con-sequences. That when the money goes, it's gone. That's it. And you can only borrow so much from people but when that's gone. That's it. Again. You didn't learn. Thick. I didn't anyway. I never think anything through properly. There's something wrong with me like that.'

You sigh and rub your face, undoing your efforts at the make-up. Louise comes over to you and stands you in front of her. She lifts your chin and examines you.

'Here, pet. Jesus, the wine's hitting you hard. Give me your eyeliner,' she says. You hand it to her and she presses her lips while she concentrates on applying it. You see how green her eyes are as she looks at yours. You try not to wobble.

'I don't remember the last time, Louise,' you say. The thought won't go away. 'It's been so long since I've gone out. I was a bit of an alco when I came to Australia. Before that even. I was using the drink to dull the way I felt. But I stopped. I did stop. I had to. I'm – I'm afraid.'

159

Gráinne laughs. She sprays a mist of perfume in front of her and walks into it. 'What are you on about, girl?'

The room clogs with that awful chemical rose scent, it makes your eye water.

'I'm not sure what to do on a night out anymore. Because before here, I didn't go out proper for a long time. A really long time.'

Louise inspects your face. She picks up a tissue, licks the corner of it and wipes the edge of your eye.

'Mascara,' she says and you pass it to her. She pumps the wand before telling you to open your eyes wide.

'What do you mean?' Gráinne asks.

'What'll I do if a lad starts chatting to me? Don't leave me on my own, will ye?'

'Sure, what harm if you get chatted up?'

'But Gráinne, I don't want to,' you say. 'I don't want to.'

Louise steps away and turns you to the mirror to examine your reflection. It looks grand but you're not too sure because of your tipsy vision.

'What do you mean?' Gráinne asks again and pauses. 'You're not a lesbian, are you? Or a frigid?'

'No,' you say and laugh. 'I fucking wish. I wish I was either. Wouldn't things be easier then?'

Gráinne gives you a funny look and raises her chin in the air.

'Nevermind,' you say to her and smile. She doesn't smile back.

Louise smears her lips with shiny sticky looking gloss and says, 'Okay ladies, we're going. Finish this conversation in the taxi.'

She rushes you out of the room, jokily whacking Mel across the arse on her way out. She turns off the light and locks the door. You stumble down the stairs to the reception, your shoes clopping on the tiles.

*

The hotel nightclub is dingy. A dirty mop smell on the sticky floor. Some of the stools and tables are unbalanced leading to more drink falling on the ground. The toilets are slightly flooded, door locks on the cubicles are uneven and so you have to lean over to hold it shut or get someone to block the cubicle from outside for any privacy.

Louise puts you on water.

'Here, drink this for a while,' she says handing a pint glass to you. She adds a straw to it. 'You're going to have two of these and if you feel like more alcohol, get it after.'

She puts her arm around your shoulder. Two guys come to the bar, one of them has a goatee, tanned skin, a plain blue t-shirt. He smiles at Louise. She smiles at him. They get talking and you stand watching them, slurping ice-water, trying not to get brain freeze or trip over. His friend tries to make eye contact with you but you turn away from him and look at the dance floor.

The club is filled with backpackers from the different hostels in the town, everyone is drinking, dancing and flirting. Some townsfolk are there too, young ones and older men who lean on the rail at the dance floor, watching and pointing.

'This place is creepy,' you say to Gráinne when she comes back to where you are near the bar. You can feel the drunkenness from earlier wearing off.

'It's brilliant craic though. Let your hair down, girl,' Gráinne shouts over the music.

You do some laps of the club and talk to some random people. Louise scores the Goatee who speaks with a heavy and charming French accent. Mel meets with one of her Irish boys. She abandoned you when you entered the club but returns later with him in tow. He's called David P and straight away when he introduces himself, you know you don't like him. He wears a gold bracelet and his pupils are black full moons.

'How ye ladies getting on?' he asks but puts loads of emphasis on the 'on.'

He bites his lip as he talks to you, asking where in Ireland you're from, pouting and feigning interest when you tell him.

'You looking for anything tonight?' he asks. His after-shave is spicy.

'What?'

'You looking for any–' He mimes snorting. 'Or a cap? Got these super strength ones up from Adelaide a while back. A half would be the same as three or four pills back home. No shit. Great great buzz. You'll feel invincible.'

'No, you're grand,' you say.

Gráinne is keen for something.

'I'm going to head off, I think. I'm too drunk,' you say but Gráinne doesn't hear you. You don't want to get any messier. You don't want to lose control.

*

When you get back to the dorm room, you take your make-up off with a wipe, the mascara leaves you with panda eyes. You get into bed and turn into the wall. The room is silent except for your breathing. You can hear some drunk hostel people outside downstairs and on the halls. Your head is banging and your stomach is uneasy. You check your phone for messages. None. You think about ringing some of the girls back home. They'd probably be getting ready for a night in Westport, deciding on who'd drive, what they'd wear, where they'd go, who they'd pull. You haven't talked to them in so long though. You don't really know what you'd say.

Don't fit in there. Don't fit in here.

You battle another wave of nausea.

Everyone's life just goes on.

You curl into a ball, hug yourself.

'It's just the drink, Fiona,' you say. 'It's just the drink.'

*

Sunday morning, you wake with the sun. You look around the room and see that Louise has the Frenchman in beside her, she's wearing the same clothes from the night before and he's spooning her, his arm heavily flung over her waist, his jaw wide open but somehow he's still graceful. No sign of Mel or Gráinne. You go down the ladder and the bunk bed squeaks a bit, waking Louise.

'Howya,' she says.

You smile at her.

'Thierry's a nice lad, a good lad,' she whispers and wipes the corners of her mouth.

'The others aren't here. I'll head out for a walk, leave ye alone. Be back in two hours or so.'

She winks at you. 'Thanks, pet.'

You like walking around the town while it's quiet. It has everything you'd need, chain supermarkets, small takeaways, boutiques, offices. It even has a newspaper. There's a hall for veterans and monuments to ANZACs who died in the First and Second World Wars and tiny parks with benches dedicated to principals and priests. The garlic factory is on the outskirts, near an industrial estate but not part of it.

You go for a coffee and croissant and read more of Dorothy's book.

Early European explorers were curious about all the unusual wildlife they saw and used to ask the native people, who are called Aborigines, what the hopping creature was. One Aborigine replied 'kangaru' which in his language meant 'I don't understand.' The explorer thought this was the name of the animal. This version of how a kangaroo got its name has become an Australian legend but isn't, in fact, true.

*

You open the dorm door to drama.

Gráinne is in front of Louise's bed. 'Who the fuck did you say it to?' She's shouting.

Louise is pleading and stays in her bunk. Her French lad is bewildered behind her. 'I said it to no one, what the hell, like. Would you calm down?'

'Calm down? Calm down? I trusted ye,' Gráinne says and turns her attention to you. 'Or maybe it was you?'

You put your hands up. 'I don't know what's going on.'

'Do you not, Fiona?'

'No,' you say and shut the door behind you.

'Well let me tell you. Around three hours ago, half-ten at night back home, my mother's house was robbed. They broke down the front door, while one of them kept a car running. They took my little eleven-year-old brother hostage. Put a fucking gun to his back. A gun, Fiona,' she pauses, squints and changes her tone, 'and this is the funny part, they went straight for, and I mean straight, for the bathroom and started cracking tiles. Does it make sense now?' She flips her attention between you and Louise. 'Well, does it?'

'Shit, Gráinne, that's mad,' you say.

'Do you think?' she says in mock horror.

'Yeah, that's mad,' you repeat.

'Yeah, mad. I'm the mad one,' she says. 'Mad to think ye were my friends. Who did you say it to? Huh? Who?'

Louise shakes her head, 'No one, Gráinne. I was hammered yeah but I didn't say it to anyone.'

'Me neither.' You put your hands up again.

'Fuck ye,' Gráinne says. 'Fucking liars.'

*

Gráinne leaves shortly after her outburst. The French lad stays on, curious. Mel comes in wearing dark, oversized shades. Her hair is fuzzy and she groans as she shuffles towards her bed. 'Sleep times,' she mumbles.

'Mel,' Louise says in a sweet voice. 'Did you talk to anyone about what we were talking about last night?'

Mel groans again and flops into her bed. 'I drank a bottle of wine, I did some lines, I did some Jaegarbombs, I did some Irish. I'd say I talked about anything to anyone who'd listen.'

A silence weighs.

Mel props herself on her elbows. 'Why do you ask?'

'No reason,' Louise says.

*

The atmosphere in the room sours. Gráinne asks to be moved but the hostel is full so she has to stay put for another week. In the canteen at work, her and Louise stand as separate as possible. You check the computer for details on the burglary but nothing is in the news. Gráinne stops speaking to you completely and avoids the dorm unless she has to sleep or grab something. She takes her clothes from the wardrobe and packs her bag, waiting for a transfer.

You meet her in the common room after work Monday.

'Gráinne, I don't know what happened or how it happened. Don't be angry with us.'

She rolls her eyes and looks beyond you to the TV.

'Don't be like this. We're your friends.'

'Are ye my friends?' she asks and stares into your eyes. 'I don't know fuck all about you. How you got here. What you did before here. You've said very little about yourself, Fiona.'

Your heart rate picks up.

'You're anyone to me. No one to me. Same as ye all. We're not proper friends. We're just using each other for company. To look popular. To not be alone. Get real, will you?'

'I don't think that way – I like ye, genuinely.'

'You're ridiculously naïve. Look, I just want to watch telly and not be disturbed.'

She sniffs and moves her head like you're blocking her view.

You walk back to the bedroom. Mel is trying on dresses for a date.

'This one?' she asks pointing at her navy polka-dotted sun dress. You nod without caring.

You think of things you should have said back to Gráinne, different ways you could have made your point, instead of just walking away. Things like you were glad you wouldn't taste her awful perfume anymore in the room. You were glad you didn't have to hear her put Louise down for being good-looking or Mel for being promiscuous. Mostly, you're glad that she's leaving because you don't want any more suspicious questions about your past.

Mel makes enough carbonara for you all after work on Tuesday but Gráinne doesn't show. As Mel brings the pots to the table to serve the dinner, you and Louise get cutlery by the sinks in the common area kitchen.

'It wasn't me, you know,' Louise says in a low voice. 'I didn't say it to anyone back home and I didn't say it to anyone here. I was with that Frenchie. I didn't have the chance to blab. It was Mel and her scumbag boyfriend. You met him, didn't you? That sleeveen from the criminal hostel out of town near the woods. The place where the dregs live and kicked the shite out of the owner. I bet she told him and he told his friends in Ireland. You know how quick information like that would go through the underworld?'

You shrug. You did suspect Mel let it slip and someone ran with it.

Mel gives you your pasta on scorching plates. Louise burns her hand on hers. She holds it for a second before flapping it about.

'Fuck sake, Melanie,' Louise says.

'Excuse me, I warned you that they were hot, babes,' Mel says. 'So, I was thinking about going to Perth soon,' she starts.

'Yeah, you give warnings, don't you,' Louise says as she pokes at her food.

168

*

Gráinne quits her job and leaves the following day while the rest of you are at work preparing the factory for the buyers' visit. She says nothing to anyone and unfriends everyone from the hostel on Facebook. She just leaves. You think about the Asian girls you stole money and bits from when you were completely penniless. You wonder if they hate you.

Was there a difference between you robbing them and Gráinne's mother hiding those jewels, or the masked men robbing her? Weren't you all the same – thieves?

Later, after you shower, you lie on your bunk and read.

Cassowaries are brightly coloured flightless birds with a large, spongy crest that protrudes from the top of their head. Cassowaries are very shy, but when provoked they are capable of inflicting fatal injuries. The second of their three toes has a long, dagger-like claw which could easily dismember a human. All cassowary species are at risk in the wild and are classified as vulnerable animals.

*

On the Thursday morning, as you walk down to your section with Amy and Si-won, you can feel the electricity around the factory. The buyers are in. The everyday feels broken because something different is happening but after a while, when you get into the monotony of the shift, you forget about them and are busy sorting.

Tommo is steaming drunk. You know it when you first sit in front of him. His eyes are bloodshot, he's a three-day shadow on his cheeks. He pretends not to see the big chunks of diseased garlic rolling by him.

'Do you honestly not mind touching that shit?' he asks.

'It's not the worst thing that could happen, Tommo. Having a smelly hand isn't a big deal when you consider what badness is out there,' you say.

He shrugs. 'The first night I came to this town, I got with a lovely Italian girl. Beaut. Black hair, brown eyes, big lips. Very sensual. I had heard the women were gagging for it in the outback. Thought I was fucking elected. Bang bang bang. I got this job on me third day and nothing with the ladies since. Nothing. Nada. It has to be the garlic. The no-fucking fucking garlic,' he says and flicks at the garlic but lets it roll down the line.

You smile. 'So you think the garlic is the reason?'

He straightens up. 'Yeah, Fiona, I'd say it has a lot to do with it. I could be in better shape but I was always on the meaty side. Working in this place though is bringing me confidence down. I'm literally down under. Mitchell. Fucking Mitchell. I reckon he eats garlic for breakfast dinner and supper. Garlic and spuds and flasks of *tae* probably.' Tommo clenches his jaw. 'Here he comes, der Führer himself.'

Mitchell has a clipboard and looks more formal than usual. He's nervy. He flashes a smile at you and checks some things off on his board.

'Everything alright?' he asks. He scans around.

'Yeah, it's grand,' you say. 'Are the buyers about?'

'They're going to come by our section soon, heard from some of the forkies. I did some study last night. On Google. Did you know this, how garlic is good for people, an anti-biotic, anti-septic, reducing your risk of cancer and toxins and blood pressure?'

'It's a member of the lily family too,' you say.

Mitchell is beaming. 'It's an anti-inflammatory and natural pesticide. The mozzies won't be at you when your blood has garlic in it. It can help control weight even though it makes things taste so good. All that. I learnt it just in case they ask when they're here.'

He's like a schoolboy itching for a gold star. You give him a smile and Tommo starts a little clap.

'That'll knock the cocks off them,' Tommo says.

Mitchell's grin plummets. 'Are you still drunk?'

'No,' Tommo says. 'I was praising you.'

Mitchell walks over to Tommo, puts his head in close to him and sniffs.

'You smell like an alleyway on Paddy's Day. You're on your last legs here. If you do anything out of order again, you're gone.' In an exaggerated Dublin accent he adds, 'Do ya bleeding understand that?'

Tommo gets off his seat and fumes past Mitchell, their shoulders clashing.

'Get back here,' Mitchell shouts but Tommo is stomping his way towards the jacks.

When Tommo eventually comes back, his eyelids are pink and puffed.

'Tommo, you okay?' you ask.

'I'm fucking sound, Fiona. Sound, now. Couldn't be better. I've a BA, a Postgrad and an MA, so I do. I'll show him, so I will. Mitchell. I'll show him. Power corrupts, absolute power corrupts absolutely. I got 510 points in the Leaving. I'll fucking show him not to talk down to me like I'm as thick as him.'

'Tommo, it's just the booze from last night that's upsetting you. Don't worry about him. His girlfriend's pregnant and he's stressed trying to get this sponsored visa. Ignore him.'

'You're a lovely girl, Fiona.'

He throws a receipt with his name and number scrawled in blue ink over it.

'Keep in touch, yeah? I'll miss working with you. I'm going to show him though, show him fucking good.'

*

After big break, you notice the suited Europeans walking around the factory with the owner and top level managers and supervisors beside them, pointing at things, putting on a show. Mitchell is trying to get their attention to come and see your section. They acknowledge him and stride across a metal walkway towards you.

Tommo is leaning back on his seat. He's thumbing his phone above his head with one hand. The other holds his

172

clippers even though he isn't trimming. You try to call him but he ignores you.

Mitchell glances at him from where he stands.

'A dog warming his bollocks in the sun wouldn't be as bad as you. Will you put away your phone and get back to work,' Mitchell hisses.

'No,' Tommo says. All Dublin. Calm.

'Tommo, just put the phone away, will ya?' you say.

'Stay out of it, Fiona.'

The suits walk down the stairs, they'll be on the line in less than a minute.

Mitchell thunders towards Tommo.

'What's the matter, Mitchell? The Dolmios and Greckos are going to see you've no authority?'

They watch the men come. Tommo leans back further on his stool. He's real elaborate now. You look down the line, even the Koreans are watching.

Mitchell goes over and snatches the phone from him. Tommo protests and he pulls his hand from behind his head, clippers perched.

Oh shite.

The supervisors and managers are talking amongst themselves but they're at your line.

'Fuck you, Mitchell,' Tommo says. 'Fuck you.' He opens the trimmers.

He's going to stab Mitchell.

Mitchell flinches and shuts his eyes.

You shut yours too. Feel hot. Sick. Why does it have to go so extreme?

You hear gasps.

A man's roar.

Commotion.

You open your eyes and look at Mitchell to see where the blade went. He wipes himself rapidly and looks up, confused.

It's like everyone cops on at the same time. Maybe because the blood starts colouring the garlic red.

Tommo has done it to himself.

He's cut the top of his middle finger off. Blood spills over the garlic. You scream but don't notice until you shut your mouth. One of the Europeans passes out.

Stuff gets too bloody, the belt, all of Tommo's hand, his uniform. His blood is everywhere. Amy screams this time.

The alarm sounds. People run around.

The boss man frowns at Mitchell and makes embarrassed apologies to the investors. He glares at you. Everything goes slow though it happens in an instant. Tommo holds his red left hand over his head and a smirk crosses his face. You guess the tip of his finger probably went down the conveyor belt. Went into the garlic paste.

His skin goes pale and he drops off his chair and to the ground unconscious.

*

'You see, Fiona, sometimes people need to go above and beyond in order to make a point. To inform and to educate. To become a cautionary tale to those that must check their stations,' Tommo says.

You're sharing cans of beer and sunbathing. You texted

174

him to see if he was okay and he invited you over to his hostel. His finger is wrapped in a white bandage. His face is still a little paler than usual and his beard is getting thicker. The sun is baking so you go into the shade every couple of minutes.

Your full line got the day off work. The factory probably thought you were all too unstable to have around the investors.

Tommo continues, 'Power can become a corrupting element in their life and they try to exert it over everyone. So I took my power back. This is the kind of thing that can make it into mythology, urban legend. It wasn't as painful as I thought it would be. The factory says they're going to compensate me, sweet eh? Insurance and all. They don't have to but I wasn't going to say no. Like, I know people will debate if I was right or wrong but whether they understand it or not, I wanted to know if this was real life and carrying consequences is part of that. That is something I had to learn and something Mitchell had to learn.'

'Bit of a hard way to teach yourself a lesson,' you say.

'Well, you know, I'd been necking white goon and raspberry cordial until half an hour before work. Might have had some effect on me thinking.'

He rubs sun block over his nose and cheeks like a cricket player. Flecks of it land on his beard. 'And I tell you wha', Fiona, probably the best thing about it – the women are already mad sympathetic when they hear about me garlic finger.'

*

Tommo leaves town and work in the garlic factory becomes like work. Long, tedious shifts with no craic. You hadn't realised how spoilt you were to have someone entertain you like Tommo did. But you get on with the job and start saving properly. You promise yourself to never be reckless with money again. You're paid quite well for regional work and do sixty-hour weeks. You don't have anywhere to spend the cash. You're aware of what you need so you'd never be in the red again.

Two Danish girls move into the dorm when Mel leaves for Perth. They have jobs doing night shifts packing asparagus in a small farm. You barely see them and barely know them. You're not even sure of their names. They are either asleep or gone.

You and Louise hang out more often. So much more you pick up her accent and say 'ach' or 'aye' in your sentences. This embarrasses you.

She goes on dates with Thierry every second evening and is falling in love. You're happy for her but sometimes you're bitter. You wonder if he'll ever go ballistic at her and deny it, say she was crazy making stories up then get her to apologise for doing that to him. If he'll ever bruise her but make her promise to tell no one because no one would believe her anyway.

When you see them together though, you stop projecting. They're a good match. He always smiles as she speaks, sometimes saying silently the words she says as soon as they come from her mouth. She loves how 'exotic' he is and melts when he does something French. They click, you suppose. They make it look easy.

They suggest you meet one of his roomies or co-workers. You could double date and though his friends are attractive, you keep turning down the offers until they stop coming.

The thought of being involved with a man again seems impossible.

*

Mitchell gets demoted at work. He's put in Tommo's position. The powers warn him that if he ever causes any more trouble, he'll be immediately dismissed.

He doesn't say much to anyone. He slams the garlic into the shoots or trims it with such violence, you think the factory will claim another Irish fingertip. You always say hello and try to make small talk but he scowls at you as if you'd been involved in Tommo's plot.

There's excitement though when it spreads through the rumour mill that the garlic producers from the region will be around inspecting the factory. Again, everyone has to put on a bit of a show. You even have a group meeting about it where you're warned to be on your best behaviour, that they never, and they meant never, wanted a repeat of Tommo.

'Mitchell, maybe today will be your day to impress them?' you say as you chop.

He sniggers. 'That fucking ship has sank.'

'Maybe not. Don't be so negative.'

He stares at you. 'It's easy for you, girl. You're just doing this work to extend your holiday here. Someone who's pretty like you and who's got an education, you're going to be fine in this world without doing a tap. You'd have the men do the tap for you, if you'd let them. Me? Well I've to fight those same men for a sniff of an opportunity. And they group up and are bigger and stronger than me. D'you know what that feels like?'

You don't say anything but your skin reddens.

'You haven't a clue what it's like, girl.'

You sigh. 'The sponsorship still might happen.'

'Don't be so fucking innocent.' He returns his concentration to the belt, to the cloves.

You don't argue back.

On second smoko, you chat with Louise and drink coffee by the sinks. There's a nice spread in the corner for the producers – canapés, cheeses, salamis, hams, breads and some different cakes and chocolates.

'Fecking broke my heart laying them out,' Louise says. 'The supervisor said we weren't to touch a thing. I do go weak for cheesecake. Supervisor said once this crew has eaten, the scraps get offered to the office girls. When they are full, the leftovers come down here for you guys on last smoko. And if anything's left, us shitty tea ladies and the other cleaners are allowed to eat them.'

'Bit harsh,' you say.

Louise laughs. 'Aye, the cunts. I've a plate full of treats in the press under the kettle. They're a bit squished from being snuck in but I don't care.'

She moves closer and shows you the mash of white cream and crumbs in her apron pocket. You laugh quietly.

The double doors open and the producers walk in. Some are dressed in suit-pants and shirts, others in mucky farm clothes with knee high socks and big straw hats. They go straight for the food and the bustle of them catches everyone's attention as they joke and chatter. You take another sup of your coffee and your arms go weak.

Jett and Rusty Fletcher.

They munch on cheese and are all smiles for the other garlic people.

You drop the cup. It shatters on the floor, the brown liquid in a steaming pool. Splashes taint tiles much further away. Everyone stops and turns. Jett Fletcher spots you. He looks in your eye. Your blood ices. He taps Rusty with the back of his hand. Rusty looks at you. A grin twinges his face.

'You okay?' Louise asks, already dipping to pick up the fragments of the cup.

'I've to head. I'm gone. I'll say bye in the hostel. I'm gone.'

*

You try to walk not rush. You can't bear to be breathing the same air as them. Your stomach lurches. You need to get away from them as quickly as possible. The siren sounds for the end of break and the factory staff come back onto the floor. You're halfway across a metal walkway. You check the lunchroom and see the Fletchers swap cards with two men and wave. They take the forkie door outside, disappearing into the sunshine.

Are they going?

You stop. You turn and turn again. Which way, which

way? Maybe you should go back onto the line but then you'll be trapped there. You don't want to be caught if they come back and walk around with the team. What would they say to everyone? What would they do to you? You rub the back of your neck. You need to decide what to do. You can't decide.

A supervisor is coming behind you. You're sweating hard.

'Hey, you, where you supposed to be?' she probes.

You scratch your head. 'Em, I was sent to collect a letter for someone over here, in the front office.'

'For who? No one is allowed off their line after smoko.' She takes a look at the clocking-in card around your neck and scribbles your name on her clipboard. 'Fiona, who sent you?'

She's like the headmistress you had in the convent.

'Mitchell did. Mitchell Dunne. He's on Section Twenty-Two with me. He's the supervisor of our section. He was the supervisor.' You've no one else to say. He might get fired over this. Or even if he doesn't, his chances of sponsorship are at risk – another person on his section causing a scene.

'Hmm,' she says and scratches the tip of her nose with her baby finger. 'Mitchell Dunne, the name is familiar. Okay, carry on to the office. Go. Move.'

You turn around and walk quickly.

'Wait, Fiona,' she calls.

Bollocks.

'Yes,' you say. You smile up at her sweetly.

'Is Section Twenty-Two where that accident happened? With the Irish?'

You nod.

'Misfortunate breed, the Irish,' she says and takes a left down a stairwell.

*

You sneak outside and scan the car park. You can't see much with the sun's glare. The hostel is a twenty-five minute walk away. Where are the Fletchers? They're going to follow. They're fucking psychos and you remember Jett's last words, echoing over the riverbank, that he'd take you apart. They'll spot you on your way back to the hostel. Your legs are shaking.

How stupid you were.

How stupid you were too to think you were far enough away from them here. This being the only big town in the area. You've to make a run for it now. If you get to the industrial estate you could try hitch a lift off someone.

You leg it.

The sun is intense and white. You get to the main road outside the car park when you hear an engine start behind you. Your bad foot pangs against the ground. You run across the road, a car beeps at you for crossing too suddenly, you don't care. You run into the industrial estate and go towards the glassy front of a kitchen showroom. You try the door. It's locked. Lunch break. Fuck. You check around. The Fletchers are indicating into the estate. You scamper to the next building. A paint shop. It's open.

A chime announces your entrance. A man reads a newspaper at the counter. He peers over the top of it. You bend and try to catch your breath.

'Sorry to burst in like this. I need to get a lift to my back-packers. Can you help me? Is there someone who can help me, please?'

He folds the paper down. He has dark skin, he might be Indian.

'Madam, what are you talking about?'

'I'm being chased. I need help. Please.'

He checks his watch before looking at you.

'Will I call the police?'

You see the Fletchers' car drive slowly around the estate. You go over to the counter. The man stares at you. You duck and peek out. The Fletchers are craning their necks to look through the window. They'll only see their reflection with that sunlight.

'Madam, are those people looking for you?'

'Don't talk to me. Read your paper. Don't attract attention.'

You peek out again. Rusty Fletcher shuts his passenger door and walks towards the paint shop. You go behind the counter, bending low beside the stool where the man sits.

'Just act like normal. Don't tell on me, please.'

The bell chimes. Footsteps.

'G'day,' Rusty says. 'You see a Sheila? Irish. Blondey. Small. She here?'

The man coughs. 'Excuse me?' he asks. He plays up his accent.

'You. See. A. Woman?' Rusty asks pronouncing each word loud and slowly.

'You would like some paint for a woman? Woman paint? Pink is good colour. Peach?'

'No, you curry muncher, I'm looking for a woman. Did

you see her?'

You hold your breath. The pressure of crouching causes your legs to judder.

'Do you wish to buy some paint, sir?' the man says in a snotty voice.

'No,' Rusty says.

'I cannot help you, sir.'

Rusty mumbles some racist slurs as he turns around. He punches a tin of paint on the way out, you hear the thump before it clanks off the floor. You're about to stand when the bell chimes again. He's back. You duck quickly.

Rusty shouts, 'Another thing, you're fucking shit at cricket.'

The door closes.

After a minute, the man speaks.

'You are safe now.'

'You sure?'

'He has gone into a building across the road. The car is outside it.'

You get up slowly and stretch.

'Will I call the police?' he asks.

You never, ever, want anyone to know about you going to the Fletchers' house.

'No. No. It'll be grand.'

If you get out of town, you won't see them again. Go much further away this time. Sydney.

'I can't leave the shop until 4.30 p.m. or I risk getting fired. If you want to sit in the kitchen through those doors, you can have a glass of water or tea. There is also a newspaper. I will drive you to your backpackers. That was a bad man, madam. I could sense his deeds. I will aid you.'

You look across the road and thank him.

In the kitchen, the shop assistant tells you his name is Arav. He boils the kettle.

'You work in the garlic plant?' he asks and looks at your pinafore and clocking in card.

'I did.'

He takes two cups down and pours tea leaves into them. The water sighs as it fills the cups. Steam rises.

'I'm sorry, Arav,' you say as he hands you a cup. He raises his eyebrows. 'I'm sorry for interrupting you. I was just really scared.'

You take a sip. It burns your lips and tongue.

He shakes his head. 'There is no need for an apology. Have those men maltreated you?'

'I was really stupid.'

He says nothing but slurps his tea. His fingers interlock around his mug. 'Are you still scared?'

You nod slowly.

Arav takes another drink of his tea. His lengthy eyelashes cause little shadows on his cheeks. He looks out the window. 'I find there are places one can never forget but there are also places one will never remember. This one is the latter. I assure you.'

*

Arav locks the shop and twists a key to bring down the shutters. He gives you a lift in a small red car that had a strawberry scented air freshener hanging from the mirror. Some girls come in and out through the front gate of the hostel. You thank him and check around the streets before running inside.

When you get to the dorm room you climb onto your bed and lay for a minute or two, trying to get your mind clear.

You pack. The eighteen-hour bus to Sydney leaves at 7.30 p.m.

*

You have everything ready and Louise hugs you. She's still in her uniform and smells of garlic.

'Fiona, my cousin Emma's in Sydney. Take her number. She'll put you up when you get there. It might be a couch or a blow-up bed but it'll help until you get a job. You'll have to chip in fifty dollars a week. It's a wee bit of a commune but it's somewhere.'

'Cheers,' you say and fold the paper with her number into your pocket.

'Do you really have to go?' Louise asks. 'I don't understand. What happened back in the factory?'

'I—,' you say and stop. You don't want to tell her. You don't want her to think less of you. 'It's nothing really. But I do have to go. One of those things.'

She nods and accepts what you've said without pressing you. You look at her and know she's the kind of person you'd like to be.

'Here.' She unclasps the chain from around her neck. She takes off the pendant that's on it and puts it into your palm. 'St. Christopher. He looks after us people travelling. He'll mind you.'

It's warm in your hand from being on her skin. 'But what about you? I can't take this.'

'Whisht. Me mammy sent me over with two of these, a bottle of blessed water from Lourdes and rosary beads that I keep in my rucksack. She lights a candle every other day too for me and me brother Caoimhín in Toronto. I'm grand for the spiritual protection.'

You close your fingers over the holy medal.

*

You get a taxi to the bus station and scan around after paying at the ticket desk. The Fletchers aren't there. You stand at the coach stop and wait, hopping up and down, willing the driver to open the door and let you board.

You look around again. Come on. Come on.

Come on.

The bus driver lights a cigarette. You roll your eyes and check your watch. Try to relax but can't. You check your watch and the door again.

'Can we just get on, please?' you ask the driver.

He doesn't reply. He keeps smoking.

A ute pulls into the station. You put on your sunglasses. Someone gets out of it. You hold your breath.

A woman.

You exhale. She walks to the timetable. The ute drives away. The bus driver is nearly finished his smoke and he nods at you.

He lets you on and you get a seat near the back. You take your sunglasses off and check your watch. 7.20 p.m. Ten

186

minutes. You wish he'd just drive. Some other passengers load on. An elderly lady asks the driver questions which he doesn't know the answer to.

'I'll go inside and check for you,' he said and ups from his seat.

No. Come back. Drive on. Fucking drive.

You give the woman the dirtiest look you can.

A car that looks like Fletchers' pulls into the station. It drives around slowly. Parks. No movement from it. You put your cardigan over your head, trying to make it look like a headscarf. 7.26 p.m.

The bus driver gets back on and gives the woman some information. She asks more questions. He answers. You put your head low. The woman makes her way to the seat across from you.

A man you can't see comes to the door and shouts at the bus driver. His voice sends a bolt of cold down your spine. 'Where's this bus going?'

'Sydney,' the bus driver says. 'You boarding?'

'Nah, mate. Fuck would I go there for?'

The bus driver says, 'Well move away from the doors. We're departing.'

'Can I take a look on the bus?'

'Nah, mate. Next bus to Sydney is at 9 a.m. Move.'

The doors whoosh and the man jumps back. They shut and the driver revs the engine. As the bus exits the station you look back as the man stands, arms folded. You meet his eyes. His head jerks and he spits to the side. He's some random person, not Jett or Rusty. Your chest expands and you let a big sigh out.

The woman who asked all the questions rustles in a paper bag for nuts. She takes one out, sucks on it, makes a choking noise for a couple of seconds and spits the nut back into the paper bag. She repeats the process.

Sometimes she fills the cup on the top of her thermos with hot water. She scoops out a spoon of vegemite and mixes it into the liquid. She groans after each mouthful.

When you're on the road for a few hours, you relax. They aren't following. They can't be. You're free of them. You send a message to Louise's cousin, Emma, who writes back three hours later saying the address of the apartment and:

'NO WORRIES MATE, JUST BACK FROM CLUB, WILL STICK SOME BOTTLES N THE FRIDGE 4 U 4 TOMORROW!!'

It makes you laugh a little and the old woman peers over your shoulder to see the text. You smile at her and she offers you a nut from her paper bag. You decline, sit back into your seat and try to sleep.

*

You flew into Sydney when you left Ireland so it isn't a big deal to work out. The apartment is near Bondi and you're conscious of how glamorous and fit people are in the city. You wear your sunglasses to hide from them more than the midday sun, which is blocked by the tall buildings.

Emma greets you. She's a trim, black-haired Nordie. She wears a pastel pink shirt tucked into short brown shorts. Her Rayban sunglasses sit on her head, holding her hair off her face. She gives you a hug and carries one of your bags. She leads you up a side street to a block of apartments.

'You must be shattered?'

You nod.

'How was the trip? I don't know how ye girls do that outback work. Horrendous, I hear.'

You say, 'Some of it's okay.'

'I paid a farmer off for mine. Six hundred bucks to say I worked with him. But it didn't even matter 'cause I'm on a 457 now.'

You know that's a sponsored visa but before you can ask, she waves her key over a sensor and the double doors unlock. A pile of 'Special Offer' junk mail litters the lobby floor and the car park door is open at the back of the building, you hear an engine and get an oily smell.

The lift is broken so you climb the twelve flights of stairs. With each floor, the place seems to get dirtier. Finally, you get to their flat and you're panting. House music blares from inside.

'It's a dive in here, sorry,' Emma says and puts the key in the lock.

The music is deafening as she opens it. Some people are dancing, others are by a table doing lines. Two couples are heavy petting. One set of them are down to their underwear and writhing on a couch in the corner. You try not to stare.

'Still going from last night?' you ask.

'Still going from last month,' she says.

She takes your hand and leads you past. Nobody seems to react to your being there except one lad with fair hair in a tight haircut wearing a plain grey t-shirt and board shorts.

He fills his cheeks with air and blows out slowly, his cheeks deflating. You notice his jaw tighten, it causes a vein to throb on his forehead. You've seen that gesture on a man's face before, it used to be a warning sign with Malley, that he was about to lose it. You get goosebumps and rub your arms.

Emma brings you into a room that has two single beds and a green lilo. 'You can put your stuff, well, anywhere you can find some space. The lilo is yours but if me or the girls aren't in bed, you're welcome to kip there.'

'The girls?'

'Yeah, Triona, Julie, Yasmin and me are in here. Yasmin's name is on the lease. She's a Scouser and the one you'll have to pay rent to. We couldn't get a lease being Irish. Do you know how much this place costs a week?' she asks but doesn't wait for an answer. 'Nine hundred and fifty, not including bills.'

'Steep.'

'No,' she says, 'Sydney.'

*

The lad who seems pissed off is on the balcony. He smokes quickly. The party is still strong and some of your new house-mates are gone to get more booze.

You go out to him. He seems outcasted. Maybe you could be friends.

He turns his head a bit to see who you are. He inhales and exhales the smoke, racing to burn his cigarette down.

'Like a fucking asylum in there,' he says. He leans against the balcony rails after he quenches his fag. He reminds you of the country boys, in for Saturday nights in town, wearing their shirts and belted Wranglers. Knocking back pints of porter. Charming and fun lads until they hit and ploughed past their limits. They became generous or dangerous, either buying rounds of drink, or hounding girls for the shift and luring hot heads for a fight.

You see where the pink sunburn of his arm meets the whiteness of his skin under his sleeve.

You say, 'I'm Fiona.'

He stares straight ahead, at the city. He suddenly turns and puts his hand out. 'Patrick,' he pauses, 'McDevitt. You probably know me. Or my brothers. They'd a huge construction firm. Eighteenth biggest in Ireland.'

'I don't think I do,' you say.

He lights another cigarette. 'You do. McDevitt Brothers. Redeveloped most of the countryside. They were big news for a while. Big news.'

You scramble your brain but there were too many names of construction companies in the Boom. You watch Patrick smoke and have no idea what he's thinking about as he looks out over the balcony, but you get an overwhelming sense of loneliness from him. You don't know how to make small talk with him though and creep back inside before it gets any more uncomfortable.

*

In an internet café around the corner, you get directions for the city libraries. You can't resist typing their name in the search bar: McDevitts. They were developers from the south-west who went bust owing 345 million euro. The brothers were a lot older than Patrick, maybe ten years or more.

You email your parents, tell them you've moved to Sydney and found an apartment with other Irish people. You think that's a consoling thing to say. They don't need to know the state of the place.

That evening Emma invites you to go for drinks in her friend's new apartment for a housewarming.

'Will it be like this?' you ask as pleasantly as you can, throbbing dance music soundtracks your conversation. You try to think of a good excuse to get out of it if she says yes.

'Oh no, this gang are doing really well. Come. Dress nice though.'

*

You change into Dorothy's purple dress and Emma wears a black playsuit. You tiptoe over the mess and leave the apartment.

Emma chats about the gang who the girl throwing the party belongs to, giving you gossip on them which means little to you. She's enjoying it though.

'So she slept with him, he said he was leaving and that was that. But the company offered him a raise so he's staying,' she says. She giggles. 'And now she's looking at him every day. Morto.'

You step into a bottle shop to buy some drink.

'How do you know her?' you ask while you get cider out of the cold room.

'I work with her in the Financial District.'

You nearly drop a bottle. 'You – you work in the Financial District?'

'Yep. I'm an advisor for a big project.'

You are stunned and wonder if many of the important looking people in the city are living in a hellish eternal house party too.

*

Her friend's apartment has a bay window where Sydney harbour lights up like a bunch of diamonds. You spend a few minutes watching it twinkle after the awkward introductions are made.

The night is close even though they have A/C running. Things are different to Emma's place. From the scent of cologne to the designer clothes and new leather furniture, the place smells of money.

A tiny mountain of white powder is on a set of food scales.

'Three grand's worth,' a guy in red chinos informs you.

'Amazoid party,' another guy says. He's bulky with muscles. They lump out of his neck, arms, chest, stomach.

People schmooze each other and you know you're under-dressed, ugly. Emma passes you a glass of punch. It's blue and has bits of fruit bobbing in it.

'Celtic Tiger's no way dead, man,' the red chinos guy says. 'It's just on fucking holidays Down Under, like. My bank account can totally prove it.'

They hear-hear. You nearly gag.

You think about the misery at home with the redundancies.

The evictions. The suicides. Ones in the signing on queue wearing hats and sunglasses.

All the parked-up cars. All the unlived-in property. All the full exile planes.

And someone at the party shouts, 'To Bertie!'

You take a big gulp of a drink and it stings your throat. It tastes of straight vodka.

'A toast to the immigrants,' the bulked up lad says.

'Keep her fucking lit.'

And you have to raise your glass with everyone else.

*

'Fiona, I like you, you're different,' the red chinos guy says and sniffs. Wipes his nose constantly. 'Come do a line?'

'Nah, I'm okay, thanks.' In one way, you're glad for company, in another, you wish he'd fuck off.

He looks at you but he isn't seeing you. 'It's free.'

His eyebrow is raised. He has a smug grin.

'I'm not interested in it. Or you,' you say in a tone more severe than you mean it to be.

He pulls his t-shirt off with one hand, ruffling his hair and unveiling a sculpted chest. 'You're missing out on this and this—' He pulls his wallet out of his pants and opens it, showing you a roll of notes.

'I'll live,' you say. Again, that tone.

He sighs and leaves, re-joining the big group. They cheer when he dances for them, a male stripper routine. You sit alone and force down more punch. It's getting easier to drink the more you have.

*

Patrick's chain-smoking on the balcony when you get back. You told Emma the travel and job hunting had you wrecked so you were going to get an early night. You were afraid you'd be rude to more of her friends. You knew you would be. Especially if you kept drinking.

'You paying fifty for this place as well?' Patrick asks.

'Yeah.'

The city is mesmerizing against the night.

'You know they make us line up for work in the morning and pick us,' he says and is silent for a moment. The vein in his temple protrudes. 'What fucking year is this? The year of No Blacks No Dogs No Irish? I left school after the Junior Cert. I been working ever since. Until – feel my hands.' He puts his hands in front of you. 'Soft. My hands are soft.'

'You not finding work?' you ask, almost afraid. You don't understand his emotions.

'I got a couple of days roofing last week. See I won't grovel and the Aussies don't like me for it. I worked with a few Maori bucks. They jumped in the river on the breaks. Came back shiny wet. "It's too hot, bro,"' Patrick copies a Kiwi accent. '"You're all pink, bro. You should join us, bro."'

He exhales noisily again, blowing the air out of his cheeks. He lights another cigarette. 'They had big lunches their wives made them. Big lads, sure. I'd no lunch. They gave me sandwiches and I didn't know what was in them.'

He scratches his cheek. 'McDevitt Brothers had 248, including the office women, on the books. Another hundred at least off the books. Latvians, Lithuanians and Polish. Sites around Munster. Charleville, beauty. A block in Limerick. Summer cottages in West Clare. I got my own six-bed all ensuite and a balcony outside Ennis. Only myself in it.'

'Wow,' you say. He offers you a cigarette but you refuse it. You haven't smoked in a long while and you don't miss them. He leans against the rails and sighs.

'Bondi,' he says and sweeps his palm across the view. 'D'ya think I give a shit about Bondi? Women? Drink? Drugs? Sunbathing? Travelling the fucking East Coast?'

You shrug.

'Fifty dollars a week, for what? Carpet. And a sheet, no blanket or pillow. Living with those wasters inside.'

You glance at the living room through the patio door. The room flashes from fairy lights hung around it. Smoke fogs. Muffled trance music leaks through to the balcony.

'See, Fiona, it's simple. If I could get some steady work, I could get on a lease, in a bigger apartment than this, fit even more in. Then I could rent it out, get myself a bed somewhere else. Keep going. It's just maths. Could get the brothers over, to work for me, I'd be on top, a penthouse suite, overlooking the Opera House, maybe buy some land in the Blue Mountains for a holiday home. Rent that out. If they'd just fucking pick me to work. I'm a great worker. Us lined up like desperate people at a dance. Holding hard hats. Trying to hold our heads up. Waiting to get asked. Waiting. This is supposed to be the place where things happen. My hole it is. Is that what you're here for?'

'I don't really know,' you say.

You'd spent too long in your bedroom. Malley hadn't got

in touch even though he must have heard that the property place you worked at let everyone go. You lay in bed most days looking into space. You wouldn't shower or get out of your nightclothes except for when you signed on, collected your dole or at the weekends when you got so drunk you couldn't name five things that had happened on the night out. You drank yourself into unconsciousness. On Mondays you suffered a black day, where the drink demons left your body and taunted you about everything. You were fragile and guilty.

When Malley got a new girlfriend, it was the biggest slap you'd ever got. How were you such a mess and he was ready to hop inside the next girl?

Every day, the news was riddled with stories of young Irish getting flights to London, Toronto, Vancouver, Dubai, Melbourne, Perth, Sydney. Escaping. You don't know where you got the will from but you walked to the Credit Union, took out your savings and bought a flight.

A plane flies by, its lights blinking in the sky.

You half-smile at Patrick. 'I didn't think things would turn out like this, that's for sure.'

*

You spend the next few days in a routine. Emma gets up for work early, usually at 5.45 a.m., so you climb into her bed which is still warm from her. When you wake again, you head down to Bondi Beach for a walk, in awe every time at how small it is for such an iconic place. You watch the sporty Australians out running or cycling or swimming.

You sit on the the hill overlooking the beach for a little while if it isn't too breezy. Some mornings, you do the full six kilometre walk to Coogee, looping around cliffs and other little beaches, climbing steps and walking sandy pathways, stopping to read the information signs on the history of the area.

You get the bus to the CBD, go to the Customs House Library near the Harbour and apply for jobs. Though some libraries are nearer to you, this one's in an old-style three-storey building nestled amongst the towering skyscrapers. The staff are helpful and it's filled with students, historians, readers and broke backpackers using the free internet to book their next trip or try and get a job interview. It's filled with normal people who are clean and sober.

You try to stay in the library as late as possible because the flat is always pumping except for morning time when they drowse off for a little bit in between partying. You can tire yourself out in the city during the day, wander through the malls and streets in Bondi Junction. In the evening, you pick up a sushi roll or cheap noodles for dinner. Try to avoid the drunk workers and Irish going to the Tea Gardens. Pass massage parlours and shoe shops and late night pharmacies. Walk around Coles and calculate how expensive everything is compared to Ireland.

When you're worn out, your legs tired, your eyes droopy, you can go back to the flat and go straight to bed.

You're beginning to feel okay here even though you still sleep in fragments. Nightmares sometimes. Other times, just an overwhelming need to wake yourself and make sure you're not in Fletchers. The girls in the garlic factory hostel had said it was worse than if you were shagging in the room, the amount of twisting and turning and moaning you did in your sleep.

You try to get comfortable on the lilo. It hurts your hips and back and sometimes, you just sleep on the ground instead.

*

You watch the rugby on the Saturday but don't drink. When Ireland win, an Aussie sports fan at the bar turns around and screams that rugby is a shit sport that Australia doesn't care about.

The All-Ireland is between Kerry and Dublin but you don't watch that. You don't care about either team and coverage begins from midnight. A non-stop twenty-hour party takes place in the flat after it, only dying down late into Monday night. You're pretty sure that no one kipping in the flat is from either county but something about watching it gives them a hyperness and homesickness that they need to drown.

You go into the sitting room after the shouting and loud music dies. People sleep on the sofas, on the ground, on each other. You plug out the stereo and the TV.

The stale fumes from the drinking, sweating and old smoke give the room a cloudy feel. You go to the kitchen and boil the kettle. Your feet are sticking onto the floor. You make a green tea, drink it out of a yellow bowl, the only clean unbroken thing you can rummage from the presses. You sit on the counter beside the sink.

The front door clicks open and someone comes into

the flat but avoids the kitchen. You can hear them cough and use the bathroom. They go to the sitting room and it's silent again.

You finish your tea and wash the bowl, put it back into the press and flick the light.

You notice him in the corner, lying on top of a sheet and with a fleecy jacket covering his body. Ear plugs jut out of his ears. His work clothes are folded, laid in front of his feet along with dusty, steel toe cap work boots. He does the same thing as you in the evenings, avoiding the flat and trying to just be here to sleep.

'Night, Patrick,' you say to him but he doesn't respond.

*

Emma's changing when you wake. She has wet hair and puts concealer under her eyes. She wears a white-striped blue shirt, a navy pencil skirt and she mouths, 'morning' when she notices you looking at her. You get ready to crawl into her bed. Your phone rings though and you grab it quick before it wakes the other girls in the room.

It vibrates in your hand as you dash to the balcony and close the sliding door behind you. It's your home house number from Ireland.

Why are they ringing you so early?

'Hello?' you say.

'Fiona, *mo ghrá*, are you okay? We got a phone call,' your dad says.

'Yeah, I'm grand. What do you mean a phone call?' You pick sleep pus from your eyes.

'A woman called Dorothy rang, extremely worried about you.'

Shit.

'What? Why?' You already know that this is going to turn out bad.

'She said you had disappeared from your job and hostel and they couldn't get in touch with you. Nobody knew where you'd gone. She was going to call the police, but she wanted to get in touch with us first. She got our phone number off her bill.'

You feel bad for not even thinking to say anything to her or Geoff and all the kindness they had for you. But you're annoyed too. Why did she go and contact your parents?

'Dad, I'm grand. I just left. Wasn't working out. I told ye in an email I was in Sydney.'

A common myna lands on the balcony. It's easy to identify him from his brown body, black-hooded head and the bare yellow patch behind his eye. He flutters about and his yellow beak pecks at the ground.

'You 'just left' a job without telling anyone, Fiona? That's not very good manners,' your Dad says and breaks your concentration.

'You don't understand. I had to go.'

'Why?'

'Because,' you pause. 'I did.'

You shoo the bird away by stamping on the ground.

'Are you in trouble out there? If you are you need to tell me and not have me and your mam killed with worry.' He says killed like kilt.

'Dad, leave it, okay. I'm fine. I'm in Sydney. In fact, a few days ago I was out with some really well off Irish people and they probably have good contacts for jobs.'

'But didn't you like the last job in the factory?'

'I did yeah,' you say. 'I just had to go.'

'Fiona, your mother wants a word,' he says and passes the phone over. You roll your eyes up to the new pale blue morning sky. The clouds are pierced with chemtrails.

'Fiona, hello,' your mam says. 'What's going on?'

'Nothing, Mam. I'm fine. Jesus. Will ye give me Dorothy's number and I'll call her to tell her I'm okay? I didn't think she'd panic. I thought she'd have forgotten about me.'

'I'd a good chat with her, Fiona. I don't know what exactly is happening but my gut is telling me something's off. She said you were 'at risk.' Why would she say that?'

'What's her number?' you ask, getting a pen from the balcony table and writing it on your hand as she calls it out.

'Fiona, what's going on? You better start talking, miss. Don't be trying to fob me off like you do your father.'

'Mam,' you pause, 'what? What do you want me to say?'

'Tell me the truth, now. What's going on? Why are these Australian people so scared? I could hear it off her. She was crazy worried.'

You don't want to talk but she waits silently on the other side.

'There's nothing going on, Mam. I don't know why she was worried. I'm grand. I'm in Sydney, I've met loads of rich Irish ones and so it's okay.'

'Fiona, there's no way that woman would have called me and spoke the way she did if there wasn't something. She seemed like a good person.'

'Jesus Mam, she is a good person, I'm not saying she's a bad person. Why ye hassling me? I sent an email. Everything is great. I'm great.' You can't control the bitterness in your voice.

'Fiona.'

'Mam, what? What do you want from me? Why are you pushing me? Everything is fine. How many times do I have to say it?'

'Don't take that attitude with me.'

'D'ya want me to tell you I'm in trouble and everything's gone to hell here? Is that what you want to hear?'

'No but you're better off spitting the truth out now instead of it spitting on you.'

'I'm not in trouble, everything's fine.'

'Fiona, what's going on?'

'Nothing,' you say really slowly.

'Fiona—'

'Mam, it's all fucking sound now. Everything is okay.'

'What happened?'

'Nothing, Jesus. It was nothing.'

'What was?'

'Look,' you say, your blood singing in your veins. 'I ran out of money. Okay.'

'And then?'

'Mam, don't push me. Don't. You don't want to hear it.'

'What is going on, Fiona?'

You run your fingers through your hair and take a breath through your nose. 'Nothing.'

'Tell me.'

'It's all over now.'

'What is?'

'What happened.'

'What did you do, Fiona?' She asks, her voice raises with the question.

'I didn't go through with it. I didn't. I ran away.'

She softens again. 'Listen, we're your parents. We're worried. We have the right to—'

'Well fucking worry about something else.'

'Fiona—'

You hang up on her.

✳

You take a seat on the ground in the corner of the balcony, looking at Patrick McDevitt's cigarette butts crushed and overflowing in the glass ashtray. You lean your head on the wall.

You didn't have sex with them, you got no money. But Jett Fletcher's fingers were in you, he sucked on your breast and you had felt something. You had been aroused. For a moment, your body wanted it. Your skin tightens with the memory.

They'll try to pool the funds for a flight home. Your mam sobbing and asking the priest for money, asking why did you let this happen, why didn't you ask for help. They'll look at you differently, your parents.

✳

You spend the morning on the balcony, crying. You let the phone ring out every time they call back. They give up when it's past midnight in Ireland. Patrick comes out for a smoke before work holding a box in one hand and his white hard hat in the other. He looks at you as he draws a cigarette out.

'You okay?'

'I'll be okay.'

He holds his unlit cigarette in his hand, puts his lighter to it, looks at you again, in your nightclothes still, your face puffy and wet, your hair in a heap. He puts his lighter down and dramatically checks his watch.

'Shit, look at the time, I'm supposed to be lining up for work. I'll smoke this on me walk.'

He tries to give you a smile before he goes back inside through the patio.

'Cheers for the support,' you say.

*

You are nothing. You're a stupid, pathetic girl. You've shamed yourself. Worse, you've shamed your family. You should have just slept with the Fletchers because it's the same, the action and the label. It's all the fucking same.

You cry so hard bile comes and you spit it out onto the red tiled ground.

You look down over the balcony, the people like moving dots. The cars are dinkies. The city is loud. You hear far off sirens and the engines of morning traffic caught at lights. If you jumped, just did it, you'd be saving a lot of people a lot of worry in the future.

What'll you do next, Fiona? You've no cop on. You're a fucking mess. What if you jumped? What if you did it?

Jump. Splash yourself off the footpath. Who'd even give a shit?

*

Your phone vibrates and you think about throwing it over the balcony. You don't want to talk to them. You flick a glance at the screen.

It's Tommo.

He's relentless and the phone rings for many counts. He isn't hanging up.

You take a massive breath and try to free the shudder out of it. You sniff and clean your face with your pyjama top.

You answer but don't speak.

'Hi, Fiona?' Tommo asks, 'You there?'

You cough and swallow. 'Yeah, I'm here.'

'Howya. Just wanted to say hello, see how you're doing? Ya still hanging with me old comrade Mitchell?'

You laugh. 'No, Tommo. I'm in Sydney.'

'Sydney? Fuck off with your Sydney. Did ye see the matches?'

'The Ireland game? Yeah. The All-Ireland, nah. I didn't wait up.'

Tommo gasps. 'Wha'? Jaysus. Best weekend of sport ever so it was.' He makes some tutting noises. 'But come here to me, I'm across in Alice Springs, with me cousin and her boyfriend. They're dead sound but – you know – they're a couple. We're renting a campervan. Driving to Darwin then around to some of the Northern Territories' National Parks. D'yeh wanna come with us? I'm not getting the second visa, I decided that day I gave meself the chop. So I'm flying back to Ireland next week. This is the last hurrah for me in Oz.'

You think about Tommo. He met you in the factory and became your friend because he thought you were nice. He didn't have to do that. He wouldn't have bothered if he didn't like you. You saw what he was capable of when he didn't like someone.

'Will you come? We've loads of room. I can't be watching Romeo and Juliet smooch and fight and feed each other and have sneaky sex when they think I'm asleep. I need a buddy. I want someone smart to talk to. Will you come? The campervan's paid for, we'll be doing it on the cheap. Come on. It'll be great craic. It'll be like the factory times except without all the garlic and wankers around.'

'I'm not sure. I'm not in great form, Tommo. Don't want to wreck it on ye,' you say and frown.

'A trip will cheer you up. Come on, you're me favourite buddy I've met in Oz. I'd love to see you. Come on with us. You can piss off if you're not having fun,' he said and paused. 'Don't think I'm a bleeding soft muppet but I miss you.'

You feel like crying again but from a better place. You look up at the sun. You scratch your face and pace around.

Tommo once quoted somebody saying that insanity was doing the same thing over and over again and expecting different results.

You can't let this side of yourself drag you down. Get over yourself.

You go in through the sliding doors and open a laptop that's on the couch. You book flights to Alice for late that afternoon; shower, change, pack. You leave fifty dollars rent for Yasmin under her pillow and a quick note to explain things to Emma.

Some of the druggies are awake in the sitting room. Holding their pounding heads. Groaning at how bright it is outside. You wonder if they saw you earlier.

Some of the alcos are awake too, washing out glasses, filling them with the cure.

It's so much easier to keep going than to face the hangover.

You nod at the ones that acknowledge you. Give them waves goodbye.

'Good luck,' you say.

'Good luck,' they say.

You grab a burger meal in the chipper and walk to the station. You hold the bag of food, unopened, in your hand and ring Dorothy. You apologise for leaving the factory so abruptly. She says the job isn't important, it's you who's important and she wanted to check with your parents before contacting the police.

It's good to hear her voice.

'I didn't want to scare them, love. If the bloody media caught it, they could broadcast a 'Missing Persons' appeal in Ireland. I didn't want that to be the first time your people heard of it,' she says.

'How did you know the Fletchers chased me again?' you say and cringe. You wonder if they said it around the factory.

'What?'

'How did you know they went after me?'

'Did they?'

'Yeah. It was okay. I got away. That's why I came up here. I don't want to ever meet them again.'

'Fiona, I didn't know you'd left because of those yobbos,' she says. 'They couldn't abduct you in broad daylight. In the middle of your work. Did you think they could?'

'They would, Dorothy. They said they'd hurt me if they ever got me again. I couldn't risk it.'

She's quiet. 'This is getting out of hand. It's time to call the coppers.'

You stand in front of the train station entrance and people swarm by. You get scraps of their different smells, the aftershave, the coffee, the spices, shower gel. They wear shiny shoes, heavy duty boots, flip flops, trainers. You see a shoeless foot and look up to meet the eye of a homeless man with a scraggy grey beard, a straw hat and a sign saying: At Least You Looked.

You hand him the meal you bought. You can afford another one. He blesses you.

You take a breath. 'What do you mean by that?'

'It's too serious. It has to be reported.'

'No, it's fine now. I won't see them again.'

Dorothy sighs. 'If you don't do it, I will. I should have done it a long time ago.'

'What? But it's done. It's all over now.'

'No, it's not. These mongrels need to be brought to justice. They do what they did and then have the audacity to intimidate you? Force you to leave your job and life? These men think they can do whatever they bloody please.'

Your skin is constricting. 'Look, I've done enough damage.'

'You haven't done anything, Fiona.'

'Christ. It's like you want me to be humiliated forever. Like you enjoy me dragging around this awful baggage – this guilt.'

'I can't know these things and not say them anymore. I'm not having it on my conscience. What if there's other girls? What if they come after you again? The police need a record of this.'

'You said it wasn't your call to make? Fucking hell.'

'They'll help. And you could get some closure too.'

'Dorothy, I don't need help,' you sigh, the thunder mood engulfs you again. 'I don't need closure. Do you think you're Mother Teresa or something? Can you not mind your own business?'

'I'm not saying this to meddle or insult you but this is bigger than you.'

'I've a flight to catch,' you say and in an icy way add, 'and I'd appreciate it if you'd stay out of my fucking life.'

You thumb the end call button with so much pressure it sticks in and switches the phone off. You're furious. You swallow past the lump in your throat a few times and raise your head. You'll meet Tommo. You'll have the craic. You'll be fine. You're fine. Ignore this. Ignore them. Get over it. You're fucking fine, why can't everyone see that?

*

Tommo meets you in Arrivals. He gives you such a big hug you think he'll squish you. His back is damp from sweat. Yours is too. You smile at him and vow to yourself to keep smiling for this whole trip. He takes your bag and leads you out to the car park to his campervan. It's painted green and blue and has 'Living the Dream' written across it in bubble font.

'Are you starved, are you?' he asks. 'I brought a lunchbox of the casserole me cousin made for us earlier if you're starving. If you're not, that's okay. I'll eat it.'

He rubs his pudgy stomach. 'I'll never be full.'

He opens the van and lays your bag on the couch in the back. The campervan is hot, the A/C is on the blink so you drive with the windows down. The wind is dry.

You eat the casserole and Tommo sings along croakily to Gotye on the radio as he drives.

'It sounds like Baa Baa Black Sheep,' you say.

'Ah, Fiona, it's the catchiest tune I've ever heard. This Gotye, he's got the emotions in him. And Kimbra is a fine thing.'

You admire the views, the craggy beauty of the MacDonnell Ranges as they stretch east and west from the city. The brownish green spinifex in the ground is dry and brittle looking but desert sharp and tough.

When you get to the hostel, you go for a nap. You bury the thoughts of your parents and Dorothy. You'll start again over here. It's going well. Tommo is fun. You'll be fine.

*

Tommo gives you some options of things to do for the evening.

'Casino? Clubbing? Could go for a walk around if you want? Because they're awful strict on boozing here. They don't want the people more gee-eyed. Clubbing might be shite,' he says and you smirk at the Dublin way he says 'shy' instead of shite.

'What's that about?'

'The strictness? They got a drink problem here.'

'Oh,' you say.

'I have my theories on it,' he says.

You laugh. 'You do? Go on, I haven't heard one of those in a while. Enlighten me.'

Tommo clears his throat. 'Well, you see, if current bio-chemistry thought is right about this, the Aboriginal people haven't the same tolerance levels for grog as Europeans, or at least for the alcohol they brought over here. We've been pissheads for thousands of years, but they got drink forced on them when the whites arrived.'

You nod.

'Cook and the Brits landed in 1770. Less than two hundred and fifty years ago. Fecking Guinness is older than that. But, just take a person, right, who is afraid or stressed out, their hormones react and change their physiological state for that moment. But say, for instance, that person gets a shitload of frights, or feels under a lot of pressure constantly, can structural changes occur in their DNA? And in the DNA of their sex cells? Thus making memories a sort of genetic code?

And if so, are the Aboriginal people still incredibly shook from within, in their chemical make-up, from the upheaval of their continent in very recent times in their ancestry?'

Tommo isn't looking at you now. His eyes are glassy and he draws imaginary semi-circles in the air while making his points.

He continues, 'Like, when you're upset and go drinking, it's real easy to go aggressive. To turn gurrier. Did you ever go drinking when you were feeling crap?'

'Yeah, of course.'

'Did it make you feel better?'

'Not really,' you say quietly. It never did. It deadened some emotion for a while but once sobriety was gone, the emotion you tried to suppress would come back stronger and consume you. You wouldn't have the inhibitions to stop it anymore. You'd be inconsolable or livid or both. All those times you made a fool of yourself when you were wasted.

Tommo shrugs. 'I know I'm simplifying but that's the way I see it. Then throw the socio-economic and disenfranchisement factors to the mix. All the hidden history. God, it scares me. What I see with these people. With this society. How do you resolve this? How do they resolve this?'

'Don't know, Tommo.'

'If there was less denial of the existence of a problem, would the problem remain as potent?'

'Don't really know, Tommo,' you say and think about the question.

Tommo smacks his forehead with his palm and blinks hard. 'Ah sorry, Fiona. You should have pulled me in off me rant.' He clicks his fingers above his head. 'I know. We could get stoned on the roof of the hostel. You can see the stars out here in the Red Centre. You can nearly touch them.'

'I don't want to smoke but I'll join you.'

'I promise I won't be intense,' he says and laughs. 'Or at least I'll try not to be.'

His question about denial replays over and over in your mind.

*

You sit on the roof and Tommo gets a cigarette paper out and pours some tobacco into the middle of it, spreads it evenly across the paper. He takes some weed from a tinfoiled wrap and sprinkles it onto the tobacco in his rollie. He gathers the cigarette paper from its corner and massages it the way across, making it smooth as he licks the edge of the paper and fastens it in shape.

He lights it up and takes a deep inhale.

'When are we heading to Darwin?' you ask.

'Ah, I'd reckon the day after tomorrow,' Tommo replies and blows smoke out. He picks tobacco off his tongue. 'Susan and Ollie want to go to some park tomorrow for the day. And I know they've booked a fancy steakhouse meal for two before they, quote, slum it, unquote, in the campervan with us.'

'I'd love to see Uluru,' you say.

'The Rock? Why? You've seen it. Everywhere. It'll be like New York, no experience because you've already had it second hand.'

'That's some twisted logic, Tommo,' you say.

'No, it's just the age old problem of perception.' He peels a little edge of his plaster and chews at it. He looks at you and says, 'Oh, alright. Since you've come all the way across the country to hang out. You know it's at least a five-hour drive?'

'I know.'

'I'll hotwire the van so in the morning,' he says and takes a deep drag. The taste of weed tints the balmy air around you.

*

You hit the road and fill each other in on life since Tommo's 'self-amputation protest'. He'd done the East Coast in a whirlwind of booze and romantic rebuffs. He speaks about it merrily.

'Fiona, you see, rejection's part of the bigger picture,' he says and ponders as he drives. 'I wouldn't appreciate the ones that say yes to me if all the girls said yes to me. I wouldn't have to improve my personality. Better myself.'

'You think people better themselves to get some?'

'The more interesting you are as a human, even if you got love handles,' he says and pinches his stomach, 'you're attractive. The more self-development you do, the more self-awareness you have and that makes you more comfortable with yourself, which is attractive. Attractive equals action,' he says and in an English accent adds, 'Get in.'

You smile at Tommo and look out the window. The sky is electric blue, the sun a dazzling yellow and the clouds are so fluffy and white that it all looks like a child's drawing.

Uluru is huge, glowing orange-red. It's the only thing out here in the desert, it doesn't make any sense after the flatness.

'Is it a bit like a burning Ben Bulben?' you ask Tommo.
'Wha'?'

'You know, the mountain in Sligo, near Yeats' grave? Doesn't Uluru look a bit like it?'

'Such a culchie, Fiona. Next thing you'll tell me the red dirt looks like the bog.'

You giggle. 'But it kinda does, Tommo. Different colour but the same bareness or something. Same loneliness.'

Tommo smiles but shakes his head and parks the van.

As soon as you get out of it, a charged feeling surrounds you.

The rock is weather-beaten up close. It has pitted holes and grooves, ribs and dips but its beauty is in that. The imperfection. The erosion. The strength of it.

You are grateful for everything that had happened to bring you to this exact moment.

You stay in silence until Tommo breaks in, 'Should we climb it?' He swats the flies away from his face.

You walk closer. You read part of one of the signs out: 'What visitors call 'the climb' is the traditional route taken by ancestral Mala men upon their arrival in Uluru in the creation time. It has great spiritual significance...'

Tommo rubs his hand through his hair and looks around him. 'No, forget I said it. Don't know about you, Fiona, you can do what you want, I'm not the boss of you, but I'm choosing not to touch that big red. I'm not getting any funky juju from old native spirits. I'm bad enough as it is.'

You shake your head. 'No way.'

Somewhere in the distance comes the rhythmic banging of clapsticks.

*

Back in Alice, you've a deep and dark sleep again, you are kneeling on a bridge. The water below is yellow. Sharks circle. Malley is on the bank and he calls you. On the other side of the bridge is a dense fog that looks and sounds like television static. You get up from kneeling. You go back to him. The devil you know.

You wake in a sweat, your body searing with fear that you were tempted to go back, that you'd betray yourself so bad. Even in a dream. You lay motionless until it's time to get breakfast. You think about ringing your parents, have the number dialled, ready to press call but you don't. You think about Dorothy, replay what you said, flinch at your hostility to her. You turn your phone off and go eat the free cereal and toast provided by the hostel.

You help load the campervan. Susan and Ollie bring sixty litres of water, three maps and a bottle of Bundy for the trip.

You start the trek north.

The road is straight and there's not much to look at out the window except the same view, continuously, a landscape isolated and burnt in the white sunshine. The repetitiveness gets interrupted by the odd passing freight lorry. If you see another campervan, Ollie beep beep beep beeeeeeeeeeeps at them and you give them a thumbs up.

Tommo points at his plastered finger. 'In case they'd heard.'

Susan and Ollie are pleasant but they exist mostly in their own little world, sharing mundane thoughts with each other that only people comfortable in a couple would share, leaving you and Tommo to arse around. You draw a portrait of him.

'Whoa,' he says when you show it to him. 'This is bleeding deadly, Fiona. You could go live in Paris and sketch people. Jaysus.'

You tut and smile. 'Stop your shiteing, will ya?'

You pass the Devils Marbles and pull in to take pictures of them but it's nearly forty degrees outside so you dash back into the van. Even with sunblock on, you can feel the sun burning your skin. Tommo compares his tan by putting his freckled arm against yours.

'Fiona, how'd you go so fecking dark? You are Irish, yeah?'

You think of the sunshine when you hobbled alongside the river. 'Don't know. Sallow skin, maybe.'

You get to a small town and park the campervan for the night. You've six hours down of the estimated fifteen it's going to take to drive to Darwin.

Susan and Ollie suggest a pint across the road at a canopied, wooden bar called Will Lalors. It's decorated with indigenous paintings on the outside.

'No fucking apostrophe. Again,' Tommo says and puts his hands on his hips. 'How do they expect ownership to be denoted?'

'Maybe there's a few people called Will Lalor inside?'

'No there isn't. All over this country, apostrophes forgotten, or never known.'

Tommo walks in ahead of you. In a loud, enthusiastic way, he says, 'First round's on me.'

The bar goes quiet. Everyone stares. It's like in a movie, tumbleweed going behind, small town people menacing towards the foreigners. You bite on the skin around your thumb nail. You look at the others who have the same god-help-us faces on.

The people in the bar start laughing.

Nervously, you join in.

'Pay no mind to these jokers. They do this to our new guests. How ya goin'?' the barman says. 'Four schooners of beer?'

Tommo raises his arms and says 'You know it, mate,' and the chat resumes in the bar.

You've a few rounds but you can't enjoy them. You think a couple of the locals look or speak a little bit like the Fletchers. Tension makes your body rigid and your thoughts go paranoid.

Any time the locals come over to ask questions about your travels or Ireland, you stay silent.

One guy in particular, wearing knee length grey shorts and a checked black and white shirt keeps trying to make eye contact with you while he talks to the group. You suck on the beer and try to control the shake in your hand. He looks like a leathered version of Hugh Jackman.

'Dublin, eh?' he says to the others. 'Beautiful city, I hear. Great atmosphere. Loved Ulysses, James Joyce was a bloody legend.'

This gets Tommo going, 'You're a man after me own heart. Sirens is one of the most perfect pieces of literature imaginable.'

Sometimes you forget how well read Tommo is.

He begins discussing Joyce and his genius and you feel the Aussie stealing looks at you.

It makes your body heat up. All the way to your face, to your scalp, the red creeps.

Susan notices you squirm. 'Are you okay, Fiona?'

You take a breath to steady yourself. 'Yep. Yep. Grand. Fine.' You drink quicker.

The man turns to face you and says, 'So are you from Dublin too?' and you watch his tongue lick the corners of his mouth in quick flickers.

'No,' you say. Your voice sounds distant. 'No, I'm from the countryside. You wouldn't know it.' Your heart races.

Stop, Fiona, he's just being nice.

You can see where his nose hair meets his beard, you can see a tiny pimple growing on the side of his temple, you can see some crust deep in the corners of his eyes. His brown eyes, his full lips, his neat haircut, his square shoulders, his broad chest.

'I might know it,' he says and smiles big. 'Try me.'

His teeth are straight except for a tiny gap between his bottom ones. He's really handsome in a rugged way.

You don't know what to do. You don't want to be attracted to him.

You try to take another drink but your hand fumbles and you spill the beer all over yourself, the glass falling and crashing to the floor. The bar goes silent again. You're wet and confused and you don't know what to do and you look at him and you look at the others and say in a loud and bitchy voice, 'So what exactly is it you want from me?' and Tommo's eyes widen and the Dublin couple draw closer to each other and the locals are still watching.

'I – nothing? I'm sorry, I didn't mean to offend you,' the

Aussie says. 'Do you need a cloth?' He points at your beer soaked lap.

'Fuck yourself,' you say.

He looks hurt and you push away from the table, the chair screeching against the floor. You hurry out of the bar into the evening sunlight.

You go back to the campervan and you don't have the keys so you crouch down in front of it, the wetness from the alcohol turning to stickiness on your top and shorts. You put your head into your hands. The sky glows above the flat plains.

A few minutes later, Tommo comes over and sits beside you on the ground. He puts his arm around you gently.

'Are you okay, Fiona?'

You don't respond.

'Fiona?'

'Of course I'm okay, why does everyone think I'm not?'

He takes his arm off you, joins his hands.

'Should I...–?' he asks. 'I don't know what to say to you, buddy. Do you want me to stay here? Do you want me to go?'

You look at him. At his freckly skin, the softness in him. He's not trying to hurt you. You try and resist but can't, the tears come thick and hot.

'I'm sorry, Tommo. I didn't mean to go for you.'

'No worries.'

'Just so – I'm just so fucked up, Tommo. I think there's something wrong with me. There is something really wrong with me.'

He leaves a silence. You blub and then suck back your breath, wipe your face.

'I'm afraid. Every day, I'm so afraid. Of the past. Of Ireland and here. Of men. Of sleeping. Of what happens next. Of myself. I'm afraid of myself.'

Tommo scratches his head.

He lets you cry.

Then he says, 'Everyone has their crosses, Fiona. It's just human. But,' he pauses and turns his palms out, 'you own them – your problems. Can you see the beauty in that?'

'D'ya remember you said working in the factory made your confidence low?'

He nods.

'D'ya think that affected the way you decided to do things? That, like, it made you more self-destructive?'

Tommo looks at you for a second and spreads his left hand in front of his face.

You laugh. He winks.

'Come on, we better go inside before the mosquitos feast on us,' Tommo says.

*

You sit in the campervan. Tommo pours some Bundy into flask lids. You tell him what happened back at Antonio's. At Fletchers'. You tell him about Malley. It's the first time you've told anyone properly about any of these things.

You switch the lantern on when it becomes too dark and place it on the table. Tommo becomes clearer, his brown hair and shadow beard.

'Ah, that lad in Ireland's a cowardly wanker. No wonder you're – you're – delicate. Should have said something to me, in the factory,' he says. His voice rises, 'and I'm fucking raging I wasn't around when those perverts were in. I'd leather them for yis. Do you think they have a new girl now?'

You are still. It reminds you of what Dorothy said. 'What do you mean?'

'Someone else?'

You think about the Fletchers' house, Antonio dropping a girl off. A girl who has no money and thinks she has no options. Her filled with doom as she walks towards the front door. You take a big swig of Bundy. Your throat and tongue sizzle with heat when you swallow.

You nod at Tommo and sigh deeply. 'They might have.'

The scene shows you something else though. Something you hadn't thought about. She thinks she has no power but she does. They've taken it. She's given it to them. Like you did.

'Would you not talk to the police, Fiona?'

'What is it with everyone and the police?' you snap. 'What could they do for me? If I talk to them, that's it, I'm done for. People will know I'm a—'

'You're not anything,' he interrupts firmly. He takes a breath. 'I don't mean you're nothing but you're the one putting the label on yourself.'

'If people found out, they'd be labelling me too. They'd say stuff about me. About my character, my sexuality. People would say my family brought me up wrong. That I deserved it.'

'Fiona, this is what I reckon. Deep down, people don't care about much more than their own lives, maybe that of their kids or their families or partners, their close circle at a stretch but after that, they're not really bothered. I don't

223

want to sound awful but it's kind of self-centred to assume they do.' He's pulling at his plaster and resticking it tighter.

You take another mouthful. This time it makes you gag.

'I'm not self-centred, Tommo,' you say and lower your head. 'I'm ashamed.'

*

Susan and Ollie come home drunk, indiscreetly whispering to Tommo to ask if you're okay. He says yeah and guides them stumbling towards to their double bed at the upper level of the campervan.

It's night time but you can't sleep. Every so often you hear howling outside. Ticking. Hooting.

You think about Malley and tuck yourself underneath your blanket. For a second you're going to do what you usually do and quash the image of him but instead you let it stay. Instead of him being a ghost in your mind, you go into the image and are the ghost. You watch him. He's in the zip-up red top he used to wear all the time, the jeans with holes, his worn out Converse. He's smoking weed. He's downing beers. He's watching TV. He looks towards the kitchen, wants a snack but is it worth the effort or not of moving. He takes another pull on his joint, decides it's not and lays into the couch, his face loses animation, his eyes slit.

It wasn't love with him. It was something painful and addictive. You wanted to fix him. You wanted to show him there was more to life. You tried to do it by sacrificing everything you had for him, all your time and energy.

But he never asked for it. He didn't.

And you kept going, a dog with a bone, you kept going until you were spent, you were as helpless as him.

You allow yourself to linger on this. You're embarrassed first then a sadness fuzzes your chest but you go with it until it passes. You feel lighter, feel calmer. His face fades from your thoughts.

Sleep comes.

*

It's the middle of the night when you jolt awake. Black emptiness is all you can see from your window. The others are snoring.

Another memory comes, you don't repress it. It's Jett's fingers inside you. His tongue on your skin. The soapy smell. His mouth, the bitter taste of it. The way you'd tingled at his touch.

You cover your mouth with your palm and jump out of the bed. You open the sliding door as soundlessly as you can, get outside away from the van. You dry heave onto the ground and wait until the nauseous feeling passes.

*

You walk around in the dark, swatting any nocturnal bugs that buzz by.

You chew at the skin loose at the side of your nails. Talking to Tommo has brought things up but it's also freed something. You're able to breathe a bit more. Take more air in. But then when you think about all that's happened you feel ashamed

225

and get short of breath. You notice it this time though, how your lungs and chest and gut react to the memories.

Why are you holding onto something that's choking you?

There's a click in your brain. You feel a piece fall into place, a pathway cleared so an idea can cruise through. You lift your head upright.

You're holding onto this feeling. You're controlling it. Why?

'Why are you doing this to yourself, Fiona?' you say aloud.

You've blamed everyone for too long. The government, Malley, the drink, your parents, that ginger girl, Antonio, the Fletchers, Dorothy even. But the truth is that it's no one's fucking fault. It's your life.

Your eyes are drooping. You wipe yourself down. Breathe. The night is giving way. Some dawn birds begin their chirps in unseen trees. Kookaburras laugh. Magpies sing. You go back to bed before sunrise.

*

The campervan is in motion when you wake. Tommo is reading a Lydia Davis book in the backseat. It's relentlessly bright and you squint at him. You're not sure if it's the light or the rum or the rough night that's caused the throb in your head. Maybe it's the idea of moving on, you joke to yourself, though when you focus on it, you feel a small flutter of hope in your chest.

'What time is it?' you ask, stretching.

'2.30 p.m. We'll be in Darwin soon. How are you?'

You yawn. 'I'm – I'm good, I think. Better.'

He smiles.

You get out of bed and fold it up and away, fix it as a seat again. You get a bottle of water from the cooler.

'Tommo, I'll be stopping off in Darwin. I won't be joining any further.'

'Really?'

'It's time,' you say and nod.

'Time?'

You nod again. It feels right. You'd resisted against thinking this way because of what it would mean for you. Exposure. Admitting your flaws. Your mistakes.

'You're not going back are you? To the farm? To catch them?' Tommo asks. He blinks rapidly.

'No. God I hope not. But I'm going to find out what I have to do. It's time.'

*

You spend the evening in Darwin chatting to Tommo. You lay on white plastic sun loungers and talk it through, what steps you're going to take. A black kite soars overhead. Some backpackers splash around in the pool. First, you're going to ring Dorothy.

You're procrastinating.

'What if she tells me to fuck off?'

'She won't.'

'What if she does though?'

He puts his palms out, spreading his fingers wide. 'If she tells you to fuck off, she tells you to fuck off. You move on. You're worrying about something that hasn't even happened. Waste of energy, Fiona.'

'Okay, I'll make the call.'

Tommo nods to urge you on.

'I'll make it.' You take a deep breath. 'But what if—?'

'Fiona, make the bleeding call.'

You nod, go downstairs and through the front door to find a quiet place outside the building.

*

The phone rings and rings and just when you're about to hang up, Geoff answers breathlessly.

'G'day?'

'Hello, Geoff,' you say. 'Is Dorothy there?'

'Fiona? Is that you?'

'Yeah,' you say and chew the bottom of your lip.

'Aw, Fiona, love, how ya goin'?' The warmth in his voice makes you smile.

'Good, Geoff, better anyway. Thanks,' you say. 'Is she in?'

'She's in the garden, we're weeding but I'll get her. It's great to hear from you. Okay, give me a moment,' he says.

He shouts Dorothy to come inside. You hear nothing until light footsteps draw closer and the scramble of picking the phone up and putting it the right way round.

'Hello,' Dorothy says.

'Dorothy, it's me,' you say.

'I know.'

Your mind goes blank. You look around, see murals of rainbow-skinned people and travel quotes on the hostel wall. *But no matter, the road is life – Jack Kerouac, Not all those*

*who wander are lost – J.R.R. Tolkien, Wherever you go, go
with all your heart – Confucius.*

'Dorothy, I – I'm so sorry. I shouldn't have spoken to you
the way I did.'

She's quiet.

'It's not been easy, trying to come to terms with everything.'

You hope she's nodding the other side. You hope she's
accepting your apology.

'So,' you say to break the silence. 'What happened when
you spoke to the police?'

She clears her throat and is hesitant. 'The inspector told
me they'd had a few complaints about that flaming creep.'

'Who?'

'Antonio. The hostel. Sporadic complaints from travellers.
They were suspicious of him. Some young boat girls who
wouldn't say too much.'

'Boat girls?'

'The mob who come here on boats, illegal migrants from
the islands. They wouldn't talk much. Cultural reasons or
language reasons or whatever. Visa reasons, probably. Too
scared.'

'Fuck. Antonio's been doing this for a while?'

Dorothy sucks her teeth. 'He's been doing it for quite
some time, I reckon.'

'Do you think there are other farmers?'

'It's entirely possible. A dealer finds those who want his
product, he makes money selling it to them. Antonio is doing
that with vulnerable people.'

You turn your head around and look in a window, seeing
your blue shirt dress, your high ponytail, your ghostlike

outline reflected back at you. You feel shaky. Chilly.

'I was so poor there, in that place. I couldn't see past it. I was so fucking stupid. Small-minded. How did I do what I did?'

'You didn't know at the time,' Dorothy says.

'I didn't know what?'

'That you didn't have to do it.'

'But what if I did know? I did but I wanted a shortcut out of the debt.' You cower, blush, but nod your head. It's the truth.

'The debt was a method of grooming you. If Antonio controls your financial state, he wields a whole lot of power over you.'

You scratch your arms.

Dorothy continues, 'Even if you consented to going out bush, it doesn't mean you were in the wrong. It doesn't matter if you agreed to it or not. If we take all emotion out of this, the problem is, by law, that a man is selling people to other people.'

Your heart is drumming. 'So, how do I go about reporting what happened to me?'

*

You ask the receptionist of the hostel about extending your stay for another night and for a room where you could make a phone call in private, with no background noise.

'I'll be speaking to the police,' you say.

She gives you a knowing look. 'This is the extension number for an office past the laundry. Nobody uses it. If you know what time they'll be calling you, I'll give you the key for it.'

You thank her and turn to leave.

'G'day,' an older man with a bright smile says near the door of the reception area.

'Hello,' you say absently. You're still thinking about the phone call.

'Enjoying the Northern Territories?' he asks. 'Leaving before the build-up?'

You nod and half-shrug.

'You wouldn't consider staying put for a few weeks. I know lots of work coming. Would qualify for your visa?'

'Not right now,' you say.

'Strewth. Even the locals can't take the heat. We got so many bloody mangos for picking and no one around to pluck them from the trees. You Irish?' he asks and you nod. He continues, 'Some of you Irish kids I meet seem dead keen on work. Take me card, eh?'

You take the card from him, read it, flip it over to see if anything is written on the back and tuck it into your pocket.

'Me bro Henk runs a farm near the Kimberley, not so far from here. It's a good place. An ace place to work.'

You thank him. He whistles a tune cheerfully and then approaches the next backpackers that come into the building. Something about him reminds you of your father.

*

You go back to the sun loungers and sit under a parasol. Tommo is splashing around in the pool and wets you as you pass. He hops out and asks how it went. You tell him. He gives you a closed-mouthed smile.

'So you definitely won't come to Kakadu with us in the morning?'

You shake your head.

It's his last trip in Australia before he flies to Dublin.

You ask, 'What'll you do back home?'

He puts his towel over his shoulders. 'I might try and use me Masters. Stop making excuses about it. Stop arsing around. Get into shape. But I might get a bar job and go on the slips. Will see what's going on when I get back. How 'bout you? Where'll you go after this?'

'I don't know. D'ya see that sign by reception? Mango pickers needed in the Kimberley region? Well there's a man downstairs talking about it, he gave me a contact.'

Tommo's mouth drops. 'You're not going back into the wilderness?'

'I think I might. Not just yet obviously but I miss being in nature and keep reading the sign every time I walk by. I feel drawn to it.'

Tommo shakes his head. 'I said before you were delicate. I was bleeding wrong.'

*

You find it hard to nod off again that night. You look around the dorm room to the doorway, the shaft of light creeping in from the hallway at the threshold. You catch yourself getting angry and stop. Breathe. You give up trying to force sleep and take your blanket to the rooftop, sit out there alone. The sky is a thick black but the moon and stars shine fiercely. The darkness brings its own light.

*

In the morning, you walk Tommo to the campervan. He opens his rucksack before loading it and passes you a brown paper bag.

'Something small,' he says.

You unwrap it. A sketchpad.

'You can do your drawings in it,' he says. 'And I want you to have these. Me mam posted them over to me but I never ate them. Hard and all as that is to believe, I'm just more a salt'n'vinegar man.' He rustles through the rucksack again and pulls out a six pack of cheese and onion crisps.

You squeal. 'You serious?'

'Yep. I'm going back to the land of Tayto.'

You give him a hug and your eyes get damp. 'You know, Tommo, I hated goodbyes so much before now. Thought they meant the end of something. But they kinda make something whole. Complete.'

He kisses your hand, 'This ain't a goodbye though, me'lady. Sure, won't I be seeing you back in Ireland? You better visit me in the Big Smoke. Even if you're a culchie and you'll probably get lost outside Heuston Station. I want you to meet me mates.'

Susan and Ollie finish loading their things and say bye. They start up the van, the fumes cling in the air as it chugs, stationary.

Tommo gets in and waves his garlic finger hand at you.

233

He blows a kiss and puts his thumb to his ear, his baby finger to his chin and mouths, 'Call me.'

You wait until he's out of sight.

'Goodbye, Tommo.'

*

At dusk, you go for a walk through the centre of Darwin. It's small, smaller than Westport. The streets are muggy and dusty. You go to the park, sit on the ground and figure out the wording of a text you'll send your parents:

Things are getting better here, I promise. We'll chat soon. Love ye x

You gather your breath. Gather your thoughts. You look up and sketch, the pencil grazes the page. Two kangaroos are silhouetted on the horizon, the sun sets behind them. Burning red and orange turns indigo as the sky deepens. The grasses and palm trees swish in the light wind. You wait for night.

THEM

Them. Hopper had to get them to a town in the middle of nowhere. A bag of MDMA caps from a motorcycle gang in Adelaide. An eleven-hour train to David P and the buckos. Hopper was no dealer. He was a delivery man. A thousand dollars for this run. That'd set him up for a move to Perth.

David P's hostel was great, mad so it was. A converted hospital out near the forest. Big common room. Few sexy looking women from around the world. A machine for cold drinks, another one for sweets and crisps. A bad swimming pool that Hopper was warned not to jump into because it was full of glass at the bottom where they'd smashed their bottles.

David P offered Hopper a pint of goon to warm up.

Hopper wouldn't turn it down with these new people, though they'd all get along in a while, he knew that much, when they'd fucking be in love with each other, buzzing off each other. But until that happened, a drink would help. Sometimes Hopper got embarrassed. People had big ideas and words and lots of them finished school or went to college. Lots of them could read good. Even the heavies. He didn't want to be thick around them, didn't want them talking about him. Hated people talking about him all the time.

David P poured a Fruity Lexia and looking at the back of the box said real loud that it was a 'delicate and fruit driven wine with luscious aromas and a sweetness on the palate.'

Fruit, wine, sweet.

Hopper thought they wanted him to say something back. Something smart. The way it went quiet after that.

So he goes, 'Sure this here is modern love. Pills and goon.'

And everyone went calm, stopped moving, stopped their lives. Hopper felt a shake coming into his hand. They were looking at him and he got scared they'd take the piss out of him but then in a big mad group they looked at each other and they laughed. Laughed for ages. Patted him on the back. Told everyone else that passed. Said he was a witty bastard. He was real clever. He was a hero.

A fucking hero.

About four goons in, they dropped some of the caps. Super strength. Very good shit.

The night went ntz ntz.

Hopper and Irish. Look at them here in Australia. Bunch of legends.

'Love you.'

'Love you more.'

Ah fuck.

'Do you know where I'm from?'

'Do you know me cousins?'

'Who do you know?'

'You don't know anything.'

The night rocked, rolled, raved, rode.

Dark skies. Pink skies. Morning skies.

All of a sudden, it was Saturday, like it had passed in a minute.

'It's way too early to skag?' Hopper said to David P. 'What ya reckon, we keep it going for the whole weekend?' If he didn't mind Hopper staying, the Adelaide bikies shouldn't mind much either.

David P nodded yeah, okay, and Hopper nodded dead on.

They dropped more caps. Buzz. Jaw. Mouth. Heart. Feet. Hands to the sun. Moving, moving. Inside the music. All morning. Remix. Hardhouse. Trance. Hear this, hear this.

They said it, 'Pills and goon, Hopper. Pills and goon.'

More ntz, hands to head, hands to the sun. Water. Wine. Jesus.

But in the middle of the day, they played Amy Winehouse. She'd just passed away. Her songs, the words – they were written for Hopper. He was in front of a mirror and his face was all fucked. His face was telling him the real truth. He missed his girlfriend and son.

But they weren't his. Neither of them.

He wanted his life to be better. He wanted his life to be okay. He wanted to be on this buzz without thinking like this. Of them. Of his parents. All the bad.

The fizzing started. He was losing the run of himself with anger. It made everything fizz. All around his fingertips, in his ears, his eyes. Fizz.

Her and the baby. The only ones that had ever loved him. Everything taken away from him.

He was back in Ireland. It was straight after 'the news' was going round and she called him in to their bedroom and sat him down. Her face white. The wee fella in the cot.

She said it, and he'd never known a sentence to do what that one did to him, even after the years with his parents, with the shades and the social workers. With the teachers and all the other bastards that'd be trying to get him.

That sentence came from her mouth, she said –

And her lips were soft and pink, her tongue was pierced, she said –

Tears ran down and off her cheeks but she didn't touch them, she said –

'It's true Hopper, he's not yours.'

And he had to move out in that moment or he'd have crashed all the house to the ground around them. The fizz would have him convinced to burn the place down with the three of them in it. The wee fella, the whiff of baby powder off him and his chubby hands, the gold earring they got him on his first birthday, he wasn't Hopper's kid and her – the love of his life – she wasn't his girlfriend but he couldn't cremate them no matter what was done. He loved them with his whole heart even though he didn't want to anymore. With all his breathing and thinking and movement, he loved them.

He was in front of the mirror in the outback hostel in Australia and it was cracked. Another twenty-one years of bad luck. His hand bleeding. His fist all bits of skin loose. His face wet. Her and the baby. The only ones that had ever loved Hopper back. Gone.

Him left with nothing but himself. Like always.

He went outside into the sun.

Someone told someone.

David P came over. 'Hopper, what's wrong, man? Are you okay?'

'Yeah,' Hopper said. 'I'm fine,' he said but he knew David P could see his red eyes, him trying not to think. To feel.

'Hopper, boy, what do you want? What do you need?' David P asked.

Hopper pinched the top of his cheeks, rubbed his face roughly. 'Play some Van Morrison. Please?'

'Who?'

'Into the Mystic. It's a song. Play it. Here will you play it? Will you put it on for me? Play it. Play it now.'

'Sound, Hopper. Anything you want.'

David P warned the others to move from the controls. It went quiet. Guitar and piano and saxaphone and Van.

Sun was sky high. They were sky high.

And they could set the world on fire. Watch it burn. Burn it all. It made it easier. When you burn it, it's gone. Then it starts new.

Hopper put the cushion off his chair into the middle of the courtyard. They were watching him. He pulled another cushion off. He put it on the other one.

'What ya doing, boss?' someone asked.

'Going to spark it. Going to fucking spark it. You in?'

And someone brought his cushion over. And someone brought his. And someone got their mattress from their bunk and next thing they'd a bonfire going. New chances wearing hot orange silk. Dancing with them.

But yer man, the hostel fella, he got wind of all his furniture and beds being on fire and he came over fucking raging.

'What in the –? You fucking cunts. You stupid Irish fucks,' he said and had his hands together on top of his head.

It was a bad auld buzz. He might have thrown a slap on

241

one of them. He shouted words in between the thundering. 'Bushfire.' 'Cops.' 'Losers.' 'Money.' 'Kill.'

He was stabbing the buzz with hate.

And so David P did it first. He rolled his neck. He cracked his knuckles. Then he squared up to him.

'What you going to do about it?' David P asked and he was jawing. He was off his tits.

The hostel fella stopped. 'What?'

'I said, what are you going to do about it?' And David P tensed and relaxed his fingers. Then someone was beside him. Squaring. Then someone else. Then someone else. And Hopper followed and stood beside them.

And they fucking showed him.

There was fourteen of them altogether. There was one of him.

The fire blazed on.

*

Back in Adelaide, after the skagging, Hopper took a breath before walking into the bikies' club. Bikies. He'd have fucking laughed back home at a gang of motorcycle heads, their silly jackets with crests and writing on them but here there was no messing. These men were mad into guns, meth, explosives.

They were into torture.

Hopper was shitting it but maybe they'd be impressed with him. Maybe they'd give him more work. He'd got the drugs up to the lads. They'd got their pay, David P had deposited it in, all in. Hopper knew that, he had the bank statement. But Hopper also knew that the rest of it was not in the plan.

He was supposed to keep a low profile. Be a delivery man. A professional. He took another breath.

The club was a strip club, it smelt of jizz-stains and drink and Hopper couldn't help look at the women swing round poles, their bodies tight and their eyes glazed over. One or two of the waitresses seemed like they were having fun, flirting with the customers, winking and jiggling their way around the tables. The rest of them looked how Hopper felt most days.

He saw the Hulk Hogan-looking bikie getting a lap dance. The boss man. He didn't want to interrupt. He could have the raging horn and Hopper'd be in his bad books even more for ruining that. Instead, Hopper stood at the bar and waited for Hulk to notice him.

The bartender was fully clothed and to Hopper's surprise, she was Irish. Hopper usually knew Irish people, not just by the skin or haircuts or accents, the hold of them was the same, the stand of them. But this one, he'd have never guessed. Maybe it was because she was working here. Because of the Catholic in them that made places like this feel dirty as fuck, even if they were a good buzz.

'What can I get you?' she asked.

'Anything,' Hopper said.

She gave him a small smile and filled a tumbler with whiskey and ginger ale. 'Have this. Are you the kid they sent to David P?'

Hopper gulped. How'd she know?

'Yeah,' he said.

She took the glass back and free poured the spirit on top of the drink until it was up to the rim. 'You'll need this so. Good luck.'

Hopper thanked her and began downing it in quick sups.

An old man stood beside him. 'Nice place here,' he said in an English accent.

'Suppose.'

'I just come for the company really, I'll miss it.' The man turned to the bartender. 'And I'll miss you most of all.'

She giggled. 'You're a charmer, Norman.'

Hopper could feel the drink swirl his blood.

He switched his attention back to the boss. He couldn't be standing around here making shite talk. He needed his pay. He finished his drink, slammed it on the counter and stomped over towards Hulk who was leaning back on his chair, the stripper's arse grinding him.

'Here, what are ye going to do to me?' Hopper asked.

Hulk looked at Hopper, the lust fading out of his eyes. He pushed the girl away and patted his crotch. 'I was wondering when you'd show, drongo,' he said. 'You were due here last week.'

He curled his handlebar moustache with his fingers. The girl sighed and put on a neon pink bikini. Hopper noticed her ribs, the way they pushed out underneath her skin. Looked like his old girlfriend's when he used to kiss her every morning after her shower. Kiss her ribs. Her chest. Her neck. The smell of the coconut gel she washed with. What he'd fucking give for one of those mornings, before she went off to work in the petrol station, before the baby woke. Her hair wet. Her skin fresh.

Hulk stood over Hopper and grabbed him by the scruff of his neck. 'Come on,' he said and dragged him to a door past the stage, up some stairs and into an office that stunk of weed. It had a giant screen for CCTV on the wall. Hulk sat at a desk messy with papers, books, a laptop, two empty tills and a cardboard box of baggies.

'You fucked up,' Hulk said.

Hopper squirmed. 'I did. I'm sorry. Things got out of hand.'

'Yeah, well the fucking narks might be on us and if they are—'

'They won't be. It was too far away. I'm Irish. The boys were Irish. Won't get linked to ye. Sure how the fuck would I know ye?' Hopper was talking real fast. 'They only gave a shite about the fire 'cause the way it spread a bit.'

'The bushfire, that's another bloody headache. Why?'

Hopper dropped his head. 'I don't know.'

'You're not getting paid for that balls up.'

Hopper's eyes opened as wide as they could go. 'Here, what?'

'You heard.'

'Ye have to fucking pay me. I did what ye asked me to do.'

Hulk rose from the desk. 'No, you minda, you messed the whole thing up.'

'We had a deal there, we shook on a deal,' Hopper said. The fizz was coming.

'You're getting bugger all.'

'A deal is a fucking deal.'

Hulk shook his head.

'We had an agreement,' Hopper said through his teeth.

'Agreement went up in smoke with that fucking bushland.' Fizz.

'Fuck ye.' Hopper punched the CCTV screen. 'Stupid fucking beards. Stupid denim jackets. Big gang on yer bikes. Big men.'

Hopper went for the laptop on the table and tried to throw it at Hulk. He missed and it crashed to the office floor. He tried to break the CCTV screen with his fist. He tried to pick up the desk.

Hulk was roaring but Hopper heard nothing. He felt nothing when Hulk grabbed him and restrained him. Hopper bit and screeched. He resisted as much as he could but he couldn't get free from Hulk's grip.

Inside his mind, he was blank.

No noise, no pain. Only fizz.

Hulk fastened Hopper's hands behind his back with a cable tie and pulled him off the ground. He pushed him towards the door and gave him a kick to send him tumbling down the stairs. Hopper's head hit the steps. His body folded over itself. His shoulder got loose. At the bottom of the stairs, Hopper spat out blood and shouted, 'Give me my pay.'

Hulk stomped down the steps and pulled Hopper up by the hair, in through the club. Some of the hair came out and Hopper fell on the ground. The girls were looking down at him. Their pointy tits. The customers were afraid to look. Hopper knew the song playing, Party Rock Anthem. He knew it because he knew the baby'd love it. He'd bounce in his bouncer to that beat. Hopper'd shuffle for him.

'You get the fuck out of Adelaide and never come back,' Hulk shouted over the music.

Hopper saw Hulk's boot come. Then Hopper saw nothing.

*

'You okay?' she said. 'Come on, wake up.' She was sawing at the cable tie. His hands got free.

The stretching of skin from Hopper opening his eyes made inside his head, inside his cheeks, ache.

It was the middle of the day, Hopper forgot. The club had been so dark. The sun out was savage. And this was supposed to be winter time. Hopper moaned and tried to sit. The Irish bartender was over him holding her bar knife.

'Will I call the ambulance?' she asked.

Hopper shook his head. 'I'll be sound,' he said and gurgled back some grit and slime in his throat.

'Do you have somewhere to go?'

Hopper shrugged.

'They'll kill you, you know. You have to get moving. There's no fucking around with them. I've seen what they can do.'

'Why are you in there? What are you doing there?' Hopper asked.

She took a noisy breath. 'I'm married to one of them.'

'Fuck.'

She scratched her ear. 'It's not the worst. Needed to go de facto. And my husband, well, he's got his moments. Can you walk?'

'I think so,' he said and she put her arm out to support him.

She looked around. 'You've to get moving. Fast. Do you know anyone?'

Hopper shrugged again.

'Yer man, Norman,' she said, her eyes narrowing. 'You chatted to him didn't you?'

'Who?'

'He was leaving today. Road trip and setting up somewhere outback. I'll ring him, he only left a few minutes ago. Let me make a call, okay?'

Hopper didn't know what she meant. He spat more of the gunk out from his mouth and lightly fingered his face, see what was swelling, what was wet. He could hear the cars on the main road. The wall in front of Hopper had posters with naked girls and music bands advertised. Vents steamed. The frying vegetables and clatter from an Asian restaurant's back kitchen filled the hot air outside.

Hopper was limping when he tried walking. His shoulder though. He'd have to get her to pop it.

She came back outside holding her phone. 'Norman – he's a customer here but he's good to the girls. Never touches them. Tips well. He's going to come back for you. He's driving through the Nullarbor. You have stuff?'

'Stuff?'

'Clothes, shoes, passport and that?'

'Have me phone and passport on me,' Hopper said and tapped his pocket. 'Don't care about any of the rest of it.'

He'd left his shite in the squat he was staying in but that wasn't a problem because he didn't have much in it. He could pick up bits again. He had never been crazy about fashion or good runners. Clothes were only clothes.

'Good. Money?'

Hopper shook his head. 'They were supposed to pay me.'

248

'Yer man seems wealthy enough. You'll be okay,' she said and gave Hopper a twenty from her bra.

'Are you safe?' he asked as he pocketed the cash.

She smirked. 'I suppose. Better go back though.'

'Will ya do me one thing?' Hopper asked. 'Pull me arm.'

*

Norman indicated into a disabled spot on Gouger Street. He was driving a blue Ford Falcon and honked. Hopper hobbled over to the car. The door was opened from the inside.

'Well, well,' he said and Hopper smiled weakly. 'We meet again.'

'Yeah,' Hopper said and introduced himself.

Norman looked younger in the daylight. Mid sixties maybe. He wore a cowboy hat as he drove. The car was cool. Norman didn't ask any questions, he hummed along to the piano music on the radio. Hopper said little. He just tried to clean himself by spitting on the sleeve of his jersey and wiping the dried blood off. His face was too sore for him to think.

*

'I'm going to Whyalla first,' Norman said. 'Will take a couple of hours. I've already booked into a motel. You're welcome to stay in my room. On the couch or the ground, whatever.'

'Okay.' Hopper answered straight away.

'I shouldn't think it wise for you to hang about in Whyalla though. It's too close to Adelaide and the bikers have another big club there.'

'I'm going to Perth.'

Norman whistled. 'It's a good little city, Perth. Plenty of work.'

Hopper wasn't going for work. He was just going.

His body had been tense and he was getting the sweats in the car. He wasn't sure if it was from being nervous or if it was a hangover. For the four-hour drive, he kept an eye on the rearview mirror. His heart beat at his chest whenever he saw a motorbike, even if it was some shitty pink auld lady scooter.

He thought about the bushfire. He swore he hadn't meant for that to happen. It was like the playground he lit back in Ireland but he'd been fizzed and out of his box that time as well. He got too mesmerised by it to stop it before it was too late.

But if he didn't get out of his box, he'd be stuck in it and it'd play back the memories. The baby's smiles. The baby's bouncing around when Hopper changed his nappy. The baby's warmth as he slept. He was a little hot water bottle.

Hopper shook himself. Tapped his head to try and get it back to the present moment. That sometimes worked. He needed to distract his thoughts.

'Why you going on this road trip anyway?' he asked Norman.

'Can I be honest with you?' Norman responded.

Hopper shrugged. He didn't care if Norman was being honest or not.

'My kids and grandkids are in Nottingham, have their own lives and I'm not essential to them. My third marriage – to a woman from Canberra – is over. She was too young.

She left. I'm retired.' He paused. 'I just don't have anything else to do.'

Hopper shrugged again. Good enough reason as any.

*

Norman checked into the motel and Hopper stayed in the car until he showed him where to go. The room was fancy, Hopper thought. A TV in front of the double bed. A couch by the door. A big dressing table with mirrors. A wardrobe. Kettle. Fridge. Ironing board and a bathroom with towels. Red curtains. Red bed spread. No cobwebs or insects. No crusty stuff on the linen.

Hopper had awful sweats, cold one second, overheating the next. His stomach was iffy and he stayed in the bathroom for a long time after his shower.

Norman had stripped off his pants and cowboy hat and was watching TV in his shirt and jocks. Hopper didn't know where to look.

'I'll order a pizza to the room,' Norman said. 'What toppings do you want?'

'Any of them,' Hopper replied. He had never been able to eat much, his stomach had shrunk over the years.

The pizza came, Norman laid the box open. Hopper sat on the bed to pick a slice. Barbeque chicken. When Hopper was done eating, he felt tired and swollen. He lay back and drifted off into a sleep.

He woke up wet. He had sweated all over his side of the bed. Norman was snoring, facing the other wall. They were nowhere near touching. The room was lit by the lamp

Hopper's side. He switched it off and the darkness made his eyes relax. He hadn't slept beside someone since his old girlfriend. And that was fucking ages ago. Jesus, he thought about it, he hadn't had the ride since. It was going six months now. He had barely thought about the ride since. That must be some sort of world record.

*

The air conditioning in the room did nothing to cool Hopper down in the morning. Norman had left but his bag was still there. Hopper opened it and had a ruffle through it for cash but found none. He looked for pills but found none. What kind of old fella was he?

He sprayed some of Norman's deodorant under his arms and down his jocks and sat on the couch wondering what to do.

Could go for a box of goon. Drink the day away.

He was sitting for a while, watching the dust dance in the sunlight, when Norman came back, full of energy and plastic bags.

'Got some brekkie, mate. Here,' Norman said and handed Hopper a beef pie. He shook the bags. 'Supplies until we get to the next motel.'

We.

Norman mustn't have thought Hopper was leaving yet. That suited him.

*

Hopper had the dark over him in the car. He felt dark about Ireland but he felt dark about Australia too. He only wanted to have a good time here but he wasn't, not really.

The car drove on through nothing. Barely any trees. Barely any hills or anything. Only a bit of scrub plants, dust and roadkill animals.

Hopper wondered what Ger would make of this. Being in Oz but being with an English person. Ger had been his best mate. His only mate, maybe.

He met Ger in a foster home for a load of fuck up kids like them. Their foster mother was an awful soft one. She'd be giving out twenty euros if they pretended to cry and told her about their real parents and the stuff they'd be at.

Ger used to love stealing cars and Hopper'd burn them out after. They'd hang around the town late in the evening. They'd nothing else to do. Ger loved to see what speed he could get to and when the Boom started, the cars got a lot faster because they were span new.

Ger knew history, especially Irish history. He told Hopper about the British and all they done in Ireland. With land and food and language and women. But mostly, with Catholics. They'd a serious problem with the Catholics because Henry the Eighth was a horndog. He wanted to have loads of wives but the priests wouldn't let him so he told the pope to fuck off and made his own religion. When the Irish didn't go with it, the British got really fucking thick. The Irish knew this so they kept it up for years and years, even though some people in the church were fiddling with the kids or beating the heads off them so Hopper didn't know if they should have stuck with them at all.

Ger told him how the Brits don't even know much of what they done in the history of Ireland because of all they done around the world, Ireland doesn't even get brought in to anything. It's 'insignificant' to them, he'd say.

He was the first person who ever said he'd go to Australia. This was miles before the recession or any of that shite. Ger wanted to go to surf because of Home and Away. But Hopper thought he wanted to get the furthest part of the world away from home. That maybe he'd feel different being himself in another place. Kind of like why Hopper came here.

Ger went down when he got caught after crashing a nice looking Passat. Should have burnt it. Should always burn them. No trace. Start new.

The fizz began to prickle. He rubbed his neck, massaged the lump down. 'Don't want this to happen,' he said.

Norman turned to him, 'Are you okay?'

Hopper nodded and tried to change his thoughts by tapping his head. It didn't work. He made a fist and hit his temple harder.

Ger hung himself in Oberstown. Hopper never went to visit him until he was laid in this plain coffin in the funeral home.

Another young lad buried in wet Irish ground.

'Why'd he do it?' Hopper asked but he knew why.

'What?' Norman said. 'What's going on?'

'How could someone like me stay in Ireland? Ireland's only sad when the brainboxes leave. Ireland never gave a fuck about people like us,' Hopper said.

Norman's eyebrows were almost touching. 'Us?'

'Me and Ger.'

Norman looked on at the road. 'Do you want me to stop so you can take a little walk or something?'

'I only want to have a good time here,' Hopper said. He'd goosebumps all over.

'Do you need medical attention?' Norman said.

'No.' Hopper dabbed the back of his neck where the sweat was going cold.

'Alright mate, your call.'

Hopper stared out the window and slumped. His mouth began to water furiously and his chest heaved. 'Shit. Shit. Pull in,' he said to Norman. 'Pull in.'

He vomited.

His limbs were weak and heavy.

'You've had a stressful time,' Norman said and patted Hopper's back as he leant out the door. 'In Ceduna, I can bring you to a hospital.'

'No,' Hopper said. He didn't deserve a hospital. He didn't have the money for it either. 'It'll be sound.'

Hopper washed his face with bottled water from the car. He took mouthfuls to rinse his teeth, his tongue, and spat on the sandy ground.

*

Hopper could see shadows of people in the corner of his eyes but when he turned to check, they weren't there. The landscape was bright and stony outside. He sat back in his seat and waited for the dread to pass. Because that's what those shadows were. His lost love, his fuck ups, his broken friends, his stupid fucking life. The dread.

*

'We could go and do something this evening, if you'd fancy that?' Norman asked as he unlocked the motel room door.

Hopper stayed silent.

'The cinema? I'll pay,' Norman said.

'Grand,' Hopper said but he didn't want to go. He just wanted to lie down. Let his body slump to the dark. Dream of the dark. Be the dark.

His parents would be laughing at him if they saw him now. They'd have told him he was worthless in Ireland, he's still worthless in Oz.

'I'm not them,' Hopper said. 'Am I them?'

'What?' Norman asked. 'You don't want to go with me?' He was changing his shirt. Hopper noticed a stitches scar from his neck down to under his breastbone. Like he'd been slashhooked.

'How'd you get that?' Hopper pointed.

'Triple bypass. Dodgy ticker.'

'The pain,' Hopper said.

'It looks worse than it is.'

'Like me.'

'Come on, cheer up. Put on some fresh clothes and join me. You can pick the movie.'

Hopper shook his head. 'I got no other clothes.'

'Well wear this,' Norman said and threw over a white t-shirt from his bag.

It hung off Hopper's body and made him seem thinner than he was.

'It's a date then,' Norman said and clapped.

Hopper rubbed his face and down his neck. He hoped that Norman was having a joke as he followed.

*

There was no cinema. There wasn't much of anything open. It was small town Australia.

'Fancy a walk on the beach?' Norman asked. He was grinning.

'Not really,' Hopper said. It was too hot outside even though it was evening. The seagulls and waves would drive him mad. Sand would get all over his trainers. Norman might try and hold his hand.

'A restaurant? This place is famous for oysters.'

Fuck off with your oysters.

'An ice cream?'

Hopper wouldn't say no to a 99.

They got cones and walked the pier. The sun was setting and the sky was glowing pink as sunburn.

'Why is it so fucking hot?' Hopper asked. 'It's nearly time for the Angelus.'

'This is nothing, it rises to the forties for most the year. Desert climate,' Norman said. He had white on his mouth from the ice cream. 'Are you ready for tomorrow?'

Hopper stopped. 'What's tomorrow?'

'We start to cross the Nullarbor.'

We again.

Norman was bringing him still. Hopper allowed himself to smile for the first time that day.

*

Norman said Hopper could sleep on the other half of the bed if he wanted to. There was enough room for the two of them to sleep on opposing sides.

'I'll lie down here, sound,' Hopper said and unrolled a blanket over the couch.

Norman turned the lights out and was snoring gently within seconds. The couch was lumpy and hard. Hopper kept picturing cobwebs being made over his face. He wiped his head and ears and cheeks but he could still feel the pricks spinning their flytraps on him. The shadows were surfacing too. The dread and the dark. Hopper wiped his face again. Maybe he'd sleep in the bed for one more night. Remember to get spider repellent next time they passed a roadhouse.

He crept over to the bed but it creaked when he got in. Norman stirred. He gave Hopper's shoulder a squeeze and turned away.

'Night then,' he said.

Even in the darkness, Hopper could see tingles from being touched.

*

Hopper had some shakes the next morning. In his hands. In his eyes.

'What the fuck is happening to me?'

Norman was reading the paper. Again he'd snuck out in the morning without waking Hopper and returned with some food and fizzy drinks.

'What do you mean?'

'I'm dying here. I feel panics. I'm sweating and shitting all the time. I'm boking. I can't breathe.'

Hopper was topless and wobbled as he stood.

Norman chewed down on an apple. 'When did you have a drink last? Or a smoke? Or any,' he said and mimed throwing something into his mouth.

'What?'

'It seems to me, you're on a comedown. Crashing. Cold turkey, mate.'

'What?' Hopper wiped the sweat on his forehead.

'Moons ago, I went to the driers. You wouldn't have even been born when I got sober.'

Hopper's chest was tightening. Sure, how the fuck, what, he wasn't on anything or addicted to anything. He just took whatever was going but nothing bad. Never with any consistency. And in Oz, it was mostly the goon.

Or the MDMA with the buckos.

Or the lithium he got off the Chinese lad in the Adelaide hostel or the codeine painkillers from the chemist for the hangovers.

Nothing bad at all.

He wasn't ever addicted to anything. Not even drink. He hadn't touched heroin or cocaine here. It was too expensive and he had promised himself he wouldn't. He didn't go near the ice they had in the squat even though it was new to him.

Tempting to try. But the ones on the crystals were ravaged. He was being healthy as a trout in Australia.

'Really?' Hopper said and took a deep breath.

'It'll pass, mate,' Norman said. He ate the full apple, seeds and core and all. 'Trust me.'

Hopper's legs were buckling so he lay on the floor. It was cooler there.

'I don't want to go in the car today,' he said.

'No worries.'

'It's boring as fuck,' Hopper said. 'No offence,' he added.

'We can hang around here if you want, I'll pay for another night?'

Hopper nodded and Norman left.

On the floor, Hopper thought about it. If he got through this, he'd be sober in Perth. Completely sober going about life. A new chance.

All the beatings he'd got were connected to drugging or drinking. All the summons.

Did she go off with yer man on the sly because of Hopper? Because of him getting so out of it? Her waiting in their flat at night for him to come home. Waiting the next morning and afternoon for him. Texting him and Hopper never bothered replying. Sure why would he, he knew where she was and he didn't want to be at home when he was partying. Would kill his buzz.

When she got pregnant, he went spare.

'Get the boat,' he said to her.

'No way,' she said.

'We can't have a baby.'

'I'm keeping it.'

And Hopper gave her hell for a while but the way her belly grew and the idea of a child – his child – gave him the hope. He wouldn't make a dog's dinner of it the way his parents had done with him. His father shuffling around looking for money and his mother always downing stuff to get away from the depression. Hopper and his half brothers and sisters being turfed between houses. Aunties, neighbours, fosters, them fucking institutions.

Hopper smartened his act up. He went on a FÁS course. He applied for a house off the council. He didn't know she had rode someone else.

Hopper wept in the motel room. The carpet smelt of cats and he could see a stain in the shape of a puddle in its fibres.

Norman opened the door and Hopper tried to get himself together but couldn't. Norman lifted him off the ground and lay him on the bed.

'It'll pass, mate. It will. That's how life goes. It passes. The good and the bad.' Norman nodded for a few seconds and wouldn't stop until Hopper nodded back.

*

Norman sat on the couch and told Hopper about the collapse of his first two marriages from drinking. The TV was on mute. Sometimes Hopper had to look at the colours on screen to get the uncomfortable out of him while Norman was talking. Norman told him about pissed beds, broken bones, nights in cells, in alleyways, droop-cock, hazes, hangovers, all the hate from his kids, from his wives, from himself. His low point was trying to molest one of his interns, a graduate called Greg, at a work party. He didn't quite remember it, just sketches – hands, skin, Greg's pale blue eyes – but he was given the choice between his P45 or a sexual harassment suit. He cleared his desk and sought help.

He recalled with tears his recovery, the twelve steps, how he adapted his life. Hopper listened on, hooked on the stories of other people's shite time of it.

Hopper told him about his life. He told him about Ger, about her and the baby. He didn't say anything about the fizz.

'Every mistake is a step of learning and growth,' Norman said. 'But the key to staying clean is to change your routine.'

Hopper sat and considered this. The quaking in his body was getting less violent. The bile in his chest seemed to be going back down. But now Hopper felt a disturbing sensation over him. He had a shower to wash away all the confessions that happened. They'd come from the inside of his mind to his mouth to the outside world, but clung onto him like smog. He was grimy with them.

In the shower, he scrubbed his skin with soap and with his nails to pry the feeling off him. The water burned.

'Will ye leave me? Will ye go?' he pleaded with the confessions.

He was whimpering.

Norman knocked on the door. 'Are you okay in there, mate?'

Hopper was concentrating. He didn't reply.

Norman joggled the door handle. It undid the lock. He opened up and Hopper looked over at him, naked and scratched, his hair plastered to his face with the water, steam fogging the room.

'I can't get them off me,' Hopper said. 'They won't fuck off.'

*

Norman made a cup of chamomile tea for Hopper and put him in bed. He said that if Hopper was still feeling this way in the morning, they'd go to a doctor.

'Do you think I'm mental?' Hopper asked.

'Not really, mate. I think you're having a tough time and you're a long way from home.'

Hopper looked down. 'Don't have a home back there.'

Norman's face was sad.

'I've no one who gives a shite about me, there or here.'

'Well, you do now.'

Hopper examined Norman. His head had fine white hair covering a bald patch. He'd lines everywhere on his face and a second chin. His eyes were blue green, kind of like the ocean by the coast. He wondered how much money Norman had, maybe he should just ask him for a loan and get out. But he was afraid to be on his own.

'I don't want to talk about any of the confessions anymore,' Hopper said. 'They're making me worse.'

'It's good to talk, mate.'

Hopper shook his head. 'No, I'm done, I'm done with them back home. I'm here. I'll get well. I won't look for anything. Any trouble. How long does it take to go across that road you're on about?'

'Nullarbor?'

'Yeah that one.'

263

'Not too long.'

'Can I come?'

Norman grinned and patted Hopper on the head. 'Course you can, mate. It would be dull in the car without you.'

*

Before they left Ceduna, Norman pulled over at a cash machine. Hopper watched from the car but couldn't guess what numbers Norman had just punched in. He did see though, Norman lifting his shirt to put the cash into a small leather purse that was strapped onto him.

When Norman walked back to the car, Hopper fiddled with the radio, pretending he'd been looking at that all along.

They left town and not long on the highway, a bunch of people were blocking the road up ahead. They were just hanging about. Aboriginal people.

'Damn Blackfellas,' Norman said.

'Why are they there?'

'No idea. Maybe it's protected land or something. Did you see any signs?'

The only signs Hopper saw showed kangaroos, camels and wombats.

'What are you going to do?' he asked Norman.

'I'm afraid this might be an ambush.'

Hopper looked at the crowd, seven people stood on the road in different places. They didn't move much as the car drew closer.

'I've heard stories of this,' Norman said and sniffed. 'They make you slow down and they kick you out of your car. Drive off.'

'Really?' Hopper said and smiled with surprise. It was a pretty good plan. 'What if they're just having a hang, chilling like?'

'Why would they be on the road?'

'Can't be bothered moving? No cars passing. Haven't seen five yet. They might be just having a play.'

Norman was inhaling deeply through his nose. He had one hand on the steering wheel and the other was over his heart.

The people weren't moving off the road.

Hopper could see some of their dark faces, their sunlit hair, their shaggy clothes.

Norman's breath was getting quicker.

'Are you okay, Norman?' Hopper asked. 'It'll be sound, just beep at them. They're not going to want to get hit. No one wants to get hit by a car.'

The early afternoon sun was brilliant and Hopper didn't know how they could stand the heat outside.

Norman was clutching his chest as he put his foot down on the accelerator. He went at rising speed towards the people, forcing them to run and dive towards the side of the road. They shouted at the car as it sped past. Norman didn't slow down until they were pins in the rearview mirror.

Hopper was stunned. 'Norman, they weren't trying to do anything to us. They were just arsing around on the road.'

'Can't take risks with the natives. We're on their land now.'

'You nearly gave yourself a heart attack.'

Norman had his breathing back but his forehead was still

sweating, despite the A/C blowing a chill air into the car.

'You can't take risks with the natives.'

*

Later on, Norman was in good spirits again. He had his annoying piano songs playing. He was wearing his cowboy hat and whistling. Hopper looked out at the dead stuff on the side of the road. Lots of kangaroos. He saw a camel being savagely picked apart by a bunch of eagles and wanted to take a picture of it on his phone but Norman was afraid of the eagles.

'It sounds like an Aboriginal name, doesn't it? Nullarbor,' Norman said as they passed another sign with Nullarbor Plain and some info on it.

'Does it?'

'It's not though,' Norman paused. 'It comes from the Latin, no trees.'

The clouds were unreal. They were like a low lying white blanket, with rips and holes of glowing blue sky underneath.

'How am I even noticing this shit?' Hopper said aloud.

'What?'

'I feel different, Norman. In my head. I do,' he nodded as he spoke. The dark wasn't around him anymore. The dread was only there in tiny scraps. Just before he dozed off maybe, or when his brain was thinking too much. The fizz was far away.

They drove on the National Highway until the border. The car was checked for fruit and vegetables which made Hopper laugh.

'Bag of apples is worse than a bag of blow?'

The car was clean and they drove on to Mundrabilla,

passed it, the road straight. The landscape never really changed but come sunset, the sky went like a rainbow.

Hopper was tripping looking at it. All the colours blending and dissolving into each other. Pinky-blues mashing reds and yellows. Injecting oranges and purples.

*

The roadhouse was small and the old woman with a moustache checking them in eyed them suspiciously. Hopper twitched under her gaze. Why was she fucking looking at them like that? She couldn't have been a bikie? Or know that hostel owner back with the buckos? Or related to someone in Ireland that he'd done over?

'You two boys staying in the same room?' she asked.

Norman nodded.

'There's only doubles in them.'

'Okay,' he said. 'We'll take one.'

'You two poofters?'

Hopper laughed. Norman fidgeted with the pen he was holding.

'No,' Hopper said.

'He's my son,' Norman added.

She kept a hawk look on her as she checked both their faces. 'Better not be a couple of poofters. This ain't that type of establishment.'

Norman coughed.

'D'ya want our fucking money or not?' Hopper said. He snorted some air. She shouldn't be giving shit to Norman.

'Try find somewhere else to stay out here, boy,' she said.

Norman put his arm out in front of Hopper. 'Leave it,' he said and turned to the woman. 'He's my son.' He handed her his Eftpos card.

'Don't take card,' she said.

Norman sighed.

'Cash only.' She pointed to a sign.

He muttered alright alright and lifted his shirt, pulling the small leather satchel downwards. He opened it and from the wad of notes, took three fifties out to pay the wagon of an auld one.

'Have a nice stay,' she said in a bitter voice as she pocketed the cash.

*

The bed was creaky in the small room. Hopper offered to sleep on the ground but Norman said nah, he was doing well in his recuperation, he should get a good night's shut eye.

Hopper got into bed and Norman turned on the TV. They watched a couple of shows but Hopper could only zone in and out of them. His concentration was off. He wondered if he should stay on with Norman or start heading to Perth. But he was having a decent enough time since the crappy feelings stopped plaguing his head and body. Norman was paying for everything and he was a sound enough fella to talk to. He just went about his day, driving or walking around trying to find some breakfast and supplies, giving Hopper cans of cola or lemonade when he got back and then hitting out on the road again.

Sure why would he leave when he had a good thing here,

Hopper lay back into his pillow and relaxed.

Norman smiled over at him. He smiled back.

*

The days and nights passed like this, driving from noon to the next roadhouse motel, having a bit of dinner and watching TV in the room. Every day Hopper was better. His bruises were faded. He liked getting up in the morning. He sat in the car and looked out at the view and most the time, he could switch his thoughts off and just be. Follow as the world went by. The burnt, deadness of it.

He saw some emus, snakes, lizards and dingoes on the road. Saw some colourful birds. Some vicious looking birds. And about a hundred thousand kangaroos. He pointed them out excitedly to Norman.

Norman asked Hopper if he'd like to drive for a while.

Hopper cleared his throat. 'No.'

'Doesn't seem to be any police about, it won't be a problem.'

'Can't drive ya see. Don't know how.'

Norman looked surprised. 'Do you want me to teach you?'

Ger had said the same thing once and they'd tried to drive a Punto, only a shite of a car, but Hopper couldn't get the jist of it. He left it to Ger.

'Maybe some other time,' Hopper said. He'd fuck-all interest. If he was going to learn something in Australia, he'd love to be a vet or something with these mad animals here.

Hopper imagined himself having a wildlife sanctuary with crocodiles and cassowaries, Tasmanian devils and koala bears. Two green and red parrots living on his shoulder. He smirked at the idea. Bullshit really. He could just about read nevermind study to be anything.

'Thickest man in First Year 3,' Hopper said.

'What?'

'Teacher said that to me once. I wasn't though.'

'So you don't want to drive? You know, the opportunities in Australia for lorry and machine drivers are bloody insane. Big big bucks.'

Hopper nodded but there were quicker ways to make big big bucks.

They finally got to a right place, a gold mine town called Norseman. Hopper was thrilled to see normal shops and businesses. Norman took the chance to replenish his funds and stopped again at a bank machine. After they checked into the motel, Hopper went with him to the supermarket. He picked up and put down loads of products. He got a whoosh off the lemons and limes, further down, the fish and raw meats, the fresh baguettes.

'You're really coming on,' Norman said to him as he paid for his basket of groceries.

Hopper nodded. He was able to think clearly.

They went for a walk around town finding the things of interest from the visitor centre's leaflets. Hopper got his clothes washed and dried in the laundry at the motel. They had a meal out in a pizzeria in the afternoon. Hopper refused the free beer with it.

It would be another few nights before they got to Kalgoorlie, where Norman was going to set up. Perth was only 595 kilometres away from there.

The end of the road with Norman made Hopper feel twitchy again.

'D'ya reckon I could be your housemate in Kalgoorlie?' Hopper said in a small voice.

Norman smiled wide. 'Thought you'd never ask.'

*

Kalgoorlie was a big gold mining town with buildings that looked like saloons from old Western movies. There was a shitload of brothels and strip clubs. Even in the normal bars, skimpies served drink in their underwear until the tip jar was full, then they got topless for a while.

Hopper and Norman went for dinner on their first evening and Hopper had the thirst on him. Thirst for a drink and a girl. Fuck. He was in trouble here. The two went together. The desire was consuming him. It wasn't seedy like a stripper's haunt. It was lively. No security or bikies or creeps. It was men having a few jars after work and women having the craic with them.

But the noise in the bar...

The banter of the workers and the clink of glass to lip. Glass to counter. Glass to glass cheers. And the girls with racks spilling over their tops. Juicy, lickable flesh he wanted to paw and taste.

He'd need a drink first.

Change your routine. Change your routine.

'I have to go,' he said to Norman.

Hopper left.

The evening was hot and dry. He took a few deep breaths and wiped the sweat off his brow. He sat on the curb, thinking about it. Utter temptation. Utter utter temptation. And he'd resisted it. He'd never done that before.

The chances.

*

They lived in a small two-bedroom detached house in an estate on the outskirts of the town. It had cream carpets and a eucalyptus tree in the garden. The smell of it reminded Hopper of the baby's first Christmas. He didn't know what it was about but Hopper and herself, they got him small gifts. Hopper lit the Christmas candle she bought and it smelt like pine trees and eucalyptus. Norman's garden.

She had the baby in a soft Santy outfit that morning. All red with white on the collar and down the middle. Had a hat and pointy soft black slippers on him. They took loads of photos on their phones. They went to church even. And the people in the church, they were looking at them and probably thinking they were a good family.

Hopper thought they were too.

She bought him a ring that year. He got her name tattooed on the inside of his arm. The whole way from wrist to elbow. Six hours of ink. He looked down at his arm, the tattoo covered over with a Chinese dragon. He tapped his head.

At Norman's they had access to a swimming pool down the street. Hopper went swimming and sunbathing most days. Norman did his work on a computer in the house.

When Norman printed off the forms for Hopper to apply for his Australian driver's licence, Hopper put them in the bin at the pool that afternoon.

*

After a month or so of living with Norman in Kal, they went out a dirt road to the Super Pit lookout. Norman thought once Hopper learned to drive, he could get his ticket for two thousand bucks and operate the machines in the mine for a living. All they did was go up and down at crawl speed, gathering and tipping.

Hopper kept complaining that the Aussies were too slow processing his form. He also complained how nobody had replied to his ad looking for work on Gumtree or responded when he sent his CV in. He hadn't sent his CV to anyone.

'You should give me a look at it, maybe it needs editing,' Norman said and Hopper agreed with him but never did.

The Super Pit was deep and wide. It was a huge hole and Hopper stopped himself making a filthy joke because he couldn't make the punchline work in his head.

The cliffs looked golden. Dust went into his mouth.

'It's kinda mad,' Hopper said. 'Gold's just something out of the ground. Like soil. Or earthworms. Why is it so great?'

Norman said, 'Well it's rare. Money is paper. Gold is gold.'

'Water's better than gold,' Hopper said and looked at the sovereign rings on his fingers. 'Definitely.'

Norman stood staring for way too long. Hopper got anxious to leave.

On the way home from the mine, Hopper noticed a billboard. 'KEEP AUSTRALIA AUSTRALIAN.'

'Damn right,' Norman said.

'But you're English,' Hopper said.

'We're the same breed,' he replied.

'Does Australian not mean the Aborigines?'

'No.'

'But they are the Australians, aren't they? The people that came from this land. Everyone else here may as well be on Working Holiday Visas.'

'No. Australia was founded as a civilised nation by the British. The Aborigines are Aborigines. Different.'

'I think your argument's fucked, Norman. Wasn't it set up as a convict colony by the British?' Hopper said. 'Ger told me that. They sent over the Irish cons and hopped them off the boat into the sharks if they died on the way. Though the rest of them must have been laughing when they got here. Imagine being sent to prison, but your prison is a country like this?'

Norman tutted and rolled his eyes.

'You've this grudge against the Aborigines and it's bullshit. Haven't seen any of them go near you. You're the one with the live-and-let-live speeches, how come you won't give that to them too?'

Norman didn't speak to Hopper for the rest of the day.

*

Norman kept rustling bags and kept talking about his recovery. He played the worst most shitest music in the car and the flat all the time, even though Hopper downloaded Van Morrison's *Moondance* album for him to put on.

Norman only played the same music, only told the same

stories, only bought the same food and drinks and shook them about in noisy bags.

He followed Hopper everywhere. He paid for everything but kept letting Hopper know that he paid, reminding him constantly.

'Stop fucking buying me stuff so, Norman,' Hopper said. 'It's that simple.'

'You know I can't do that,' Norman said. He was rubbing his chest. 'That's why you're still here.'

'What? Yes you can, just don't. It's easy. You quit pints. Surely not spending money on me has to be easier than that.'

'Our paths crossed. For the moment, our journeys are intertwined and I don't want to jinx my future.'

Hopper refused all gifts, food and money from Norman for three days but gave in when he needed to replace his sun cream.

Norman was clingy. Too clingy. It was time to move on.

*

Hopper brought Norman to a cathouse. He had saved some of the spends Norman had given him. It was a sleek set up and they could book into different themed rooms – Oriental, Mediterranean, Tropical Paradise, Safari. Hopper reckoned they should go with the standard rooms. After all, they were there for the ladies, not the wall paintings and decorations.

'This is fucking amazing, isn't it,' Hopper said.

Norman nodded but was pale-faced.

The madam came out to speak to them and find out their

'needs' and Hopper wanted her but knew she was too good for him. He loved how her straight black hair swished when she talked. He loved the swell on her hips and arse.

She showed them a catalogue and Hopper was on a semi.

Norman was coughing and acting weird.

'Are you alright, Norman?' Hopper asked. 'Are you going your own age or young one? The mature women are unreal. What ya reckon?'

Norman coughed again but this time at the end he made a high-pitched throaty sound. He was holding his chest.

'Are you okay, Norman?' Hopper asked again. 'Norman?' He turned to the madam, 'Maybe you should call an ambulance?'

*

Norman was sent home from hospital after they observed him and ran tests on him for a few hours. They said it was a scare. Not a heart attack. They told him to relax and stay away from stressful situations. When Norman was sitting up in his double bed back in the gaff, wearing his shirt and jocks, Hopper brought him in some water and a cheese sandwich.

'The excitement got to you, eh, old boy?' Hopper said, passing him the tray.

'No.' Norman had his head low. 'The jealousy did.'

Hopper took a few minutes to think about this and then he left the room.

That night, he went back to Norman's room and stripped down to his jocks. Norman looked at him confused. He climbed into Norman's double bed and turned to him. 'You've been awful kind to me.'

'Don't worry about it,' Norman said.

'I've calmed down, the fizz is gone. I don't barely have it anymore.'

'Barely have what?'

'I owe you for the accommodation and food,' Hopper said.

Norman waved his hand across the bed. 'No. You don't. It's been a good time.'

'Yeah it has,' Hopper said. He scooted further into the bed, closer to Norman.

'What are you doing?' Norman asked.

Hopper's thighs were against Norman's. They were hot and hairy.

'What are you doing?' he repeated.

Hopper went to unbutton Norman's shirt and he pushed his hand away at first but then he let him. His breathing quickened. Hopper undid the shirt and pushed it on the ground. He lifted the leather satchel and threw it near the door. Norman was in his vest now. Hopper could feel his horn. He took it in his hand and played with it. Massaged it. Gripped it and moved it up and down, it was silky and fat. Norman lay back into his pillow and gasped. Hopper went faster until his wrist was strained and the sheets were wet.

Norman fell into a deep sleep after. His snoring was loud and steady. Hopper got up and dressed silently. His hands fumbled around on the ground until he found it. He picked up the satchel and unzipped it. Six hundred and fifty bucks.

Hopper snuck out the door and into the night.

*

He hitched a lift to the airport with a miner flying out. A new chance. This time, he could make a go of it on his own. He could see Perth on the horizon and she looked beautiful.

*

He shouldn't.

*

Her face was pierced. Her cheeks. Her eyebrows. The middle of her nose like a bull. Her lip and ears. She was in the airport café and he knew it looking at her. He tapped his head. He walked around her table twice before stopping at it, fresh coffee and pastry smells mingled.

'What are you selling?' he asked.

She looked up from a glossy magazine. Her black eye make-up sparkled. A New Zealand accent. 'Excuse me?'

'Have you got anything?'

'This is a fucking airport. Do I look like a complete idiot to you?'

Hopper checked around him and noticed all the security guards and announcements everywhere.

'Where you going?' she asked, her eyes on the magazine. She licked her finger and flicked a page. There was a big picture of the Beckhams, looking in love and happy, with a new wee baby beside them.

'Perth.'

'Me too.' She inspected him. 'I know people in Perth.'

Hopper smiled.

*

And her nipples and her clitoris were pierced too.

He'd needed to be with a woman.

Ruby brought him to her rented apartment overlooking Cottesloe Beach. They smoked a small bag of weed.

He needed to remember who he was.

She was from Christchurch and made a lot of cash working in the mines, cleaning dongas, the places where the miners kipped but she didn't want to talk about the job, wrinkling her nose when Hopper asked her. She only talked about the sweet cash she earned.

'Bloody needed that pay. Told men to rack off twenty times a day. Way they bloody looked at me. I was meat. Intimidating place for a chick. Ninety per cent male. Bloody intimidating.'

'Don't be getting thick,' Hopper said and kissed her nose. 'Just come here to me.'

He buried his head into her neck, nuzzling her soft skin, inhaling her scent, the sweet on it, the perfume, the female.

*

Hopper woke to the sound of rain outside. He hadn't heard or felt rain in ages. He got out of bed, Ruby was still under the sheet, her tattooed shoulder bared.

He went to the balcony and opened it, the rain poured heavily on the roof. The ground was splashing and Hopper put his head out into it.

Ruby came in to see where he had gone. 'You're a bloody madman.'

He washed his hair in the rain and drank it.

She kissed him and he'd felt pure joy for a moment.

But moments like that never lasted long for Hopper.

*

'I can't get into something with you,' Ruby said. 'I'm just out of something. I want to stay out for a while. Reconnect with myself.'

'Sure why would you be with me so?'

'I think you've got a good heart.'

'Do ya?' Hopper said, his eyes narrowing, the walls closing in on him. How could he? All he done. All the bad. All he fucked up. 'Really?'

'Yes, definitely.' She nodded, smiled.

His body relaxed like something huge had been taken off him.

*

Ruby got rid of him after the weekend.

Hopper sat on a park bench for the afternoon and wondered what to do but his mind came up with blanks. Perth had been his only plan. Get to Perth. He spent the last ages trying to get to Perth. Since he left Ireland he was trying to get to Perth. Now he was here, he didn't know what to do.

He was empty.

He shouldn't have gone smoking with Ruby. He'd have to stay strong and not get in touch with her, though every time he took his phone out, he wanted to text her. He walked around the park and decided to check into a backpackers, whatever one he could find first.

*

He came across two Irish lads in the hostel's smoking area. There was a breeze in the night air. They saw him passing and shouted.

'Hey, you, where you from?' The smaller one said. 'I'd know from the head on you, you're one of ours.'

'Dundalk, ye?' Hopper replied. He itched the palms of his hands and noticed the three goon boxes on their table

'I'm Murph from Mayo and me man here is Shane from Galway. Are ya gooning?' he asked. His eyes were twisted from drinking.

Hopper hesitated. 'I – I wasn't going to. No. Trying to stay off that stuff.'

'What do you mean?' Murph asked.

'You know, just, not. I don't think I should drink. Don't really...' Hopper talked but he was losing his voice. He didn't want to say he was trying to go sober. Not to these two. Being on the wagon was as humiliating as being off it.

'Will you stop, here, Shane, pour this Louth man a drink,' Murph said.

Shane emptied a beer glass, shaking out the last few drops onto the floor. He poured some white goon into it. 'There you go, sir.'

He handed Hopper the drink.

He shouldn't.

But they were watching him. They were his age. They'd keep chatting to him. He finished it quickly, which they cheered. His blood warmed. He felt good. He remembered this. They filled his glass again and he took a seat beside them on a metallic deck chair.

*

The lads told him about fucking up their interviews for the mines.

'Like, we didn't know they were going to get urine samples.' Murph was accusing in his tone. 'We'd have prepared ourselves adequately if we knew.'

Shane said, 'Yeah we wouldn't have been flute acting last weekend. Imagine running on a treadmill in our fucking borrowed suits and shoes for the fitness test?'

Hopper shook his head. He liked these lads. He wanted them to like him.

'Look at those mares,' Shane said and pointed to a table of foreign women.

'Would ya shift any of them, hey?' Murph asked. He slapped Shane in the shoulder. Winked at him. Shane sniggered.

Hopper took a big swig of his goon. 'I'd shift the lot of them. I'd do worse than that to them.'

The boys laughed.

'Rides.'

'You go talk to them so, Hopper,' Murph said.

'I would but I don't speak their speak. Anyway would ya look at them and look at me. I'd say your boy here has the best shot.'

'What about me?' Murph was mock insulted. 'This man's been breaking hearts and beds around Australia.' He slapped Shane's chest again. 'Getting us into fine messes.'

'Here, will you fuck off telling everyone my business. You don't be complaining when you get the spare friends or the free stuff they give me. Hanging tight and getting all me benefits without any drama.' Shane shrugged. 'Sure, I don't know, they come to me. They give me gifts. I don't do fuck all.'

'Why don't you talk to them?' Hopper asked Murph.

'Ara, me heart is taken.'

Hopper understood that.

'There's this unbelievable London one, talked to her earlier. *Sionnach*, so she is. Asked her if she'd any Irish in her, she said no, asked if she wanted some and the way she laughed, man, no lie. Me lad is restless thinking about her. Shane, you talk to them.'

'No,' Shane said. 'Well, I will, but let me have a few more of these first. Pints of confidence.'

'I'll fucking talk to them,' Hopper said and got out of his seat. He went over to the group. 'Any craic?'

The giggling and chatter from the girls stopped dead and they just eyed Hopper. It made him uneasy. He tapped his head.

'I'll take that as a no,' he said. He went back to the lads. 'Shower of stuck-up…'

Shane nodded.

Murph said, 'Get this testicle another drink.'

*

They got locked together, slurring stories of misadventures. When the lads mentioned the drug binges they'd gone on, a light went off in Hopper. The world changed. It gave him a break. He wouldn't have to try anymore. He had his way in.

He told them stuff he shouldn't have but he trusted them. He even offered to get them acid when they said they'd never done it before. He'd have to ring Ruby and see would she find some for him. The three of them drank until they were told to shut up by people trying to sleep in the dorm nearest the smoking area.

'Night Hopperoo, me auld flower,' Murph said and almost tripped down the stairs.

Hopper tried to creep into his room and make as little commotion possible. Them buffer lads, they were sound. They would be mates, like. He lay on his bunk looking up at the ceiling, the room dark except for his dormmates' charging phones and blinking laptop lights.

Norman had been sound but Norman didn't count. Ruby was sound too but she didn't count either. Hopper had the warm in his chest, been a long time since he'd had real friends. It had been a long time since Ger.

*

He'd a splitting hangover in the morning and so he stayed in bed until it was late afternoon. The boys came looking for him.

'D'ya want a game of pool, Hopper?' Murph asked.

He joined and they played for a few hours. The lads went to 'scab' a dinner. They said they'd try grab a meal for him too. They were meeting again for some pints that night.

'Money's a fucking nightmare to keep a hold of over here,' Murph said. 'I'm literally pissing it out of me. I'm gonna call it alcomy. I turn money to urine through a process of drinking.'

They told Hopper about a job a Donegal lad had offered them.

'It's up the back arse of nowhere. John Anthony or whatever he's called is a fucking potato head. Total prick but we can ditch him there. Easy enough if we're working all the time. Won't have to talk to him.'

'He'd probably feel like punching a bag of potatoes too, tough cunt,' Shane said. 'D'ya wanna come, Hopper?'

Murph said, 'Huh?'

'Where?' Hopper asked.

'On the job? Yer man is looking for Irish fellas to go and work on a mango farm for the harvest. They want us 'cause we work hard,' Shane laughed, 'or at least we have the reputation of hard workers. Sounds like a doss too. Easy. Hopefully some easy women. Chance to save some money. Perth has me paupered.'

'Chance?'

'Yeah, sure come on with us. What would you be doing here?'

'Shane. No,' Murph said.

'Sure why not, like?' Shane said.

Murph raised his shoulders. 'Just.'

'It'll be grand,' Shane said and turned back to Hopper. 'Do ya wanna come?'

Hopper nodded his head.

He was in on the job and he was in with the lads. All above board, clean work. His life was falling together. At last. That faith Norman used to go on about. Have faith things will work out the way they're supposed to. Put your life in the faith. This was faith. Things were really looking up. It was time for him to get a real job like every other bastard going.

*

John Anthony was a fat-headed thug. Murph called him a latchego.

Hopper had no interest in him and he'd no interest in Hopper. They knew the likes of each other already. Hopper, growing up near the border, had come across Republican muscle bastards before. Power tripping. Tricking lads off the estate into dirty work for cheap gear.

John Anthony didn't shake Hopper's hand when they were introduced. Hopper heard him mutter 'spide.' The fizz stirred. But Perth wasn't for trouble, that wasn't why he was here. He ducked out of his way.

*

He was lying in his bunk when Ruby contacted him for a 'business meeting.'

She was waiting at a chip shop near Cottesloe. Hopper ordered fried hake, chips with vinegar and ate using a fork so she wouldn't think he was rough. He smiled at her.

'So, you said you might be interested in getting to know some people around Perth?'

Hopper shrugged.

'Well, I had an idea. As you're already aware, I've some connections but I'd really like to get some other ones. Bloody over working in the mines. Prison camp. Easier lives to live, bro, easier methods to make good money. Wouldn't mind a way into the backpackers, is it big?'

'Grand size. Probably sleeps 200. Why?'

'Sweet as. I need to get a rep in the hostels. To direct the travellers to me. A go-between. Understand, bro? Someone I could trust. I'd give you a nice cut.'

Hopper laughed. Of course he fucking understood. But he'd agreed to head on to the countryside. 'Look, I'm no good to you. I don't know too many here yet. The ones I do know, I'm leaving with in the morning. Me and my friends are going to some mad mango village. I'm staying out of trouble from now on. But it's a decent business plan. Good luck with it, Ruby.'

She sighed and broke eye contact but he didn't care. He was going straight. He was going to be a farmer.

'Want to get baked so, Irish, since it's a going away party? Hit some clubs?' she asked.

Sure why the fuck not.

*

Hopper hadn't slept. He went straight from the chipper to Ruby's to a few bars and nightclubs to the beach to smoke more weed.

He said his goodbyes to her, tried to kiss her again but she resisted. She gave him the acid in tinfoil.

'Gratis,' she giggled. 'For free, my friend.'

He walked slowly to the backpackers, filled his small bag and went to the car park. The early morning sun hurt his eyes.

John Anthony was bulling. Hopper pretended not to notice, he put his bag in the boot.

'How's things?' Murph asked, his eyes were bloodshot and a fine whiff of drink off him.

'Devil a bother.'

Murph grinned.

'Travel light?' Shane asked.

'Don't need much more than my jocks and a couple of t-shirts,' Hopper said and scratched his head.

The lads filled the car, John Anthony made the air go different around him when he got in. Hopper touched the tinfoil in his pocket. He didn't know when he'd take it or if he'd just fuck it out the window. He shouldn't be touching psychedelics. He wasn't right for them yet. He'd never really been right for them.

*

The car journey upset him.

He slept for the day part of it, except when they stopped – to take pictures, for food and after making shit of a kangaroo. During the night part, he was flooded with thoughts of Norman. It reminded him of Norman being in the car. He'd been bad to him. All Norman'd done was get him out of a spot and all Hopper'd done was fuck him over.

The boys had argued but John Anthony made everyone shut up with his aggression. Hopper just stayed quiet. Guilty quiet. He'd smoked way too much last night with Ruby. He'd to stop fucking smoking. It made him too paranoid.

He shouldn't have touched Norman.

Was he gay?

He wasn't gay. Sure Norman wasn't either. He had kids and wives and hung out in strip clubs.

Neither of them were.

It just seemed like a fair way to say bye. Maybe take the sting out of robbing him.

Then there was Ruby. She wanted him but she didn't. Being with her only reminded him who he wasn't with. It was like someone scraped out his heart when he thought of his old girlfriend, her getting it from another man.

He hit himself in the head but he couldn't shake the bad feelings of them. Them over here. Them back in Ireland. Jesus what was he at?

All the times Hopper thought the wee fella had features

like him, the same nose or the same hair. He loved when people agreed.

He massaged his shoulders. His temple. They were going to be in this fucking car forever and he was going to get stuck with these fucking thoughts. He wiped the back of his neck.

Her and the baby.

She moved back in with her mother. He wasn't allowed see the wee fella after that. Because he'd been cruel with the stuff he said to her and about her around the town. But she had been cruel too.

Would the wee fella even remember him?

'Fuck this,' Hopper said. He was done with this thinking. He'd been in the car for too long. The dark was all over him. He shouldn't.

'I have that acid ye know,' he said and checked his pockets.

'What?' Murph turned around from the front, amazed.

'Will we take it? There's another six hours in the car, like.'

John Anthony said, 'How long does that shit last?'

Hopper lit his phone and unwrapped the tinfoil. Shane smiled at him and put his hand out for some like he was receiving the holy communion.

Hopper rubbed his nose with his sleeve. 'I don't have any liquid, just tabs. Should be mild enough. Three hours maybe. Five max.'

Complete horseshit. It'd probably go for at least ten hours. He'd not been off his head properly in months. He was buzzing with the idea of it.

Shane smashed his straight away. 'Been driving all fucking day. I deserve this.'

Murph took a tab.

John Anthony said, 'Do what ye want but be fit for when we get to that farm or I'll fucking kill yis.'

Hopper smirked. Dead on.

*

After an hour, or two hours, or maybe less, time felt slimy until the dragon in Hopper's tattoo started to move. It peeled itself off his arm and floated in front of him. It had a green snake-like body, coiled and scaled. Little sparks and flames flared from its nostrils as it breathed. Hopper opened his eyes and smiled at it.

*

The dragon spoke Chinese. Two whiskers coming out of its mouth swirled in the air. Hopper knew it was his guardian.

Nobody else in the car could see it, he checked. Murph was staring out the window at the sky. John Anthony was looking at the road. Shane was leaning back into his headrest.

But then Hopper looked at the dragon and down at his arm.

MARIE

His first tattoo. Uncovered. He gulped. He had been hiding from her name. His old girlfriend.

Hopper scratched his head. His neck. His ears. He tried to shake the dread in his heart. He didn't look at his arm again, he kept it stretched away from his body. The dragon hovered still and Hopper noticed something burning under its chin. A pearl.

John Anthony turned around. He was talking but his words were all jumbled.

'Wolf – Shotgun – Dundalk.'

The dragon hissed at him.

Hopper started to get worse. He was seeing colours, dangerous colours. Ones that couldn't be there in the dark, ones that made the panic noise in his chest.

Shane said, 'This LSD is a bad batch I reckon,' and it echoed until Hopper caught the words, the meaning of them.

Did he think Hopper was trying to poison him or something? Or maybe Ruby was trying to poison Hopper? Would she?

He was scared. He was really fucking scared.

'Straight for you, Hopper,' John Anthony said. 'Pyschopath – petrol – wee weird Aussie - knife?'

The dragon hissed louder.

They were all laughing. Even Murph and Shane. His friends. Everyone. Always laughing at Hopper.

Why did everyone always laugh at him?

The dragon opened his mouth and a great flame lit a scene in front of Hopper. The more they drove through that desert, the closer they were going to hell. Only badness was waiting for them at the farm. Nothing would be the same again. Hopper could see that clearer than anything, through the orange flames. It was as clear as being hungry or as being sad. So much trouble ahead.

The dragon showed Hopper visions of a neck – his neck – in front of a big hole. A place like the Super Pit. Norman was there. A knife slit across the skin. Norman's cloudy white spunk oozed out of Hopper instead of blood. A baby cried.

MARIE

The others were laughing. Still. Hopper couldn't breathe. His arm. Still showing her name.

The car had walls. Hopper felt around. The dragon flared some light and Hopper found the handle.

He opened the car door.

He got free.

*

He came to in a tree but didn't know how he got up there or how he didn't fall out when he was asleep, if he did sleep. His hands and arms were scrapes and insect bites. He was clinging to a branch, body across it and legs dangling but he couldn't shake the fear off, even hours later. The dragon was back on his arm.

Hopper stayed on his branch. Birds flapped and landed above him. The air twisted into itself and looked like itself but different, like chipper oil on water.

His skin felt like it was melting.

He had to find the others and tell them the vision he had – continuing on that straight road in the red dirt wasn't the way.

But he couldn't find them.

*

Did they go? Did they go to the mad mango village without him? Would they?

No one would do that on anyone, sure Hopper got them the acid, they'd invited him, they knew he wouldn't know where he was now. He'd just freaked out, he was sound. Some bad tripping but the way out of that is through.

Were they around somewhere? Looking for him? Getting some help? He was doing a job with them. They brought him with them.

Were they gone? Hopper looked around the bush. Trees and birds and the road off further. A track road. Not the main road.

Where the fuck was he? Where the fuck were the lads? Murph and Shane. His friends.

They were his friends.

He called out for them. He called until his throat went too dry and just made cracks when he shouted.

He looked around, the sun was beating down on him. They were definitely gone.

He was left with nothing but himself.

Like always.

*

Hopper followed the track. He was thirsty. So fucking thirsty. He got fizzed about the lads and punched some tree trunks. Split his knuckles. Punched his head. But the thirst took over and that was all he could think about.

He kept trundling through the desert. Parched. Water. Fuck. Water. Collapse. Fade coming. Water. Gold was bollocks. You couldn't die without gold. Water though. Need water.

He spotted an old Aborigine. He rubbed his eyes to make sure.

The chances.

Hopper asked him for a wee drop of water. The sunshine had dried his insides. Needed a drop of sunblock too. The colour red off him. Burnt alive in the heat.

*

Hopper couldn't understand why Norman and some Australians were such bastards to the Aborigines. Yer man was as nice as anything when Hopper approached him. He didn't speak much English but Hopper didn't speak the best of it himself at times, especially after hallucinogens. They put holes in his talking. Holes in his thinking.

The Aborigine made his hands say, come on, follow me. Hopper followed him and they went down to this big open bit of desert with a few burnt-out cars. There were loads of kids and women with not much clothes between the lot of them. Some of the kids were chatting and jumping around Hopper when they saw him, asking questions in a different language. All Hopper asked was for water.

'Water, lads. Water. Any chance?'

He stuck his tongue out to show them. It was coated white. All the juice was sweated out of him and into the desert sky.

A woman came back with a jug for Hopper to drink from and the jug was lovely with its bright yellow, red, orange dots and shapes. It was what snooty ones go on about, go walking around big halls looking at, pointing at, going 'Oooh, yooaaah,' at. The jug was art. Hopper was proud to be drinking out of art.

The water was better than anything he'd ever tasted before. He drank it greedily and thanked the Aborigine and his family for being so sound.

He said, 'Come on The Town,' and punched the air, just for the laugh because they wouldn't know it. But they still smiled, their teeth moon white on their dark faces.

They had an old telly which was showing a news report that all these lads who lived in Libya and Egypt and that part of the world had the fizz. But it was too hot to watch TV, so Hopper walked around the place having a look in the tin-roofed houses, trying not to be a spare prick.

*

In the late afternoon, the Aborigine man got a hollow piece of wood with holes in it and put it on top of some brown grass he'd piled up. His wife put her hands over both sides of the wood. The man got a stick and stuck the bottom of it through the holes. He worked it round and back the other way, up and down. Hopper's eyes got bigger and bigger. He had it.

Smoke.

The Aborigine kept going. Up and down, backwards and forwards. More smoke. The brown grass, she took it. She took the spark and lit.

'Fucking nice one,' Hopper said and the Aborigine nodded. Hopper took out his lighter from his jean's pocket. Put his thumb on the wheel and lit that up. Held down the red tab to keep the flame going.

'This is the way I do fires, boss,' Hopper said, the metal going hot near his thumb.

The Aborigine nodded again and took a lighter out of his shorts pockets and sparked that. He held his flame up too. Hopper gave a big laugh.

*

At the night time, he stayed with them sitting in front of the campfire. He didn't talk much. None of them did. They just watched the fire's show, it going high and wide and low and dipping and flaring and shimmying across the air.

The Aborigine went, 'Wimberoo?' and the kids screamed and jumped excited. He passed on leaves to his wife and she took one and passed them on. All the kids took one and they gave Hopper the eyes to say, 'You as well.'

He took one and passed the pile on to the little one that was beside him. The Aborigine picked three of the kids and they stood over the fire warming their leaves until they started to bend. Then they put them into the hot waves of the fire and the leaves flew into the air. They cheered for each other. The kid beside Hopper didn't win but she was clapping anyway.

New go.

The Aborigine picked Hopper, a different kid and a teenager. They stood and did the same thing.

His leaf shot up, 'G'wan,' he roared at it and the kids laughed.

The teenager won. Hopper didn't know what he was supposed to do, so he just gave him a small clap.

After a while of playing and chilling, the kids got sleepy. Hopper was sleepy himself. The woman brought them away leaving him and the Aborigine in front of the fire. Hopper shook his hands because he was sound but as well as that, he was a good dad to them wee ones. Hopper wished he was his dad when he was small. He had a pang thinking that he was once a dad himself.

The Aborigine squashed a jumper inside another jumper and pucked it into a rectangle shape. He passed it to Hopper and put his hands together like he was praying against his ear.

'Pillow?' Hopper asked and he nodded. 'Thanks, boss.'

The Aborigine walked away to his wife and kids. Hopper took a deep breath, concentrated on the fire and went asleep to the crackle and pop of wood and grass burning.

*

The Aborigines gave him some fruit and the whole family hugged him the next day when he said he'd be on his way. The mother was playing country and western on an old time hi-fi, a big box of a radio Hopper hadn't seen since him and Ger robbed one from the electric shop in the town when he was twelve.

They gave him a bottle filled with water for the walk.

'Ye're awful sound,' he said.

When Hopper was off, he got back to the main road and found the teenager hiding from the sun behind a tree. He was sitting on hard dark coloured grass, doing a bit of glue. Hopper watched him inhale. He sat beside him and was offered a huff.

'I dunno. I really shouldn't,' Hopper said.

The teenager offered it again and Hopper hesitated, sighed, took it. They lay against the tree and the world went almost perfect for a few seconds.

'Sometimes wonder,' the teenager said.

Hopper turned his head to face him. He was the first to speak English. It sounded strange coming out of his mouth.

'Sometimes wonder, is this what my country felt like before the Invasion,' he said and took another huff.

Hopper shrugged. His face was numb.

The teenager offered him another, his eyes and mouth all fuzzy. Hopper stood when it wore off. When he said he'd to move on, the teenager offered him the lot of it, plastic bag and the big tube full of industrial strength.

'For you, brother.'

Hopper didn't want to be rude and he didn't want to stop now so he accepted. He took the biggest drink of water and it was like kettle water with the heat of it so he left the bottle on the ground.

Unsure of what day it was or which direction he had come from, he followed where the sun was starting to go down. That must have meant south, or did it mean south when everything was upside down here, he wasn't sure but he kept going. He didn't give a fuck anyway 'cause the auld glue would keep him lit for a while.

*

Hopper was soothing the goosebumps off his arms and wincing 'cause he'd rubbed at his sunburn too hard. Boiling and freezing all in the one go. He was on the straight road to Perth. It was the middle of the night maybe. Gone mad cold.

And there they were, two big strong kangaroos. He could see them because of the moon.

They were standing ahead. Not bouncing. Still, but looking away. They smelt like horses and their muscles reminded Hopper of horses too but horses sitting down and ready to spring. Not the horses to make glue from. But their faces looked a small bit like the hares they'd have the greyhounds chasing.

The nature of the world was funny like that.

A spider sometimes looked like a crab. A lizard looked like a tree and a hippo like a whale. Sometimes, people looked like dogs with big eyes and tongues panting when they were hungover dying for water. Or pigs with snouts hoovering everyone else's drugs without paying. Or sharks, with mad teeth to rip you apart, like the State, pretending to help ya out but shredding the shite out of you and your family when you think you're safe.

Hopper said to the kangaroos, 'Hey. Hey,' real quick until they turned around, their top paws a-tingling.

They looked mad curious, clicked at each other.

The big kangaroo goes, 'What's the problem, sir?' with a soft voice on him like David Beckham.

Hopper's eyes opened wide. He laughed. 'Are ye fucking Tan kangaroos?'

The big kangaroo turned to his wife kangaroo and said, 'I can't understand a word out of that fellow.'

'Ah, here,' Hopper whispered. 'I'm not that fucking bad. Only sometimes.'

The wife said, 'Come along, now,' like Victoria Beckham. Posh. She clicked her lips and the two of them started down the road.

Hoppin'.

They went on like that for a few minutes, Hopper scratching his head, blinking and deciding if he'd go with it.

Sure he'd go with it.

Why wouldn't he?

He asked the kangaroos, 'How is it ye are the Beckhams?'

They both halted suddenly, looked at each other and the wife clicked. 'Well, we figured we wouldn't scare you if we spoke like this.'

'I'm not afraid of the Queen or any of her crew but I hope ye don't think I'm English too?'

'Not at all, sir. We was just assuming the identity you put on us,' the bigger kangaroo said.

'I don't know what that means.'

'It means,' the wife said, 'that you picked it. But don't be afraid, just come with us.'

'So ye're saying that I've put those voices on ye? Why?'

'I don't know, you tell us?'

Hopper didn't like football or clothes. Why would he pick them? Something scratched at his memory. The airport. Ruby's magazine.

'Now concentrate,' the big kangaroo said. 'Why are we here?'

Hopper started groaning. 'This is more of it, isn't it?'

'Concentrate.'

Hopper's throat went dry. 'They fucking left me. I thought we were mates but they went. Don't want to cry. Don't. I been through worse but I was stupid. Stupid.' He whacked his head with his fist.

'Concentrate,' the kangaroo's wife said.

'Why are ye doing this to me?' Hopper asked. 'I don't want to think about them. The fizz will come.'

The moon was so big he could see the dents and potholes in it.

'Concentrate.'

'I only want to have a good time here in Australia,' he said. 'That's the only thing I wanted.'

'Thoughts that you have are generated by you,' the wife said. 'It's not the event but how you interpret the event that's important.'

'How do you mean?'

'The way you think about what happened.'

His brain pulsed.

'You decide,' she said.

'I decide?'

'Yes.'

Hopper saw some movement in her. Inside her. A small kangaroo poked her head out of the belly. She sprung onto the road. A tiny version of them. She nodded at Hopper. She was mad cute. Her mother clicked and purred against her head. The baby Beckham hopped beside them.

Hopper stopped walking and started swallowing real quick. He didn't want to go with them anymore. He didn't belong with them.

Once, or more times, he wanted to pretend just once, he had a look on Marie's Facebook page, just for pictures of the wee fella. Just so he could know he was okay. It was awful hard to turn love off. It wasn't like a tap. In that way it was the same as the fizz. Hopper couldn't get much of a power over it but the fizz did go. It came on strong and then died. That was the difference. He was still coming up on love. Only thing he knew for truth, it was the worst drug out there. The most dangerous shit going.

The baby kangaroo jumped back in its mother's stomach-pouch. Hopper's face was wet from crying and he dried it with his hands.

The wife kangaroo said, 'Have you noticed what we do?'

He threw away the bag and the tube. The moon was finishing and the daylight would come soon. He scratched his head. This time he couldn't get rid of the headache when the fumes wore off. 'Hop,' he said and hoped they wouldn't laugh.

'Yes, but to where?'

'I don't know where. Do ye migrate or one of those things?'

'Concentrate. Where do we hop?'

'Ye hop there,' he said and pointed down the road. 'Ye hop in front of ye. Forward.'

'Forward. What does that mean?'

'Come on, I don't know,' he said. His head was beginning to beat. 'It means ye don't go backwards?'

They clicked and tutted and purred to each other. They smiled at Hopper.

'Oh,' he said and stopped, putting his hand over his chest. He knew what that meant.

The big one said, 'It's time for us to go now, Hopper.'

'Goodbye, my friend,' the wife said.

Hopper laughed and said, 'Goodbye,' and when the

words came out, they echoed. They were proper words that made noise on the outside. It was only when he could compare them to the way they were talking that he realised none of them had said a thing out loud the whole time until then.

*

The kangaroos left and it was day again. Or afternoon. Hopper might have passed out somewhere on the road.

It took him ages to take a piss and when he did, it was coming out nearly brown. It hurt so much behind his eyes he screamed to relieve the pain.

He tried to take cover from the sun but there wasn't anywhere to go. His head started rolling and swelling and he thought it was going to balloon off his body into the sky.

The last thing he remembered was the puke coming before the fade.

*

The kangaroos came back. 'Hopper, get up. Get up. Follow us. Don't let go.'

But all he could do was groan and his face was wet with sick. It was puddled around the ground beside him.

'Hopper, come on. You don't have much time left.'

'Am I dying?'

They clicked at each other and turned to him. 'Yes.'

He struggled to sit. His head was making a drumming sound on the inside and he could feel the side of his face twitching. His hands were all shaking and he couldn't see properly. Everything was blurry like his eyes were open in the river. He couldn't get up.

'Hopper, come on,' they said.

'I can't.' More sick was rising from his stomach. His legs wouldn't work.

*

This was the end. He could feel it.

Sun was life.

Sun was fire.

Sun was death.

*

The blue sky was moving. Hopper's head was bouncing. He was being lifted, arms over two men's shoulders. They had his back.

An engine was running.

'Get his legs. His legs. Watch him. Open the door of the truck.'

It was cool inside. Cool breeze. Water at his lips.

'You're gonna be alright, mate.'

An Australian voice.

*

They brought him to a shack place that looked like a halting site but was full of Australian lads. They had big teeth in their mouths and big black guns resting by their feet but Hopper wasn't afraid.

They filled him with water. They left him in a bed in one of the caravans. He was asleep a lot. He only knew that when he was awake. They kept water beside the bed. They checked on him.

*

He woke again and felt a lot better. He yawned and touched his head and shoulders and chest, his legs. He played with himself for a minute or two but decided to stop. Bad courtesy to be wanking in someone else's bed. He looked around the caravan. The lads were outside. Hopper took a breath and went out.

Four of them were sitting around watching the big red sun go down. They looked like brothers with their blondy mullets and teeth. The radio played guitar music.

Hopper didn't tell them about the kangaroos. 'I don't know who found me. But I – you know – I—'

'No worries,' one of them said. He had a beard.

'Thanks, like,' Hopper said and looked at the ground.

They offered him a green deck chair.

Hopper asked, 'Which way is it to Perth?'

One proper funny looking brother, his eyes very near together in his head and a big long jaw that didn't look stuck onto his face said, 'I'm driving to the city in the morning, mate. You can keep me company if you want?'

Hopper blessed himself. 'Grand.'

He was shown the inside of the trailer properly to see

where things were by a brother with a cracked front tooth. The heat was different to outside. It had nowhere to go in here. Dead heat. Hopper wiped his eyebrows and the tip of his nose. He was shown the bathroom, how to get the shower working and the 'dunny.'

'S'alright?' the cracked tooth asked.

'It's fucking beautiful,' Hopper replied.

The cracked tooth fried a big chunk of meat and the smoke fogged around the trailer. When he added an onion in and turned the meat over, it all noising and cooking and making that smell in the air, Hopper said, 'That your dinner?' and was mad jealous.

'No, mate,' the cracked tooth said and elbowed him in the arm. 'It's your dinner.'

He cooked the meat, got two big slices of white bread, lettuce and put them on a plate. All laid out nice like in a chipper. He gave it to Hopper.

'Eat outside, mate,' he said. 'Too hot here.'

Hopper followed him out and went back to his deck chair. He nearly spilt drool onto the dinner he was that excited. He ate the lot of it quick and put the plate under his legs when he was done, rubbed his belly and grinned.

The beard one handed him a tin, drops of water coming off it from the cooler. 'You're a fortunate bloke.'

The beer was sweet.

He nodded at them. 'I know I am.'

'How long you out walking, mate?'

'No clue.'

When Hopper was with the black ones it was maybe a few days or even more than a week ago or it might have been

307

the day before. Who even gave a shite about time keeping? It wouldn't change the type of time you had.

The gas blasted onto his tongue, into his belly and he burped good and loud. That set a few of the others off belching.

'No swag?' A different one with nothing wrong with his face asked. 'No mob? No Sheila?'

Hopper shrugged.

The cracked tooth raised his can. 'No worries.'

He toasted that.

*

Hopper had a few more cans with them and once they got used to him, he told them about Ireland, about the twenty-six counties they definitely had at home and how mad it was that if you took all of Ireland, the north and south, it'd fit at least ninety times over into Australia. That's how big Australia was. That's how small Ireland was.

'We should go to Ireland some day when they forget about me on the books back there,' he said, inviting the lads to visit. That was only common manners but he didn't really have a place to bring them to.

He had nowhere anywhere.

His chest seized with the sting of it.

The brother with the beard picked up his gun and shot at a big crow that had landed on the fence. The noise almost broke Hopper's ears. He screamed and jumped out of his seat.

The others laughed.

Reminded him.

Maybe these Australians were going to reject him too? Like everyone. Pretend to be his friend, abandon him when he trusted them.

'Why don't ye do it so?' Hopper said.

'What?'

'Ye're fucking planning. Trying to trick me, aren't ye?'

'You need to calm down, mate,' the one with the jaw said.

'Ye going to fool me, yeah? Let me think I'm safe is it?'

'What?'

'Going to trick me into something. Make a joke of me after?'

Hopper raised his fist. Fizz was speeding through his blood.

'I said, calm down, mate. Don't be a fucking cunt.'

The others loomed around him on their seats. Hopper checked their faces. They'd do it to him. They would. That's what all this show was for. Make him think they were friends then piss off on him and laugh their heads off about it forever.

'Sit the fuck down, mate,' the beard said. His voice was deeper.

Hopper sat down for a moment before jumping up and going for him. 'Fuck ye,' he said as he decked him into the head. It cut his knuckles he hit him so hard.

The others jumped out of their seats.

'Come on,' Hopper said, motioned them on, deafening with fizz.

He tried to fight the lot of them. He shouted the worst abuse he could think of. He insulted their mothers, their heads, their caravans.

He wrestled and scratched. The noise was far off. Shouts. Skids. Feet and boots and sandals against his skin. Flesh banging.

'Come on,' Hopper said.

He wanted them to beat the fizz out of him. He was pure weak but he wanted it.

He got a good tidy puck into the nose and it toppled him backwards onto the ground. He lay down. The blood trickled back his throat. Metal taste. He closed his eyes.

The kangaroos – they hopped forward.

They moved on.

The fizz faded thinking about that.

The Australians stopped fighting him. He stopped asking them to.

'You alright, mate?' the lad with the cracked tooth asked eventually. He'd his hand out to pick Hopper up. He hauled him onto his feet.

'No,' Hopper said and walked away from them, bleeding. 'No, I'm not.'

*

Hopper stumbled down the road. His eyes were hot with the threat of tears. He walked on, not having a fucking clue where he was going, half-drunk, bloodied, busted up, alone. His chest was trying to shatter on him. His lower back had a dull throb that made him feel sick when he remembered it.

His skin was blistering. His lungs were dry. He was lost.

He heard an engine get louder in the distance. Some honks.

He turned around. The mosquitos were bastards as dusk set in. The truck was behind him. It slowed.

'Mate, she'll be right,' the one with the jaw that was driving to Perth in the morning said out the window.

'What?'

'You don't know where you're going, bro. Get in.'

Hopper looked at him. The jaw's face was blank.

'You sure?' Hopper asked.

'Sure as shit.'

Hopper smiled and went to the passenger side. He climbed in slowly. His body was in bad shape.

'I'm sorry,' he said as the jaw did a U-turn.

'It's over now. The past is gone.'

'It was the noise. After what I'd just been thinking about, being nowhere, when the noise happened – I don't know how to explain it. Except, d'ya know when you'd lose the run of yourself with anger?'

The jaw looked at him. 'Rage blackout?'

'Yeah. Maybe one of them. I call it the fizz.'

The jaw nodded. He knew. 'Mate, you're fucking hard for a small fella.'

Hopper nodded. 'Have to be.'

'You want a stubby? Grab one from the esky,' the jaw said and pointed at the cooler on the seat between them.

Hopper opened the lid. Some bottles of beer were bobbing around in the watery ice. He plunged his hand in, grabbed one.

But he let it go.

He took his empty hand out, wiped it on his jersey and drew in a long breath.

*

Kangaroos hop forward.
Kangaroos hop forward.
Hopper hops forward.

*

In Perth, Hopper worked for his accommodation. Easy. Hoovered the floor and stripped some bunks in the morning. Sprayed the showers with blue stuff. Emptied the dishwasher. Wiped counters. Got free breakfast and internet too. The weeks flew by with this new routine.

He got talking to a load of new people. Ones from Scotland, United States, Bolivia, Finland, Israel, Ghana, Turkey, Vietnam, Taiwan, Austria, Mexico, Indonesia, Algeria, Tonga, Brazil, Canada, Uganda, Japan, France, Guatemala, Slovakia, South Africa, Greece, China, Poland, Italy, India.

He fucking knew loads of people now. He had loads of friends. He was learning so much off them and he was getting them whatever they were looking for. He wasn't a fucking saint, like.

He got in touch with Ruby after a week of being back. He explained jobs and the countryside hadn't worked out for him. Doing deliveries was what he was good at. Skilled at.

He wasn't trying product anymore though.

He kept his relationship professional with Ruby. They shook on that. He did want to ride her again but he'd wait until she was on for it. There were loads of other sexy women in the hostel anyway. There were loads of them that were sound too.

Ruby was dead on to work for. She paid Hopper fairly, gave him freebies which he sold and she praised him for his work. He was a valued employee. And she'd never beat him up or get someone to beat him up if she had a problem. She called him over to her apartment to discuss it.

When he passed things on to the travellers, he gave them a warning. 'Too much of this stuff and you'll be the same in the head as me.'

They'd laugh. He'd laugh. But he totally fucking meant it.

*

He was in the kitchen when he saw a girl. Irish. Definitely. Her eyes were bluer than the Castletown River on a fine day. He didn't talk. Just watched her. She concentrated on cooking her bolognese. The flame massaged the frying pan.

One of Hopper's dorm mates, a cowboy from Alabama, said hello. 'We're going to have a few beers, will you join us?'

'I'll get a cup of tea and hang out.'

'What are you staring at?' the Alabaman asked.

'The fire,' Hopper said, pointing at the pan, getting entranced again by it.

'Hey? Hey man?' the Alabaman said.

Hopper got a jump and was back in the steamy kitchen. 'You joining us?'

'Yeah,' Hopper said and tapped his skull a few times.

He followed the Alabaman to the common room and

forgot about the girl until she was frozen on the stairs, holding two empty plates, gawping at him. He gave her a small wave. She gave him a slight nod of the head and went downstairs before rushing back empty-handed a few minutes later.

The Alabaman tried for a second time to convince Hopper to be a jackaroo on a cattle station in the Wheatbelt.

Hopper took a sup of his tea. 'I can't, I said this to you already. The countryside and me, well we're not meant for each other.'

'I don't know why you won't just come along. It sure will be an adventure.'

Hopper gave a chuckle.

'Why you hooting? Why not join me?'

'I got some things going here,' Hopper said and it was no lie. Ruby's next ambition was to get introductions to the new Irish, especially to the boys off their swings from the mines. Them loolahs were mad for buzzing and they had all the cash in the world for spending.

Besides, he liked Perth. It was tiny and isolated but at the same time, it had it everything even if it shut down early as fuck.

He got a shiver through his whole body.

'You okay, Hopper?' the Alabaman asked.

'It's like someone's just crossed over me grave,' Hopper said and shuddered again. He felt like he had to turn around.

Murph.

Murph was racing down the stairs, his bag on his back. The girl chased after him. Them. Hopper had a big sensation across his chest that it was something to do with him. Why they were running away. The fizz stirred at seeing Murph. Hopper inhaled and exhaled deep until it passed.

*

He went outside for a ciggy and a coffee later. Black swans flew overhead in a v-formation. They were long necked with slow beating wings. Hopper smiled as they trumpeted to each other in the air. He tried to take a photo of them on his phone but he wasn't quick enough. Black swans. Who'd have believed him?

He sucked on the cigarette and blew the smoke out the side of his mouth. A car pulled in. Hopper watched as the girl from earlier got out. Murph was in the driver's seat. She gathered her stuff.

She walked towards the entrance gate of the hostel. A solemn look on her face.

Abandoned.

He knew that rejection. The fizz came back stronger than earlier. It itched in Hopper's fingers.

It reminded him of how they fucked off on him.

Murph was grinding the car into gear, accelerating.

Fuck him.

Hopper dropped his cup. His cigarette. He ran, hurdling over the hostel's wall, hopping the path to the road. He shouted at Murph and ran without thinking in front of the moving car.

The impact of it lifted him with a thud onto the bonnet. The braking dropped him. He was sprawled on the road. The headlights dazzled. The fizz was spreading through him.

He'd forgotten how alive it made him feel.

Murph jumped out of the car. 'What the hell, Hopper, you ran straight in front of me?'

Hopper pushed himself up off the ground. 'So it is you?' he said and wiped his hands. He wriggled his fingers. 'You know me? Who I am?'

'What are you playing at? I could have killed you. Christ.' Murph was looking up at the sky.

'Why'd ye go?'

'What?'

'Why'd ye go? Ye went. Did ye go without me?'

'Hopper,' Murph said and sighed. 'I don't want to get into this.'

'Did ye even look for me?'

'Yeah – we did, it was too dark.'

'So ye just left?'

Murph gulped.

'Ye did. For sure. I didn't know. Did ye tell anyone I was out there?'

'Hopper, Jesus, it was a bad thing.'

'Ye didn't tell anyone. Is that 'cause ye didn't reckon my life equal to yers?'

'What? No, it was all fucked. We didn't know what to do.'

Hopper said, 'When I got back I asked people. I asked them what it meant, when I finally got back and I was half-fucking demented, with second-degree sunburn and kidney failure, I wanted to know why.'

Hopper could see the girl in the shadows, watching like the dread.

'Where the others?' Hopper asked.

'Shane's in Sydney, or on his way. John Anthony's...'
Murph shook his head. Crossed his arm over his chest to
the other shoulder. 'Are you okay?'

'Well, I got here in the end. I thought we were mates,'
Hopper said and the fizz tried to come again. 'You made
me think we were.'

The girl stood closer. Coughed.

'Where you going?' Hopper asked.

'Away. I got to go away,' Murph replied.

'Do ya?' the girl spoke. She stood next to Hopper.

'Look, what do ye want from me? All three of us to go
off together, a big happy family in Margaret River?' he said,
switching his glance between them. 'A slut and a junkie
helping my fucking case. What sort of set up are ye after?
Are ye both so thick?'

'I'm not a slut,' she said.

'I'm not a junkie,' Hopper said.

'Why'd you have to be like this, Murph?' She shook her
head.

'You left me to die,' Hopper said.

'He leaves everyone,' she said.

'Hopper, you didn't see what it was like, and up in the
farm, I thought you were there. I knew you'd be fine. You're
a scavenger. The rat head on you. And now it's fucked, Jesus,
and my money. All my fucking money is up there.'

'That's what you're worried about?' The girl spoke slow.

'Yeah, of course, there's thousands,' he said. He stopped,
'No, it's not all I'm worried about, come on.'

'Swear on your mother's life,' Hopper said.

Murph sighed. 'Just let me go, will ye. Everything's ruined.

317

And it was you who started it, Hopper.'

'I done nothing.'

'You gave us that shit acid then you lost the plot.'

'Ye asked me, persuaded me to go,' Hopper said, 'and then ye fucked off.'

Murph sighed. 'You don't know what fucking happened. Who wanted you around anyway? It was Shane who asked you and you ruined everything.'

'Murph, stop,' the girl said, putting her palm out.

'Get off your high horse, Fiona, he's a degenerate.'

Hopper clenched his fingers. The fizz swelled.

'You don't know him,' Murph said.

'You don't either,' she said. 'Who are you to be throwing stones?'

'He's dirt,' Murph said to her.

But Hopper'd never been cleaner. He didn't want to choose the fizz tonight. He'd go down for it. He wasn't afraid of prison or deportation or nothing like that, he was afraid of going back. To the way he was.

'Dirt,' Murph repeated looking Hopper dead in the eye.

Hopper was electrified with anger but he walked away. He looked back, Murph and the girl kept arguing with each other.

Hopper knew what he was going to do. And it was his own self deciding. Not the fizz.

He walked up on the curb but turned suddenly. He sprinted towards the car, hopped into it, locking himself into the driver's side. On the ground, there was loads of shit everywhere so he grabbed a newspaper and scrunched its front pages. He took his lighter out, lit the paper, held it up to the roof. It quickly took the flame.

Hopper laughed.

Murph and the girl turned around outside the windscreen and looked in. Their arms dropped.

The heat.

Hopper got out of the car and shut the door. The roof alight.

Murph shouted. He went towards the driver's side.

'I wouldn't open it. The air will feed the fire and she'll blow,' Hopper said.

Fiona stood unmoving, wide-eyed wide-mouthed.

Murph ran to the boot, it squeaked open. He threw his bag onto the road. Hopper was smiling.

'You lunatic. D'ya think this is funny?'

'I do, yeah,' Hopper said moving towards Fiona. He'd bring her off the road. The fumes weren't good for her lungs.

Murph swung a punch at Hopper. He caught his ear.

Hopper roared instinctively. He wouldn't give in to the fizz but he wouldn't give in to a spoiled buffer bastard either. He shoved Murph.

Murph stumbled backwards but regained his balance after landing on the bonnet. He pushed himself up and charged.

Hopper ducked out of his way like one of them fancy-clothed Spanish buckos to a wild bull. But he turned to see Murph's shoulder connecting with Fiona, sending her small body back, going backwards more than down, falling.

Her head hit the ground first. Hit the edge of the footpath with a crack.

Blood trailed from her mouth. It looked black.

Jesus.

Murph's hands went loose by his side. 'Oh fuck,' he said real high-pitched.

Hopper bent over her. She looked gone. Her eyes were all eyeball under the lids. White.

Murph looked around, his top teeth were covering his bottom lip. 'Fiona, are you okay?' He shouted at Hopper, 'Is she breathing, did you check her?'

Hopper put his ear to her mouth. Couldn't hear anything. 'Dunno.'

Murph held his face in his hands. 'Not my fault – not again. I can't—' He stopped, still for a second. He looked at Fiona, at Hopper and wiped his eyes. 'I just can't…'

He shook his head and turned away, silent. Scooped his bag up. He limped first but broke into an awkward run and ran.

Ran like fuck.

The car headlights were still on and the fire was steady, hissing, sizzling. Had other cars passed? Hopper couldn't recall. It was a quiet enough street but more people were coming over for the look. Asking about the car. Asking about the girl.

'It's sound. It'll burn out. We'll ring for help if things don't improve, okay? Give us a chance, she needs space,' Hopper said. He sat down and cradled Fiona. He put his hand in front of her lips. The air was slightly humid, cold again, humid, cold, humid.

Breath.

Her voice was crackly when she came round. 'You're Hopper?'

He nodded.

'My head,' she said and put her hand to it and when she took it away it was streaked.

'I think you were concussed,' Hopper said.

'Jesus, look at my car.'

The upholstery was all aflame. Choking black smoke pillared from it.

Hopper ignored the people who came over so they moved on. Found each other. He was focusing on Fiona.

'It's your car?' Hopper asked.

'Yeah. I bought it earlier.'

He scratched his head. 'Sorry. I'll get ya back for it.'

Her voice had a shake. 'Is it going to explode?'

'No, no. That's only Hollywood stuff. I done this a million times when I was younger. Doesn't look like she'll spread to the engine. Should smoulder out soon. As long as she got no air.'

'It's dangerous,' Fiona said. 'We're in Australia, like.'

'I know. I know.' Hopper cringed. 'But it'll melt everything inside the car and die out. Probably. Promise. I'll pay for the fire brigade if they have to come.'

'Where's Murph?' she asked, one eye squinting like she was looking at the sun. She touched her head again, sucked up air as she moved her hand.

Hopper shrugged.

'He didn't?' She lifted an eyebrow. 'Did he go?'

Her chest was rising and falling. Made him think she might be crying on the inside, like he did sometimes.

She turned away. 'Just when I'd started to get myself together.'

'What ya mean?' Hopper asked.

'My life, I thought I'd begun to sort it out. Then all this,' she said and pointed weakly at the car.

Hopper nodded. Reminded him. All his stumbling around. How he didn't know if he could go on. If he should.

'Fiona, don't be worried,' he said and took a deep breath. The words formed all clear in his brain, like they came from somewhere else. 'Because it's not the event but how you interpret the event that's important.'

Her face was lit by the streetlight. 'What?'

Hopper paused. 'Some things that happen to you, events, you can't choose. D'ya get me?'

She stared him in the eye.

'It's all chances. Look at us. How we're here right now, what were the chances? We'd never have got talking back home. No way. I'm not looking for you to say we would. I'm being real.'

Hopper finally understood.

'Events are chances,' he said, 'but thoughts aren't. All what happened happened. The past is gone. If it went good or bad or how ever way, doesn't matter. It's only going on in there anymore,' he said and pointed at his forehead. 'You pick what to make of it now.'

The skin round her eyes crinkled.

He put his hands up. 'I mightn't be making that much sense on the outside. A kangaroo was the one who told me. I was fairly out of my box at the time too.'

She nodded. 'It makes sense. But...'

Hopper waited.

'I think I tried to make the same mistake again.'

'You see it was a mistake?'

'Yeah.'

'You know why it was?'

'Yeah.'

'Then you pick what to make of it.' He raised and dropped his shoulders. 'Hey, before this goes all wrong – tomorrow, come find me, I'll show you around, I been in Perth a few weeks now and know the run of it.'

'Are we in trouble?' she asked.

The commotion was getting too loud. Too many people were descending, hungry for the story, asking what the fuck was going on. Demanding. Why was the car burning? What did they see? What happened?

Sirens sounded in the distance. The flames kept chomping.

Some backpackers chatted and made jokes and took pictures. Neighbours from down the street were out for the look.

Fiona got up from the curb still holding the back of her head. People gathered around her. She pointed at the car, shrugged.

'I done what I done,' Hopper said but it was lost in the noise.

He watched as she moved through the crowd, answering questions. The fire glowed. Hot orange silk dancing. The cloudy night sky was clearing for stars. Hopper felt the warm. He unzipped his top and slid it down to check his right elbow and the side of his arm. Skinned, road-burnt. The dragon on the flipside was wild and ready.

ACKNOWLEDGEMENTS

Thank you to:

All my family and friends from Claremorris and beyond who have supported me as a writer, you know who you are. My agent Sallyanne Sweeney, and editor Neil Belton, for believing in this book.

Michael Naghten Shanks, Shane Mac an Bhaird, Noel O'Regan, Rosaleen McDonagh, Cathal Sherlock, John Wallace, Dave Rudden, Gerard McKeown, Ian Sansom, Glenn Patterson, Iris Curteis, Mayo Arts Council, Tyrone Guthrie House, Varuna Writers' House, Arts Council of Ireland – for earlier draft and professional development advice.

All the good people I met while travelling Oz.

Alice Walsh – the first reader of the whole book, for editorial suggestions and unwavering encouragement.

Sarah Hession – for the title and the invite to Australia which changed my life.

Jennifer Reapy – for having faith in me and how life goes on; a sister, friend, inspiration.